The Shadow Kingdom And the Land of Nines

The Shadow Kingdom And the Land of Nines

The Chosen Ones

Inabis P.M.

Rev. date: 01/03/2023

To order additional copies of this book, contact:
Xlibris
844-714-8691
www.Xlibris.com
Orders@Xlibris.com
539734

CONTENTS

for my wife

Chosen ones, you are hope
Chosen ones, downhill slope.
Chosen ones, turn the sky
Chosen ones, need to try

ACKNOWLEDGMENTS

I wanted to write this novel series in a different way. But did not know how. So, it took time. Many days, nights, weeks, months, years went by. Still, I did not know. Finally, it took some shape. The initial draft started to change. And now, here it is. The finished product. The book: The Shadow Kingdom and The Land of Nines. The first one in this series.

Many thanks to my wife and my children for your support and to my many friends who took time to read the initial draft of this book at an early stage and gave me invaluable suggestions. Thank you!

Thanks to the Xlibris team, its editors and especially to Kaye Parsons for patiently waiting for many years to make my dream come true.

CHAPTER I

A fateful voyage starts

Not long ago on an early Tuesday afternoon in the month of May, a cruise ship named *Adora* was in the port of Canopus. It was preparing for a long voyage across the ocean to Cassiopeia. The large cruise ship, grey, blue, and light purple in color, had extremities to complement the experience. These ranged between three pools to twenty-four-hour dining facilities complete with multiple bars and bands. *Adora* could accommodate more than four thousand passengers in small, medium, and large rooms with windows and balconies. The ship had large family suites with a veranda and an attached kitchen. Among the guests were travelling dignitaries from countries including King Orion Vulcan and his beautiful wife Zenithia Vulcan. With a long ponytail, short hair, a rugged face, and a well-built body King Orion appeared more like a fighter. His tall feature, respectable appearance and strong persona would impress anyone at first sight. King Orion had the in-born talent in sword fighting and martial arts that made him famous.

The Vulcans. The Vulcans that are famous. The Vulcans that people rarely get to see or experience to talk to. The Vulcans, the people from another planet. The beautiful and strong Vulcans.

The Vulcans occupied two most expensive suites. The spacious ocean view suites. Suites of the size of a basketball court with every amenity. Lounges, private pool deck, separate bedrooms with attached bathrooms. The personal attendants with their own rooms. The adorable Vulcans. With exquisitely beautiful dress, humble nature, and slow-paced delivery of speech. The Vulcans.

People knew about them, Knew about their humility. About their cruelty. The Vulcans, the living legend.

Vulcans spent millions on humanitarian crises. Helped the flood victims, the crippled, the homeless. Helped the unknowns, the weak, the unfortunate. Yet they never stopped from throwing away their fortunes on extravagant expenses. Or from torturing or killing people whom they never trusted. Anyone who came on their way. A rare combination of both. The famous and the infamous.

People thought they were great. Others had a different opinion.

Adora was carrying a mixture of people of different nationalities, complexions, and origins. Onboard were professional photographers, taking and selling their pictures. The bars packed with people, disk jockeys amusing them. Movie theaters playing movies. Sports arena with wide open invitation for young adults. Swimming pools with spa. Broadway shows entertaining people. Tattoo shops free for clients. With so many activities and thousands of people the atmosphere in the ship was vibrant with energy and color.

Two young kids, a fourteen-year-old boy Tyler Osbourne and his sister, a twelve-year-old girl Ella Osbourne were going to travel in the same ship along with their guide. These two orphans had been living with their foster parents in Eridanious. An epidemic recently broke out in the Canopus chain of islands. Tyler and Ella came to visit their ailing relatives: their uncle, aunt, and the cousins. However, their visit did not turn out that well. The relatives had already died from the disease. The heartbreaking news shocked them.

Tyler had short black hair, fair complexion. His charming

thoughtful face with a Roman nose made him get attention at the very first look. A medium-sized boy with a round head and high cheekbones, Tyler was growing up to be a determined individual. His big inquisitive blue eyes were always searching for answers.

Ella was a charming girl, full of energy and enthusiasm. She had long black hair, big eyes with long eyelashes, a dimple on each cheek and a smiling face. An intelligent girl Ella had lots of questions in her mind. As tall as her brother, she had a darker but still bright and attractive complexion. Her beautiful face, big green eyes, prominent eyebrows, and a small star mark next to her left eye close on her forehead, made her special. She had an expression of concentration on her face.

The fourteen-year-old boy Tyler was unmindful and afraid of the unknown. His twelve-year-old sister Ella had a stronger personality.

Tyler, Ella, and their guide, Ryan, spent one night at a neighbor's house in Canopus. Ryan Major, a farmer from Eridanious, was their family friend who lived across the river in Eridanious. With a beautiful wife, two daughters and a son, he had a happy family. Due to an emergency, the kid's parents could not come, and they reached out to Ryan at the last minute to go with the kids as a guide.

Early in the morning, they all left Canopus to take the return voyage. It was a long distance. The sudden outbreak had completely disrupted the communication system. They could not find any carriage to go to the port even after waiting for a long time.

"Let's start walking." Ryan said. "But I doubt we will be able to catch the ship."

"It's quite a long distance and we have been standing here for almost an hour." Tyler said.

Suddenly a horse driven carriage appeared at the end of the long road.

"Finally!" Said Ryan.

The carriage drew near. It was full of people, people even hanging from the sides. There was no space for them to get in.

They stood there and waited for a while.

"I know a shortcut." Said Tyler. "Follow me. We will take the boat ride."

Tyler led them down the hill to the river Indisa. One boat was sitting on the riverbank.

"Get on the boat. We have a nice tailwind." He shifted the anchor. "Indisa heads to the ocean. We will get off at Lacerta, a small town. Close to the port. I know this route. We took this route when we went for fishing in the ocean. An easy route to get to the ocean.

The boat sailed. It moved swiftly downstream. It passed by grocery stores, farms, fishponds, dirt roads, green forests, bazaars and many other beautiful places and greeneries. The deep dark forest was hanging over the river. Kids were running on the side of the river chasing after the boat. Two kids started throwing stones at the boat for testing how far it would reach.

"Watch out!" Screamed Ella.

A huge snake was hanging from a tree branch that was dangling over the riverbed. Tyler pushed his oar to move the boat to the middle of the river. The snake was still hissing, but the boat was out of its reach, and it did not jump.

It is good that we could take the river. It will take a while, but we will be able to catch the ship." Said Ryan.

"Yes. At least we do not have to spend another night here." Said Ella. Her face was still sad. She was having a tough time coping with the loss of their relatives.

"Go, move to the other side." Ryan shouted. "Push, push your oars harder.

Tyler and Ella quickly maneuvered the boat to the other side.

Four hours later they reached Lacerta.

They started running. By the time they reached the pier, the ticket booths were closing. The last-minute pieces of cargo were loading.

Ryan went up to the gate. "Luckily, we already have bought out tickets in advance", he murmured.

"Have you got your tickets?" The ticket-clerk, a big man with a sharp smile and long beard enquired. "You people are late. I am not sure if you can purchase them anymore."

"Yes! We have our tickets!" Ryan replied.

"Alright, show 'em!" The man chuckled.

"They are just in my…" Ryan reached into his pocket-and suddenly turned pale.

"Um, just a moment please sir…" Ryan began checking all his pockets.

"What's wrong?" asked Ella,

"Oh no, don't tell me you forgot 'em!" The Ticket clerk said sarcastically,

"No ticket, no ship'n."

"No, wait, I think I have them," Ryan said pulling his hand out of his shirt pocket,

"Oh, wait until you find those tickets, I think what you are holding in your hand are old tickets." He was glancing at the old tickets that Ryan searched out of his pockets. "I'm not sure if you got any…"

The ticket-clerk chortled.

"Of course, we forgot our tickets. Why wouldn't we? Our luck is great!" Tyler said hysterically.

"I hate this island," Ella was annoyed.

"I thought I had them. I remember checking already when we started!"

"Sorry folks…I'm not sure if you could get in, ship leaves in an hour, so I got to pack up and get on board, best of luck to ya folks!" The clerk slowly stood up and began packing his things.

Ryan backed up and stared at the kids. A responsible man, Ryan knew if he couldn't get them on board, it would be hard for them to find a shelter for the night anywhere nearby.

"I have an idea, lets hop the fence" whispered Tyler slowly.

Ryan rolled his eyes; the gate was at least twenty feet in height.

"Tyler don't be stupid; we have to come back tomorrow and buy some tickets then."

"I'm starting to hate this island too." Tyler groaned.

"I literally said that a minute ago." Ella stated.

Just then a truck rolled up to a cargo checkpoint, not too far from the civilian's gate. In the distance Ryan noticed a steward with a scanner and an iPad. Ryan immediately got an idea.

"Follow me." He said in a low tone. Ryan didn't want to miss this ship, even if he must do something stupid.

They began moving swiftly towards the cargo gate, which was about a hundred feet away.

"Follow my lead," Ryan continued. If his idea worked, they could all get on the ship.

They walked up to the checkpoint and found the steward.

"Hi, my name is Ryan. We are late. Sorry!"

Ryan made a unique face of apology.

"Here are our tickets." Ryan handed him the same old three tickets from their trip to the island. "We could not check in at the gate, sorry, these two are my, um, nephews, I'm here to show them how cargo works on a cruise ship."

"Sounds good to me," The man answered, glancing at the papers in approval. "This way please."

The Steward paused. Taking another look at their tickets, he said meaningfully, "No worries. Let me check something."

The Steward pulled out his ticket scanners and scanned them. The screen showed the words *expired* in big red text, but it prompted him to a new screen with the new tickets and room numbers. He stared at the screen and then turned back to Ryan. "These are old tickets. Do you have the new ones?"

He stared back at the screen and a smile appeared on his face. A giant 'PAID' sign popped up on the screen. "Oh—wait. Found it. You are all paid, no worries!"

Ryan was still searching for the new tickets with a murmur.

"Let me print out new ones for you," The steward said, "this ship is going to leave very soon." He printed out new ones from his scanner and matched their faces with the pictures on the tickets. Then he handed the tickets over to Ryan and said, "Please follow me."

They followed the steward across the checkpoint and up the ship doors. He led them down to the fifth floor.

The cabins were getting full. Families were busy settling in or opening their bags and carriers. Folks were having a fun time.

They were strolling through a babble.

"Did you guys get lost on your way here?" The steward asked.

"Yeah, sorry, we got lost on our way to the port." Ryan grinned.

The steward stared back at the tickets for a moment and then took another turn.

"We are almost there."

The steward guided them through another turn and ended in front of a cabin. "Here you go. This is your key. Relax, and enjoy your stay!" He smiled at Tyler and Ella as he pushed the door. It propped open. He handed them the keycard.

"Make yourselves comfortable!" added Ryan. "I'll see you in a bit."

"Now let me find your cabin." The steward stared up at Ryan.

"I believe it is two floors above."

They turned in the hallway to get to the stairs.

Tyler and Ella walked into their room. The door shut behind them. They peered into their cabin.

"I can't believe we are finally here."

"And we got a nice place." Tyler said in a pleasant voice walking into the room.

"We must thank Ryan."

"It's pretty crazy that he pulled this off." stated Ella.

The cabin had a sleeper couch and two other pullman beds

along with a sofa and a coffee table. It came in with all other usual amenities.

"I'm tired, going to sleep." Ella jumped on the bed. Tyler sat on the sleeper couch looking out through the window toward the draw bridge. The rest of the cargo were going in.

"What is that? The huge thing they are loading!" Tyler yelped. He was looking out of the cabin window toward the front of the loading dock.

Ella was listening. She jumped up on her bed and ran to the window. They stared outside. An enormous wooden crate was going in with the help of a crane. The loading crews were trying hard to load the crate. But each time they brought the crate closer to the ship, the crane lost its motion, stood still for a few seconds, and then moved back to its original position. After multiple failures, the manager asked the crew to load the wooden crate into a huge truck. The loaded truck rolled over the drawbridge. Slowly the truck reached the middle of the drawbridge, then it stopped functioning.

"Something weird is happening! The crate might be too heavy to carry." Ella reacted.

"They are loading too much stuff. They always do. Look how long it is taking." Tyler remarked.

"Let's take a walk." Ella said.

They walked out of their cabin and moved toward the hallway to have a better look at the loading dock and to watch the ocean. They sat down in a coffee shop on the deck and ordered for drinks.

A discussion broke out between the crews at the loading dock. A few skippers showed up. With their permission, one of the crew members affixed the truck to a chain link in the ship. The chain link rolling, the truck was inside. Everyone was relieved. A few more cargo waiting: a few cars, ten motorcycles, and three boats. All finally loaded after this.

The rest of the loading operation went smooth. At last came the food stuff, spices, flour bags, many other packages, drinks, and other food supplies. Soon the loading was completed. It was almost evening. The purple red sky was smiling over the calm blue ocean. The last crimson sun rays were making a canopy of golden ribbons across the horizon as it was setting.

Tyler and Ella turned back.

The evening drew in. The ship was about to start its voyage.

Yet almost another extra hour passed before the horn sounded.

The ship moved.

"Finally! I have been looking for you guys. Let us have our dinner." Ryan showed up.

"Sure." Ella and Tyler said in unison.

"Let us go to the deck. There is a nice restaurant. I think you will like it." Ryan said.

"Certainly, why not? We would love to." Said Ella.

Their evening dinner started with appetizers and three drinks.

"They have international dishes and the regular ones. What would you like to have?" Ryan asked while Tyler and Ella were looking at the menu.

By the time they had finished the dinner with chicken tikka masala, chicken makhana, goat curry, channa dal, naan and lassi, the ship started moving. The sun was setting in the west. A beautiful red golden canopy was reflecting over the waves and reaching towards the heaven. The night moved in. The starlit sky was visible above the beautiful calm ocean. The ship sailed peacefully.

"I must go back to my cabin and get warm clothes. It is getting chilly. You need to go back to your cabin too. Go and take rest. I will catch up with you tomorrow morning." Ryan left.

Tyler and Ella waited for a little while and then slowly walked out of the restaurant.

"Let's take a tour across the ship." Ella said.

The appearance and amenities available in the ship made

them enthralled. They lost their way twice when they entered the kitchen area, but finally found their way out.

"I feel sad about the whole thing…. our aunt, uncle and our cousins are all gone, wish we came earlier." Tyler was talking with an absorbing tone.

"It is sad, incredibly sad. The pandemic. Please, let us not talk about it." Said Ella.

It was a long walk around the ship. For next few hours they walked through all the sixteen decks in that large ship touring across the floors before they finally came back to their cabin. Tyler sat on the Sofa. Ella sat on the bed and gazed outside the window. Their guide Ryan stopped by.

"Where had you been? It is getting late, and I was worried. It is a large ship. All kinds of people travelling. Stay close to your cabin. Would you?"

He stared at them for an answer.

Then said, "it is time to go to bed. Have a good night's sleep folks!" Ryan advanced to the stairs to return to his cabin.

The cruise ship continued its peaceful voyage. It sailed calmly across the ocean for next few days.

One afternoon, Tyler needed to have a drink.

"Hey, do you remember which deck we are on?"

Ella had a far-off look; she was trying to catch the last glimpse of the sunset over the beautiful island they were passing by. The red colored clouds splattered across the horizon created a stunningly magnificent mosaic platform over the landmass. The early afternoon shadow was mixing with the green trees, fallen leaves and the golden hello to make a beautiful image at the distance.

Tyler concluded that Ella did not want to talk now. He decided to go ahead exploring a bit by himself. As soon as he opened the door of the cabin, Ella shook her head and stared surprised.

"Where are you going?" she asked.

"To get a drink." Tyler said.

"I would like to come along." she replied.

They left their cabins and came to the staircase. Up the stairs they went to the upper level to a café. Loud music was coming out of bars packed with people. They ordered their drinks.

"It is an amazing experience. I love it." Said Tyler.

"Me too." Said Ella.

No one was in a hurry, all spending their time leisurely. Chatting with friends, relatives. People travelling alone had found a friend or a companion. Couples were watching the clouds or sunset over the ocean. Kids glued to their phones on chats or on video games had little time for anything else.

After a while they left the café and decided to go to the other side of the ship.

Soon they lost their way.

"Uh, we came down that hallway, right?" Ella asked in a confused voice as they were holding the bars and leaning toward the ocean.

"Hey!" A voice called them from the behind.

Tyler and Ella turned. One uniformed crew officer was talking to them.

"Let me introduce myself. I am Captain Baker. Nice to meet you." The tall officer dressed in white uniform and a cap came forward with a big smile. Tyler and Ella were pleased with his warm handshake and the appearance.

Brilliantly dressed two other crew members were standing next to him. "How do you like our ship? Having a fun time?" Captain Baker asked.

"Oh yah! It is wonderful to know the ship and its people." Tyler and Ella said with confidence in unison.

"Great." The captain came forward. "One thing we try to do every time we sail, is to take a tour across the ship and introduce ourselves personally to everyone. We have not met you. Our mistake. Sorry. So here we are. It is nice to meet you. Let me introduce you to Anik and Devan, two of our crew members.

Others are busy running the ship." The captain paused. His voice was cracking.

"Now, if you want, we have some afternoon activities going on at the upper decks. Do not forget to check them out. It is fun." Another officer said.

"Nice meeting you!" The captain and crews smiled.

"Thank you. Good to meet you too!" Said Tyler and Ella.

The captain's associate handed them two brochures about the cruise ship.

"Here you will find the route we take and names of all the small or big islands we sail by. The names might not look familiar to you. The brochure includes all the in-house activities in our cruise ship with a clear map of the floors. It might help you to get to your place swiftly."

The captain and his team turned and headed another way.

"This sounds great. We are sure going to have great fun this evening!" remarked Ella.

"What?" Tyler asked. "You were so morbid a few minutes ago."

"Shush!" Ella said examining the brochure. "Hey, look we can do some of these."

Tyler paid attention and noticed something that immediately caught his eyes on the brochure.

"I have an excellent event coming up right now. Rock climbing. Time? Oh, my gosh! Right now. It starts in fifteen minutes. Got to go!"

"Hey, wait!" yelled Ella, but Tyler was already gone.

Tyler sprinted to the stairs and ran to the back of the ship. At one side the participants were getting ready. One of the crew members was penning down the names.

The competition began. Tyler was in a good mood to rock climb and did not show any sign of slowing down. A beautiful girl drew his attention. He could not shy out of making an impression in front of her.

Soon the next round of the competition began. A few judges were seated. Among them he noticed King Orion Vulcan, and his wife Zenithia Vulcan. Tyler won the first place two times in a row without much of a difficulty. The girl Amba finished second. A few weeks ago, on the same event, Tyler had difficulty to get to even 3rd place in Eridanious.

"You are good." Smiled queen Zenithia.

"Yes, he is." Commented King Orion. The stout and strong king laughed and honored him with the medal in the victory stand and shook his hand. Tyler stared at his eye. He felt happy to receive the medal, but something made him uneasy. He watched tears rolling down Amba's eyes when she was presented with her medal. With a tearful smile she received her honor. Tyler couldn't stop looking at her beautiful but sad face. Now Tyler wished Amba received the medal.

"Are you alright?" He asked.

"I'm fine. But it is just that I am never used to being second." Amba replied. She wiped her tears with her elbow and smiled.

"I understand. But there will be another round tomorrow." Tyler said. Give it a shot. You might…who knows."

"I'm in 7259, 9D. Which one is yours?" Tyler asked.

I'm in 6259, 9D. That's exactly below yours." Amba smiled.

They started walking, came to a cafeteria and sat down to continue their conversations. Tyler felt his heart was pounding as he touched Amba's hand while handing her over the glass of a drink they just ordered. His voice became deeper.

Ella already guessed where Tyler could be. She went straight to the arena but could not get there before the awarding ceremony or when Tyler was heading to the victory stand. She was happy to hear the announcement that Tyler made the first place. By the time she arrived there, Tyler and Amba had received their awards and decided to go to the cafeteria to get a drink. It took Ella a while to discover and join them.

Six more days passed peacefully. In the meantime, Tyler and Amba became close friends. Amba invited Tyler and Ella to have breakfast with her parents. Amba successfully finished with gold in her last two events.

It was late in the afternoon on the ninth day. The ship was approaching the coast of Eridanious toward Cassiloneia. Light rain mixed with heavy winds came in. About three hundred miles north of the bay, the ocean changed its form and color. The setting sun on the horizon brought out an envelope of magnificent display. The drizzle, the crimson sun and the wavy ocean made it a spectacular sight.

Captain Baker watched the situation for a while and then ordered for an early dinner with light menu. He wanted people off all the decks. He was smelling something different out of the abrupt changes in the wave and wind patterns.

He was aware of the news that broke out about the development of a cyclone approaching in their direction but was unaware of its exact location and strength.

"The wind is gaining strength; we need to watch out for those clouds there." The captain expressed his concern to his fellow officers.

"We need to get the passengers off the decks. Quickly serve them a light dinner and ask everyone to go inside." His trained eyes were searching for the signature of any disturbance in the skyline that might be looming.

"I will ask the operator to make the announcements." The crew member ended his sentence looking at the captain's eyes. The wrinkles on Captain's concerned face made him worried.

People started having their dinners. Soon people finished eating and went back to their cabins. But some decided to hang out at the bars. Others went to the theaters. The passengers were not happy with the idea of an early dinner and had questions in their minds. The atmosphere inside the cruise ship seemed peaceful, relaxed, and enjoyable. Many people even fell asleep in time.

Two more hours passed. Out in the ocean, the wind steadily gained strength with increasing tides and heavy rainfall. The eventful night drew in. The spiraling huge waves were hitting the ship hard. The crew were toiling to keep the ship on course.

The vast ocean was roaring. It was pitch black. The ocean swells began approaching one after another. The gushing wind and surging waves were hammering the ship hard from every direction.

The ocean that appeared so calm and peaceful changed. More colossal waves rolled in. The huge cruise ship with thousands of passengers now appeared tiny. It sporadically lost direction.

The passengers who were awake sensed something was going on.

Soon announcements came on the speakers: "Please stay inside. Do not leave your cabin. We are in the middle of a nasty storm. Your captain requests everyone for your full cooperation. Please, please stay where you are. Do not move." The flashing emergency red lights were on.

The few braves that decided to hang out in the bars cracked jokes about another 'Titanic'. The bar tender did not mind serving them. Some folks got terrified once the news of the storm broke out. Women at the theater were crying holding their children dearly.

"Mom, are we going to die?" The five-year-old daughter stared at her mom's face and asked. "I'm scared!" Her three-year-old brother was crying.

"No! Nobody is going to die. We will be fine." The mom pressed them close to her heart.

Others consoled them with prayers, patting their backs or giving them hugs. But everybody thought this phase will pass soon.

Afterall, the ship was close to its destination, Cassiloneia. Cassiloneia was only fifteen hours away.

As the storm intensified, lightnings were visible hitting across the ocean. At the control room, the captain and his colleagues were struggling to deal with this sudden cyclone. They were listening to the radio announcing the intensity of storm. By midnight, the storm had reached category five. The ocean became brutal, the crew now lost every control of the ship. They were now afraid and realized the ship was in real trouble.

"How far are we from land?" Captain Baker asked. "Follow the guidelines of 1-2-3 rule. Try to avoid the tropical cyclone. We need to stay out of 34 KT wind field of this storm."

"Around two nautical miles sir I think!" replied the officer in-charge.

"Too close, we are in a rocky sea floor. Need to move further away toward the ocean." The second officer screamed.

"Yes, stay further out!" Yelled the Captain.

The second officer immediately asked the control room to act. The ship slowly turned to its starboard side. Suddenly, a fierce wind rattled the ship, while a gigantic wave pushed the vessel high up in the air. The ship continued moving as it tilted sideways almost fifteen degrees. Then it smashed on the side to a rocky bed underneath. The heeling caused the ship shuddered to a halt. Instantly there was a trembling sound. The water started gushing into one of the basement compartments through a gigantic hole.

Most passengers were asleep at the time, but the loud crashing jolted them awake. They fell on the floor, while others had difficulty to stay in one spot. The passengers still on the deck, were about to scream. They fell and began rolling down on the deck. Three or four people toppled into the ocean. People ran for safety. They grabbed chairs, railings, or anything they could to save themselves. In that pitch-dark ocean a complete anarchy broke out across the ship.

"I'm not sure if our ship will withstand this cyclone!" One man shouted to his wife staring at the ocean while holding to a rail.

"What do you mean? This ship is huge and has travelled all around the world. Adora cannot sink!" King Orion shouted from the other side standing by his wife. They came out of the bar. Even with their unsteady legs, they were unmoved by the situation.

"They say Adora is mightier than the ocean!" Queen Zenithia screamed from his side.

"Of course, my darling. Nothing can touch the Vulcans!" King Orion laughed.

"Hmmm, as an engineer, not too sure if there is any truth to it! Not now at least from what I see." The man replied in an alarmed voice talking to his wife.

"No! Everything will be fine! We are going to be all right." His wife said in a low peached voice. But it was hard to understand if she was confident.

"Nothing, I tell you nothing will happen to Adora. Our ship will be fine. Relax!" The King was upset this time. He heard their conversations. He moved close to the balcony as he was trying to gauze the roaring thunder across the horizon.

"It's rough out here." Zenithia took the king back to his suite.

The disk jockey standing in the big bar addressed the crowd again.

"Just stay where you are. It will pass. Give it time." He was standing behind a huge table attached to the floor. His voice declared he had little faith about what he was trying to convey.

The captain heard the news of the hole in one of the chambers at the bottom of the vessel.

"How much time do we have?" Asked the Captain looking at the second officer in a calm but anxious voice.

"At least two to three hours! These isolated ballast chambers in this vessel, all are airtight. Water cannot go anywhere. Our ten super-pumps should be able to take care of any disaster!" Replied the officer.

"But we need to work on buoyancy! Balance the weight of the other side! Ask them to fill an opposite ballast tank to keep the ship balanced." Captain Baker ordered.

The crew members were trying hard. With water gushing in, they had limited options. They were hoping the powerful pumps would be able to handle any of the problems. Then another huge wave might put the ship back on deeper water. But they were unaware of the events that were unfolding. Such strength of a cyclone took them by surprise. The storm had already derailed the ship from its path. The gushing wind made the situation worse. The crew members were trying their best to map the ship back to its sea lane. However, thundering cyclone and tumultuous ocean made them powerless. The captain stared at his compass; he was feeling the tension that made him uneasy.

"In order to survive, we must withstand this storm. We must. One way or another we need to stay in this area. We need to have enough sea-room and steering way in this cyclone. Don't give up." Captain Baker shouted while his tone revealed the gravity of the situation.

His only anticipation was if the ship could float back, it would withstand the strong waves for a few more hours, the storm might lose its intensity and change direction. By then, with some luck, other rescue teams or coastguards would arrive, and the ship could survive the disaster.

CHAPTER II

The Unfolding Episodes

Tyler fell from his bunk onto the floor when the ship smashed on the rocky bed underneath.

"Oh no, what's going on, Ella?" he screamed.

As he was trying to regain his balance, the lights went off and came back. Finally, he stood up. Still holding one side of the bed. Ella managed to stay where she was. She grabbed the rail in time. They stared through the cabin window. Most of the lights were out. People were running around everywhere.

"What's wrong?" Ella shouted.

"I doubt if our ship is moving at all!" Screamed Tyler.

"Are we stuck? Did our ship slam onto something?" Questioned Ella.

"Don't know! But something must be wrong." Tyler agreed as he was looking out for some favorable answers.

The emergency exit signs were flashing. After a few more minutes, most of the lights came back. But then they started to flicker again.

"Something is not right. ...look!" Shouted Tyler.

In that dim yellow light, Tyler and Ella spotted a strange scene through their glass window. Passengers were running, screaming, and crying. Scattered across the ship in the middle of that stormy weather were many cabin mates, officers, shipwrights, and seafarers trying their best to keep the crowd under control. It was hard to understand what they were saying from the speaker in the room.

"What's going on? Are we sinking? What should we do?" Yelled Tyler.

"We can stay here and die. Or we can go out and check what's going on!" Ella remarked in an awful voice while trying to stay up with a farm grip on the cabin handle. She was busy with frustration putting her belongings back on the table. Things got scattered across the cabin floor.

"Let's get out of here!" Tyler's voice drifted. "Where is Ryan? Our guide? We need to look for Amba and her family too." His anxiety for Amba was evident.

"Good luck with that. I don't think you can find him in his cabin unless he is still there waiting which I doubt." Answered Ella, "Let's go and look for them."

They opened the door, came out of the cabin, ran through the chaotic corridor. The catastrophic scene everywhere made them nervous. The storm was coming down hard through a broken window. They got soaked immediately. They managed to get down the stairs and reached Ryan's cabin.

The room was empty, no one was around. The floor was messy, everything scattered. People were crying in the neighboring cabins. The area was chaotic, and many were in shock.

"He might have left already." Ella said thoughtfully.

"He must be somewhere." Accepted Tyler.

"We need to move. He might be up on the top deck." Answered Ella.

They ran up the stairs to another deck. People were in a hurry. "We're closed." Screamed the girl in a café. "Closed," said another bartender while shutting down the bar.

Tyler and Ella searched for Ryan almost everywhere: bars, theaters, huge multi-purpose ball rooms and cafes. People were scattered all over, kids screaming and running with their parents.

Tyler and Ella went up and down from one deck to the other as they continued their search for Ryan.

As they moved to the bottom of the vessel, water was filling up the chambers they noticed. A few crew members were hastily trying to restart the pumps. In that dire situation nowhere, could they find Ryan.

They took a turn while going up.

Up they went two more decks. There they found the first officer and the captain. A crowd in shock was listening to their speech. An emergency battery powered flood light was keeping the area lit. The first officer was also explaining. Nobody was listening to them. It was getting difficult to control the anxious crowd.

"I request you all to stay calm. We are doing everything. We can solve this conundrum. A lower chamber of the ship has been compromised, water is gushing in. But we are sealing it off. Soon, the ship will regain its balance. Once the storm moves out of the area, we can sail again." The captain announced. His voice reverberated across the ship. He stared exhausted and concerned.

"Oh my God! Are we going to die?" Screamed someone in the crowd.

Lightning flashed. In that light people realized the ship was not tilted anymore and started moving after it regained its balance.

"Please stay calm! The first officer standing next to the Captain shouted. "Just stay calm. As our Captain is saying, we will be able to withstand this storm. We desperately need your help."

"No! No one is going to die. Nothing would be able to sink us. This is an enormous ship. Adora can withstand many, many, cyclones. Don't panic. We already sealed off the bottom chamber." The Captain reiterated.

"Ten of our super-power pumps are working at maximum capacity. We sent out many "SOS" messages to nearby ships. We got some responses already." Before the Captain could finish his sentence, lightning struck another corner of the ship, and a fire began. Instantly the crew members ran to the spot to snuff out the fire. That part of the ship experienced serious damage, yet nothing critical. The ship was being tossed in the stormy ocean like a toy.

The passengers reached out for anything they could to hold and stay steady. Some leaned and grabbed the person standing next to them. Others grabbed the railings, doorknobs, or handles. Many were rolling over the floor.

A series of lightnings struck across the ocean. In that light, every person on the top deck watched a strange scene. The ship tilted on its side, dipped side wise and then floated again. Then it stopped moving. It was stuck in a halted position facing a huge rocky island.

"How did we get here? What is the name of this island?" The captain asked the first officer in a low voice.

"Don't know! Not on our map Sir! This is a busy sea route we are travelling. There should be many other cruise ships or cargo ships." Explained the first officer.

"Hmm, not a good sign. Need to stay out of this rocky bed as far out as we can!" hooted Captain Baker in an angry tone. He was careful not to speak out loud or show any signs of his anger to the public.

"Get me into the radio. I need to talk to the passengers."

"I know it's a bit scary. I know what you all are thinking, but the ship is not going to just sink. We have some time in hand to empty the ship. But don't try to jump off the ship. It is a stormy night. This is a volcanic rocky seafloor, there are hidden rocks. You can't just jump into a stormy ocean. You can injure yourself or even die. We have plenty of lifeboats. We will start boarding if we must and only when we are ready." Finished Captain Baker. His voice faded away in the mist and rain. Heavy storm was now hitting every corner of the ship with all its force.

"But, when?" Someone screamed out of the gathering, looking around, "Tell us. When?" Others echoed with him.

"Soon, we are looking into that. It is difficult to do it now." Continued the Captain, "please try to stay calm. If no help arrives within the next hour, we would like to vacate the ship in an orderly manner. You will hear the announcement. We're getting the lifeboats ready and going to announce all the directions. Don't forget to follow the instructions when you get to lifeboats. Always fasten your seat belts. We have twenty-five hundred passengers and eight hundred fifty crew members. Our stock of lifeboats and life jackets is plenty." Captain Baker finished his speech in a commanding voice.

"Watch yourselves, try not to fall! Hold on to your rail tightly." A voice told them from behind. Tyler and Ella looked back and noticed Ryan standing behind them while they were listening to Captain Baker.

"Where have you been?" Asked Tyler.

"I'm here now. Trying to understand how we can survive this ordeal. But you two must stay here. It is easy to get lost and I will never find you. Do you hear me? Stay right here and don't move. Ok?" Ryan admitted in a nervous voice. Then he ran to another part of the ship in a hurry. Tyler and Ella could not see him anymore.

Another announcement came in, "be careful! We should be able to vacate the ship and board you all in time. A difficult task in such a hostile weather. We are waiting to see if the wind speed reduces. We will announce when we are ready. We will not leave anyone behind and will take you all. But we ask you to follow the rules. When you empty the ship do so in an orderly fashion. Please stay in a line. Allow the children, women, and elderly to get on the lifeboats first. Our crewmembers will guide you in boarding but be patient."

Horror and chaos broke out all around the ship. Fear and anxiety took over everyone's mind. Fear. The fear that asks you to run. Anxiety. The anxiety that tells your time is running out. Time. Time is everything. Time that you can never buy.

Some people stayed inside their cabins and didn't want to come out to the deck. They were hopeful that help was on its way. With frequent lightning striking across the ship a few more fires broke out in different parts of the ship. Like the previous ones, the fire-crews moved in extremely fast, and they were out in a few minutes. The rain helped to put out the fire as well.

Yet the situation was getting out of control. Out of fear and desperation and without much thinking, some people were acting erratically and even didn't hesitate to jump into the ocean.

Tyler and Ella waited at the same balcony for some more time. But there was no Ryan.

"Let's get to the other side of the ship." Ella screamed.

They ran through the partly tilted ship to take another look across the ocean over the rails.

"It doesn't look good." Said Tyler. "We need to look for Amba."

"I don't know how long this ship will survive." Ella argued.

They ran and ran, searching for Ryan and Amba. Ella spotted Amba standing in a line with her parents.

Right then a tsunami type wave came and swept people away along with Amba and her parents. Amba's parents fell into the ocean. Amba rolled across the deck and was falling into the ocean. Ella caught her hand just in time while looking out at the roaring ocean and its ferocious waves with anxiety.

"Hold my hand tightly." She screamed.

Gusty rain was hitting their faces in full strength.

"Hang on! Tyler screamed. He was trying to regain his own balance. He threw a rope at Amba, tied the other part on a railing.

Ella was losing strength. Her hands were slipping.

"Get the rope. Catch it." She screamed.

While looking beneath at the ferocious ocean, Amba managed to gather all her strength and catch the rope.

Three of them ran to get into a line. Huge lines formed at different corners of the ship for boarding the lifeboats. But due to the storm and heavy wind, people in the lines were moving all around.

"It will take too much time to get to the front. By then the ship might sink." Screamed Ella. "Need to find another way to get into a lifeboat."

With no time, they had nothing in mind except getting into a line somehow.

"Look, another line just started forming and crew members are asking people to get in the line. Amba screamed. "Let's go that way."

"Great idea." Ella screamed.

They were able to get into the line. Crew members were looking after the boarding operation. It was a challenging task to get people moving in such stormy weather.

A sudden gust of wind and heavy rain came pounding the ship hard. People lost their balance, slipped, rolled down and fell into the ocean. Lines fell apart.

Scattered people ran around in that dimly lit ship. Panic took over the entire ship.

Another wave smashed on the other edge of the ship. It tossed Amba onto the railing. Tyler and Ella flew high up in the air and dropped on the top of a cable. They both were injured, but nothing serious.

They ran to another side of the ship. The area was a cordoned off with a door, 'restricted entry.' They crashed through the door.

"Look, Lifeboats!" Screamed Tyler.

A few lifeboats were stacked. A sign next to them; 'Emergency use only, Do Not Touch' was hanging.

"Come on! If this is not an emergency, then there would never be an emergency." Screamed Ella.

"This is our only chance." Tyler quickly grabbed Amba's hand and picked up a bundle of rope from a stack at a corner.

"You go in first." He requested Amba.

Amba stared at his eyes. With tears on her face, she kissed him on his lips and managed to get into the lifeboat.

Tyler and Ella jumped in. "Fasten your seatbelt." Screamed Ella. Tyler began pressing random buttons.

"Which one is it?" He shouted.

"Must be this one." Amba said with a concern.

She stared at the last green button on the distant right.

Tyler looked at her, kissed her again and pressed the button.

Immediately the lifeboat got unlatched from the ship, fell into the ocean, and started moving.

The lifeboat wobbled and shook. It dipped, and then surfaced and dipped again.

"Are we sinking? Screamed Amba.

"Hold on tight. Either we are saved or will go down." Shouted Ella.

The lifeboat surfaced again. It spanned and started moving.

"I can't see anything!" Tyler screamed, "Which way are we going?"

"As long as we steer away from the ship, we will survive." Ella screamed.

The cyclone was coming on hard. Their modern enclosed lifeboat was twisting, turning, and being tossed like a small toy amid the stormy ocean. They were only hoping the lifeboat was moving in a different direction away from the ship.

But they did not realize the storm was bringing their lifeboat close to the rocky sea floor.

The lifeboat was moving fast. It took a rocky turn. Many times, it went under water, then resurfaced. Then a strong wave and the gusty wind threw it high in the air and it smashed against a dangerous rocky mountain rising above the ocean. Amba's seatbelt came off. Next, she was flying high in the air and fell on the rock her face down. A huge wave crashed into the rocky mountain.

"Amba, Amba….where are you? Screamed Tyler.

"Amba……Amba……are you there?" Cried out Ella.

There was no more any trace of her. She was gone. Only more waves came at high speed. The damaged boat was now far away from the rock as it was being filled with water and on the verge of sinking.

In that encounter, Tyler and Ella almost got killed.

After a long stormy ride, Tyler and Ella and a few crew members were the only survivors to escape the sinking ship alive.

The two young kids were now at a loss! Their half-submerged lifeboat was drifting away.

"I can't stop thinking of her!" Cried Tyler. "We just lost her."

"She is a great swimmer. Hope she survives this storm. I'm not sure even if we can survive today."

"I don't see any other boats nearby. I think they all are scattered in every direction or drifted away from each other due to high winds."

Tyler and Ella were nervous. They were shaking in fear and desperation.

"Look there is a huge fire! Lightning just struck the ship!" Ella screamed. She pointed at a distance over the ocean.

"The ship is sinking." Tyler shivered as they watched the ship falling apart and sinking in front of their eyes.

"Our boat is damaged too! We need to get out."

They were looking at the holes and damage on the boat. Everywhere water was gushing in. Tyler had been removing the cold water with his bare hands, which was a race against time. Half of the boat was now under water and was barely floating.

After fighting the storm for almost an hour, Tyler and Ella got completely exhausted. They were seeking out everywhere for help, but couldn't see any boats, ships, or vessels. No one was there. Then abruptly, the storm picked up wind and changed

direction. The situation did not get any better, the clouds and
winds gathered strength. Lightnings were flashing. Huge waves
pushed them to twenty feet high above the sea level and dropped
them back. It continued for a few minutes. After a while they
came close to the edge of a mountain. Suddenly their boat
gained speed.

"What's happening?" Tyler screamed at Ella. "Why did we
speed up so rapidly?"

"I don't know!" Ella yelled back while gasping for air but
trying to stay calm as she was working hard to keep the boat
going in the same direction. But her humming oscillating voice
got thinner and thinner as it travelled with the winds across the
ocean.

In a short while, they came close to a waterfront, where the
Rocky River of the Eridanious Island met the ocean with great
strength. Many tall waterfalls were gushing into the ocean with
a roaring sound.

The speed of the small boat increased. Tyler and Ella stared
ahead to the point where water from another river was gushing
in. Their tiny lifeboat was now being tossed here and there as
they approached the delta. Within seconds their boat was upside
down. Tyler and Ella were thrown out into water. As they were
getting drowned, the boat got sucked in by a whirlpool, smashed
alongside a jagged rock. Their small lifeboat broke into pieces
before they could do anything.

Ella was bruised in her head. She lost her consciousness for
a few seconds. Her forehead was bleeding. With more injury
to her arms and legs she was about to drown. As she was going
down to the ocean floor, she heard her mother screaming at
her, "Ella, my dear Ella, wake up! Wake up my baby! Wake up!
Wake up!" With a jolt she came to her senses and started moving
her legs. After a long fight, finally she came to the surface to
breath fresh air. It was a close call!

Tyler was gasping for air. He was frantically trying to stay
afloat. With gloomy and terrified eyes, he could not find his sister.

He screamed, "Ella, Ella!" His cry was reflecting everywhere in that dark and gloomy ocean. But Ella was nowhere to be found. Right then Ella came up to the surface and touched his back.

With lightning striking across the sky, these two fearful souls stared everywhere for help.

Tyler was hurt too, but his injury was not too bad. With his injured right hand and bleeding left elbow Tyler took shelter behind a rock, where the water was shallow. As he turned his head, he noticed Ella was struggling to stay afloat. After securing the rope tightly, Tyler began to swim toward his sister. He leaned over and grabbed Ella's hand. She was moving away into the whirlpool. Fortunately, after a struggle, they escaped with the help of the tight rope.

Tyler dragged his sister behind the huge rock. It was not easy for them to stay there for long with waves hitting. With every moment passing, Tyler understood his strength was weakening. He was beginning to feel the pain and was losing his grips. Tyler turned toward his wounded sister. He understood Ella had been seriously injured as her eyes were now closing.

"Come on Ella, come on!" He screamed. He took his sister close to his chest and tried to wake her up.

Lightning struck. They waited there for a few minutes. An enormous wave rolled in and tossed them out into the open water. Tyler swam while tightly holding her sister's hand. He fought to keep his sister's head above the water. Tyler merely managed to float, swimming on his side while holding his sister with one hand. Fear and desperation were prominent on his face. Uncertain and exhausted, Tyler stopped fighting the waves. His only hope was to keep his sister alive and to bring back her consciousness soon. After fighting the storm for some more time, the waves took them to an area where the water was comparatively calm. Tyler turned to his sister. Ella was awake now and was swimming on her own. Her arms were now fighting for staying afloat.

Tyler was a bit relieved, but he stayed close to her.

With their heads above the water line, they stared up at the night sky lurking gloomily in front of them. The storm was coming down heavy on them with frequent lightning strikes and drizzling at that early hour in the morning.

"How are you feeling?" asked Tyler.

"I'm feeling better. I am alright." Ella replied in a moaning voice.

"This isn't too bad! We might be near a land." Tyler gasped and commented to keep up the spirit of her sister. He stared around. But in that drizzling early morning it was hard to see. They understood they were drifting away from each other.

"Come on! Hold my hand tightly!" Tyler screamed at his sister while stretching out his hand toward her.

But an enormous water current moved them apart. Lightning was flashing across the sky.

"Don't give up. We need to stay close." Tyler screamed at his sister who was now far away. He was swimming toward his sister and stayed with her.

A piece of wood from the broken ship was floating in the ocean. They rushed to get a grip of the log without delay. But the tiny piece of wood was not much help.

"Hope someone will appear soon to rescue us." Tyler's trembling voice echoed across the ocean.

"I pray we get some help from somewhere." wished Ella.

At a distance, Tyler saw a movement. Something dipped and floated again on the ocean surface.

"There is another log, let's go get it," Ella shouted. Tyler swam nearby. He moved toward the log.

Little by little, they moved closer pushing the current. They grabbed the wooden block submerged into the ocean. They could feel it was enormous.

As they were holding the wooden block, lightning flashed across the sky and flooded the ocean surface. In that glow, Tyler and Ella examined the picture of a half-submerged mahogany colored wooden frame. An ancient throne, a gold seat in the middle, was beaming with golden light in front of them under the water. The bright light coming out of the throne was so strong they had to close their eyes. The light sparked across the ocean and then made its way and absorbed into the bodies of Tyler and Ella. The wooden frame turned back into the same old chair.

Tyler and Ella dropped their jaws in awe. By then they took their hands off and were just floating beside the old chair.

"Must be from the ship, probably that large box they were boarding remember? Ella commented.

"A few minutes ago, the wooden block looked like an ancient throne. Now the block appears like an old chair! Don't get it!" Tyler announced.

"You got to be kidding," Ella pleaded.

"We are in the middle of the ocean with nothing to help us to get to the shore, and all that turns up is a wooden chair cum throne!" Tyler said.

"Who knows! But not too bad for us! At least better than nothing bro! Be thankful!" Ella said.

"The ship must be gone. Everyone must have died." Tyler remarked gloomily as he turned his eyes to a distance.

"Yah, but right now, all we have is this chair, so we might as well put this to good use," persisted Ella in a high-pitched voice while trying to stay afloat at the same time.

"Okay, but what should we use this amazing chair for?" argued Tyler while rolling his eyes.

"We can use the chair to stay afloat, and we'll use our hands to paddle our way through, so we don't have to be stuck here," assured Ella.

"Oh yes, that will work miracles," protested Tyler sarcastically. "I am tired now, we have been swimming for quite some time and we're so exhausted!" he said, trying to point out the obvious.

"Fine," said Ella. "I'll paddle through, okay? Now just grab the chair and stop arguing," gasped Ella with exasperation.

They grabbed the wooden frame with firm grip. But Ella was having difficulty to get a solid grip!

"Hold tightly! Don't let this go!" screamed Tyler.

"I'm!" Screamed Ella. She grabbed the handles of the chair with her hands.

Unexpectedly, they realized about a unique sensation for a moment once they touched the wooden piece this time. They let the wooden frame go. Then touched it once more. A spark of electricity went through them. Instantly they felt better. All their worries and anxieties were completely gone. Right then, a series of lightning struck the ocean. In that light, they glanced at their surroundings.

Tyler and Ella got the touch of the beauty of that stormy ocean for the first time. A blue light enveloped their surroundings that flooded the ocean and the ocean floor. The whole ocean area was as bright as day light. They could not believe how beautiful the ocean could be with all the tumultuous roaring waves, and category five storm lurking in the sky. Streams of silvery golden blue light were coming out of every part of that throne and were beaming out to the heaven. In that reflection, Tyler and Ella stared at each other. They were watching the real picture of a throne, a throne carefully carved on the mahogany board with a gold seat in the middle studded with diamonds. It had handles and legs decorated with sparkling jewels. Two golden snakes wrapped around the throne. Neither of them had realized, the throne belonged to Anishand Nalland, the great great grandfather of Anish the Great from the Rigororiyan Dynasty of ancient times. Ella and Tyler became a bit more conscious and felt better of their situation. With firm grips they decided to stay with the throne.

"Don't lose the grip. This is our only hope." Repeated Tyler.

Soon they realized the throne was not sinking with their weights but was moving. The partially submerged throne was moving fast. In fact, the throne was taking them further and further away from land deep into the ocean, that they did never realize.

Tyler moved little by little to see if he could get into a comfortable position into the throne.

"The throne seems enormous, Ella. I can't stay like this. My hands are losing grips. Let's see if we can sit on it. I don't think the throne is going to go down," Tyler commented.

"Are you out of your mind? We'll sink and die!" Ella said frantically.

"Come on, trust me on this." said Tyler convincingly.

"Fine, but we can't fit ourselves." explained Ella.

"What? "Asked Tyler.

"I mean—"

"I know what you mean," listened Tyler while thinking for a moment.

"Hmm . . . perhaps we can wish for it?" smiled Ella.

"What?" said Tyler.

"Wish for it—you know, it's a thing you do when you really want something," Ella persisted.

"I know what a wish is! But do you think the wish will work?" asked Tyler.

"It's worth a try," remarked Ella, shrugging her shoulders at the same time. "We always did this trick when we were in trouble. Remember?"

Chapter III

The Mysterious Throne

In the middle of the ocean in that stormy night while lightning streaked across the sky, Tyler and Ella closed their eyes. They grabbed the handle of the throne with one hand and did their prayer with a firm handshake with the other.

"Oh *Angel, help us if you could*
Help us Angel, you know you should!"

"Please make room for us to sit on you!" They uttered.

As they wished, the throne moved slowly, and they could feel the enormous seat popping up in the middle.

"Wow! It's massive!" said Tyler thoughtfully.

"I told you. Our tricks always work!" Ella exclaimed.

They had no time to think. First Ella climbed into top with Tyler's help. Then Tyler got himself positioned. They were happy to see the throne was not sinking with their weight.

"See!" Tyler reminded. "Nothing to worry about." He stared at his sister and noticed Ella's hands suddenly slipped and her head slammed on the side of the throne.

"Ella, Ella!" Tyler screamed. But there was no answer. Tyler got nervous.

"Oh my God! Please don't leave me. Wait. Stay with me! "Tyler screamed; panic was overtaking him. He thought his sister was dying. "Help me, God!" His fearful voice was being blown away by the heavy wind over the ocean. Tyler pulled his sister and checked if Ella was breathing. Ella was unconscious, but she was alive.

By then, the storm had receded a bit. Nevertheless, drizzling continued. Unexpectedly, at a distance, Tyler noticed a rescue ship. It was not very far off.

Without delay, Tyler jumped out of the throne. He began to swim. On his way he was pulling the throne with his other trembling hand. The ship's searchlights were reflecting everywhere. The lights fell upon them for a few times. But they went unnoticed. Nobody came to their rescue.

Tyler continued screaming, "Stop, stop, help us here! Save my sister, come, please come! Please!" He broke down into tears. His voice pattered in the murky ocean…it had no strength… tears were rolling down his defenseless face!

He managed to come close to the ship and looked up. People were on the deck chatting. As the search lights fell upon them, one of the crew members even noticed something in the water, he stared back over and shook his head. But the ship continued moving. Tyler tried but failed to grab the Jacob's ladder of the ship to stay with it. The ship slowly moved forward and disappeared in the distance leaving them behind in that dark stormy ocean.

Treacherous waves were crashing into each other and tossing the throne like a toy. Tyler was feeling light-headed, tired. He rolled into the seat, took his sister's hand, and fell asleep. He was unaware of the journey that he was now making into the land of mystery with his unconscious sister. In his mind, Tyler knew, the morning was imminent. He was optimistic his sister would endure this fateful night.

A little time passed. None of them knew, they had been split from his sister. The throne had made a replica of its own. Each was being carried separately side by side. A pair of hands came out and held them tightly to their seats. The thrones were drifting away swiftly deeper and deeper into the ocean to an unknown land.

The unfathomable, mysterious Eridanious Sea surrounded by mountains and forests from either side was still under darkness. The night was not over yet. The thrones were now moving through the ocean at enormous rapidity to take their passengers further and further away from the mainland. After some time, the thrones came to a remote corner of the ocean where the ocean met the forest. The thrones slowed down and came to a complete halt. Many pairs of hands gradually came out of the thrones and wrapped up Tyler and Ella.

Tyler woke up to a surprise to find his situation. But his sister was not there next to him.

When Tyler found out his sister was not there, he began to panic. His pale face was searching for Ella everywhere in the dark ocean. He did not know Ella was not too far from him and was being safely carried away in another throne as she was being soaked by enormous waves just like him.

Tyler tried to get off the throne but could not move. He wanted to make himself free. Tightly held in one position by many hands that came out of the throne to cover him, he started screaming.

"What's going on?" Tyler grumbled and stared around. The throne was now moving like a small boat.

Tyler was searching for a way to get to a land. The precipitation had stopped. In that early foggy morning, Tyler hardly realized his situation and just stared at the ocean and sat there speechless in fear and anxiety.

Suddenly, his throne began spinning rapidly. Tyler felt a massive pull downward as the spinning throne was going down fast.

A whirlpool circled around the throne and began to take the throne deep down. Tyler could not believe he was alive; he was going down and down as the light was getting thinner. The drag he felt was unbelievable. Tyler gave up. A velvet of darkness engulfed him. He managed to have some air left in his lungs and to keep his eyes open.

Tyler discovered the throne was being pulled alongside something. He touched it and felt a smooth surface like glass. As he went down, the throne and his body leaned touching the glass wall. He tried hard to push himself away but got more and more glued to the glass wall.

Tyler was almost out of breath as he felt his body wobble vigorously. He watched the throne had been shrinking while he was sitting inside it. Tyler was trembling in fear. He watched powerlessly as his body attached to the throne began to roll down like a ball glued together. Tyler was about to wriggle, and a noise came out of his mouth with some water.

"Am I in a dream, awake or having nightmares, or dead?" Tyler thought. At this point, his body and the throne were no bigger than a golf ball.

Before he could realize, he was pushed down by a huge pressure of water. The whirlpool of water forced him deeper and deeper into the ocean against a glass wall. Even at this stage, Tyler could think quickly and watch all happening around him. As lightning had been striking across the sky, he witnessed his glued body to the throne spinning at an enormous speed. Then the glued mass knocked the glass wall with a heavy force. A tiny hole was created on the wall. The throne and Tyler glued together passed through and landed on the floor of a dimly lit room. Tyler watched, the hole on the wall filled up immediately by itself and all water that passed through vaporized. The little throne came off his body automatically. The throne regained its original shape and size. The sparkling beauty of the enormous throne lit up the room for a few minutes as it stood there. Then the color began to fade, and the throne turned into an old ordinary chair. The chair stood up by itself like a machine, rolled back to one corner of the large room next to a table. A few more palatial chairs were visible. There was no trace of water. No one would ever imagine this chair was ever wet and was floating in the ocean minutes ago. All this happened within seconds in front of Tyler's eyes.

Tyler stared at the throne for several minutes helplessly and lost consciousness. As he was fainting, if he would have turned his head he could see, his sister was getting transported at the other corner of the same room. The replica of the throne attached to Ella's body, came off and regained its shape and size. Then it also transformed into a throne and stood there for a few minutes with all its beauty of sparks and jewels. Next the color faded, the throne turned into a palatial old chair. The old chair rolled back to the other grand chair that transported Tyler, merged with it to become only one majestic chair, and sat next to the table. It had no resemblance to a throne. Ella was completely unconscious and did not watch any of these.

Tyler and Ella were within the four walls of a half-lit room. Their wet, small, frigid bodies lay there for many hours. Neither of them knew they had been transported into a hidden old Kingdom of Rigororiyan Dynasty hiding under water to fulfill a thousand-year-old prophecy.

CHAPTER IV

The Golden Dome of Magic

The Osbourne family was not a native to Eridanious. Linda Osbourne and her husband Jay Osbourne had been living in Eridanious for quite some time. Known in the neighborhood as a happy family with a comfortable lifestyle, they still had something missing. They had no children.

Jay was a doctor in the local hospital. Linda was running her Yoga classes at home. Any extra time, they dedicated for aid organizations.

Linda, the mother of two adopted young kids, Tyler, and Ella, was a lady with lots of energy. A woman in her mid-thirties, Linda liked to invite people to her home and serve them with lots of food, snacks, and drinks. She never imposed her ideas on anyone and was eager to listen. With her open mind, an attractive, and stylish look, she was able to make an instantaneous positive impression on people. The story for adoption of two children, dates to their rescue mission when they visited Canopus some years ago. Linda and Jay went on a mission to a distant land named Canopus. There they found two lovely young kids Tyler and Ella. They decided to adopt them.

Now Tyler and Ella were away on their trip to Canopus. On such an evening in May, Linda and Jay had been sitting on their balcony looking out at the ocean spreading across the horizon.

The crimson color of the setting sun was sweeping away over the waves. A mystical sound of gentle breeze was swirling around their huge house facing the blue Eridanious sea.

"Do you still remember our experience that day Jay? How we came across Tyler and Ella? It was simply by chance…by God's grace. I thank God every day for this opportunity of having them." Linda said in a brisked voice with humble tone. Her eyes became watery. She poured some coffee for Jay in a cup and handed it over to him with some afternoon snacks. Then took a tissue to wipe her tears.

"Oh yes! It is such a sweet incident and still a vivid memory!" Jay answered.

'I could not forget how bad it was! It was just by chance. Really never thought we would go anywhere on that gloomy drizzling morning." Linda detailed.

"Um, indeed! We are so young then! We arrived in Canopus the day before. It was our first expedition with that international humanitarian aid-group. Our mission was clear. Save the people. Start vaccination, distribute food and water. Contain and clear out the disease." Jay reaffirmed.

"We had to work hard and earn their trust. But from the beginning, I was kind of sure. They desperately needed the medicines." Linda said tearfully.

"The contagious disease was spreading so fast. It killed many more people in just one month, more than the total number of people died in last ten years in that area. Without the help from our aid group and other organizations, I doubt they could ever survive that pandemic." Linda continued.

It was a dark time. A time of uncertainty. A time when every part of the society feels vulnerable. An unknown fever was rapidly spreading across that distant archipelagos Argo-Navis and its adjacent areas Canopus, and Berenices. The pandemic took its toll by claiming many people's lives. While many thousands had been dying every day, many more lost their jobs and livelihood.

The devastating picture was prominent across the country. It is during this time, Tyler and Ella lost their parents.

Linda and Jay were right. In those fateful days, the unknown virus was spreading rapidly. It claimed many thousands of lives across Argo-Navis and Canopus.

Once they arrived, it took a few days for Linda, Jay, and their aid-group to get to know the area, the people, and the community. The climate was not very welcoming. Strong winds with occasional rain were sweeping across the islands. The sun was rarely visible. On occasions, it came out only to quickly disappear again behind the clouds. No one could predict if or when the weather was going to get any better.

As the day began, Linda and Jay were out with their team. Distribution of aids started. It was a hard-hit area of Canopus. Food and medicine started flowing to families. Doctors and nurses were checking the sick, and the infected ones.

On such a gloomy morning, a stagecoach drawn by six white horses galloped by them down the road. It came to stop in front of a two-storied house at the cul-de-sac. Six people, three tall handsome well-dressed men and three exquisitely beautiful women came out of the carriage. All with partially covered faces and long saffron cloaks. Their bold appearance, stout and strong bodies had a bright golden glow. One, a bit older man was leading them. His deep eyes were sparkling behind the covered face. They were carrying two little kids, a girl, and a boy.

"Is Analyn there? Analyn Glory?" The leader asked from outside the house.

A middle-aged lady Analyn, deep wide eyes, high cheek bones, long black curly hair with a beautiful face rushed out of the house.

"Who is it? Yes, I am here. What can I do for you?" She had three other kids, one big boy named Borealis and two little girls Cosmos and Azalea following her. Her husband Isaac, black and white beard, short hair, a rounded face, and long nose came right behind her with a cigar in his mouth.

"Analyn, these are your sister's kids. Their parents died a week ago. Now they are sick. They might not survive if you don't do something or act fast. They can't make it without your help."

The big old man with long grey beard and long hair had a high pitch voice. But the man appeared happy, peaceful, and content. His hidden smile could tell that everything would be fine.

"What happened? Oh my god! Tyler and Ella! Poor babies!" the lady screamed in a loud blare while crying. She turned toward the people in the wagon and asked, "May I ask who you guys are? Or who told you to bring them here?" She picked up the girl named Ella in her arms and touched her forehead. "Dear god! You are running high fever!"

The kids appeared weak and frail. Her husband picked up the boy, touched his forehead and checked his pulse.

"He is very hot too. Looks very weak." Isaac said.

The kids were barely awake. With swollen red eyes, scrubby faces, dirty clothes, and muddy hair they looked very sick. They were too young to understand what had been going on. The boy Tyler was only four and the girl Ella was two years old.

The strangers stared at Analyn and her husband for a few minutes with a fixed look, then went back to their carriage. Except the chubby old man.

"May I come in?" The man asked.

"Sure! Please come in!"

The man stepped into the house, closed the door behind him and stood in the middle of the long hallway. He had a grave face.

Analyn ran after him and asked, "Thank you for saving them, bringing them here. But what's going on? And who are you guys and where did you come from?"

The man shook his head. He leaned over toward Analyn to offer her a piece of blue golden cloth neatly folded. The bright blue cloth with golden borders had a shining white star and a red chakra sitting on top of each other in the middle.

"What is this? Could you please tell me something?"

"Take it. Let me explain it to you."

Analyn stared at his eyes for a few moments. She was surprised. Yet, she humbly accepted the cloth. Unfolded and stretched it. At her touch, the cloth lit up. It sparked at the middle with ripples in beauty, but it had no end. Fourteen palaces of the Rigororiyan Dynasty were visible. All submerged under the ocean. Seven on one side belonged to the Shadow Kingdom and the Land of Nines. Each with a distinguished beautiful color. In the middle was appearing and disappearing a floating tower made of golden stone. It reached out to the heaven from the ocean floor. It had no end. On the other side were standing seven gloomy looking palaces all grey and black under the name of *Kingdom of Obsidian: The Seven Palaces of Fire.* Moving colorful fourteen different stones were lighting up the palaces. A force field was keeping the ocean water far high above the kingdoms or the palaces. Beneath the ocean water was visible two safely guarded kingdoms full of people that had everything from sky to forests, lakes, mountains, rivers, roads, gardens. Birds flying in the sky. Soldiers riding galloping horses. Wild animals running in the forests. A red golden glowing chakra was moving rapidly over these fourteen palaces. In a few seconds, the glow subsided, and the cloth turned back to a normal cloth.

The man explained, "It is the story of a Wizard Saint King Atheshand Nalland Rigororiyan. His two sons, Anish Nalland the Great and Rishaan Nalland and their kingdoms and the Rigororiyan Dynasty. A deep long story. Everyone is seeking the power of the Endless stone. Thousand years of legacy of curse, hatred, love, and cruelty. A Prince under spell of an indefinite sleep. All the fourteen stones are watching. Keep it. *'The Golden Purple Dome of Magic',* they call it. This has magical powers. It will protect the kids. It belongs to them. In time they will claim it. You will need it now. You do not know us yet, Analyn. You do not have to. Time will come and you will know." He continued.

"People call us as the 'Enigma of Six, the guardian angels of the universe." He took a long pause. His eyes were glowing with light.

"When lives are in danger, no one is important than those lives. You need to save these kids. Their lives are too valuable. They cannot protect themselves on their own. They are too young. Someday they will. That day will come. And they will protect many others. Until then, you need to take good care of them." He stopped. Everyone stared at the kids. The kids were sound asleep.

"Once the boy turns fourteen and the girl turns twelve... they will be completely invincible. Nobody could harm them anymore. But right now, someone is looking for them. He wants them dead. Watch out for a one-eyed man with a deep dark scar of the image of the Scorpion Devil King Sculptor on both his cheeks. He also got a tattoo of the Devil King on the forehead. Controlled by his master's will, he wants these kids dead. The dark expert in evil, who wants to control a dark land! With many of his spies. The one-eyed man, already here, is one of his spies.... somewhere... looking for these kids. He could be anywhere and could be everywhere.

"What do I do with this cloth?" Analyn enquired.

"This is not just an ordinary cloth Analyn. It is made of a forcefield. Place this cloth over the kids when you put them to sleep or want to protect them to make them invisible. You or your husband if you want him to, would be able to see through and break into the barrier to get to them. If needed, you could share this special power with someone you trust. Now close your eyes and stretch your hands." Analyn closed her eyes.

A bright spark of a yellow golden plasma started to form on the chubby man's palm. It traveled around her body and then finally settled on the chest of Analyn and then disappeared.

Analyn felt a pull for a few seconds and then she was fine. In those tiny moments she travelled through all her past. She found herself standing in front of a long passage that had no end. Then she noticed herself being born, her childhood, her sister, her friends. She met their loving parents, their neighbors, and their neighborhood. They were happily living with their parents. It was a great time, a beautiful land, under the rule of King Anish Nalland The Great. Then she noticed King's father, a Wizard Saint King. A tall man in saffron dress with a mystical voice and magical powers.

Then she came across his other son, Scorpion King Sculptor. Dark time, dark days. The dark Scorpion King Sculptor's soldiers came through their land and burnt down their houses. They raped the women and children and ravaged through their entire land.

Her time travel continued. She observed how she got separated at an early age from her sister as she was running to flee from the torture and massacre of those soldiers. One of her cousins pulled her out of the rubble and they had to run. The family she lived with went into hiding deep in the forest to elude the dark King and his soldiers. One night her parents sent a messenger who came on horseback to their cottage at night and she got reunited with her family.

It was a peaceful life for her for a few years. Then the dark night came. The dark soldiers from King Scorpion were back. They burnt down their whole village. She and her sister Andromella were picked up from the wreckage by one of the night guards. He was kind enough to throw them on the bank of a sandy river.

"Now go, run. Run if you wish to live. And never turn back." He whispered and disappeared in the darkness. The half-moon was burning in the western sky. Analyn stared at the eyes of the night guard. His face looked familiar. "But who was he?" She asked herself and repeated the same question to her sister again and again. To this day she remembers her name and asks the same question, 'who was he? The Messiah?'

"Now go, run, if you want to live. And never turn back." The voice whispered at her ears haunted her again and again. From a distance they watched their parents burnt alive as their house crumbled ablaze. They crawled to the river, found a boat. After rowing all night, they came to the nearest island Argo-Navis and crashed on the shore. Next morning one farmer discovered them alive. He took them to his home and introduced to his wife."

After learning everything, his wife said, "you can stay here. Our house is small but can accommodate two more. You might not have plenty, but enough to eat, and drink. In exchange, you are welcome to help us at home and in the fields."

Time passed. Slowly they grew up.

Her flash-back continued. Then they met two handsome guys and got engaged.

She watched her beautiful sister Andromella. She remembered all her hatred and fight with her sister. Remembered how she hated her for her exquisite beauty. Analyn was now being pulled into a dark tunnel…away from light and happiness… her beautiful days ended…. she got hooked into drugs in a cozy party. A reflection of her wasteful years. One such evening she was in a party and an argument broke out with her boyfriend Isaac. How close they came to killing themselves one night. It all started out in a bar. It was a sweet evening just like any other evening to start with. After a few drinks they felt happy and cheerful. But then Isaac fell for another girl and approached her for a dance. From the distance Analyn watched them in close. They were kissing and enjoying each other's company. Devastated Analyn could not take it.

On their way back, she did not utter a word. Once they got home, she started drinking, and so did Isaac. Soon things turned ugly, they started yelling and hitting each other while taking drugs. They started having nausea, vomiting and heavy itching. Soon their breathing slowed, they fell ill and became unconscious.

It was her sister Andromella who saved them. Yes, it was her. Her sister came by that night with her boyfriend Volanos just to say hello and to have a few drinks. Fortunately, the door was open. They discovered them senseless on the floor gasping for air and rushed them to the nearest hospital.

All vivid memories....then she watched her sister Andromella getting married to Volanos. Tyler, and Ella were born. The following year she tied her knot with Isaac and moved to Canopus.......................she had her own children....and moved on with her life.

Then the epidemic hit. People started dying everywhere.... the bright moon got darker. A dark age began. Analyn was now regaining her consciousness. She could feel a pair of dark eyes watching her. She could not see the face or could not say who it was. She screamed in fear and pain. Scared Analyn woke up sweating. She was breathing heavily.

"Wow! What a dream!" Shouted Analyn. She woke up still shivering. She felt sad and remorse. She noticed the chubby man's eyes were fixed upon her. Her husband Isaac was holding her.

"It is the dark force. The dark master that you just experienced is looking for them. You can't protect them for long. Just not possible for you here. We need to send them to a faraway land. To someone we can trust. A distant land where they can take refuge from the dark master and his evil forces." He stopped.

The old man turned, "a young lady and her husband will be here. With a distinct sign of a lamp on her chest you will recognize her that will only flash in your presence. Yes, once you see her, you will recognize. We will call her the lady with the glow. She and her husband. They are coming. They will ask you for adopting these kids. Allow them to adopt the kids. Do not refuse! Only they would be able to save the kids." The old man stopped with a smile.

Analyn and her husband were listening with their heads down. By the time they looked up, the old man had left. Analyn ran behind the carriage. She broke into tears, "tell me what to do...I am afraid. Tell me...tell me..."

"Protect them.....send them far and away...give away for

adoption that is the way…remember the lady with the glow … her husband by her side. Do not hesitate to hand them over… to their new parents…the kids will be safe. They are here for a purpose… to fulfill a prophecy…. give them away for adoption… remember the lady with the glow and her husband….save them…they will be safe …they will live…..” The charioteer had already signaled the horses. The last few sentences flew across in the air like an echo toward Analyn….. the galloping carriage disappeared in the horizon.

Jay and Linda noticed the carriage coming and leaving from a distance. They had no idea exactly what had been happening that morning.

Analyn glanced at Isaac's face. She felt the pulses of the kids, and asked him in a rugged voice, "take the kids and clean them. Give them a hot bath, would you please? I will get the meals ready. Borealis, Azalea and Cosmos, you all go and finish your showers. Would you?"

A dark brief smile showed up on Isaac's face. With a nod he took the kids in his arms. Borealis, Azalea and Cosmos followed their dad with a babble as he moved and took the stairs.

The night fell. A night of love, hope and happiness. A night of suspicion and hatred. A night of desire, loathe and despair. A night of darkness and anxiety. A night that can create and destroy.

As suspect and anxiety grew among people, they started talking. And they started to complain about the spread of the disease. And they started to be motivated to drive out the cause of the disease. Then the morning came. The morning that takes away grief. The morning that brings the light of desire to live again.

But that didn't matter. Because there was a cause. A cause to be upset. A cause to be angry. A cause to scream and scream and scream until you understand that it is of no use.

A crowd gathered in front of Analyn's house. And started shouting. They did not have any reason, yet they did. They had been blaming Analyn and his family for giving shelter to her sick niece and nephew. One man had a dark scar on his right cheek and had his right eye covered. He was limping and had a stick in his hand.

Analyn had a daring spirit. The spirit that made her complete. The courage that drives us to excel and conquer. The courage that brings us joy and happiness even during shadows and darkness. She knew how to control a crowd that knows little. A crowd that only looks for poking into the unfortunate moments of others.

She shouted back in a firm and clear voice, "if you knew every life is precious, then you won't scream. If you knew how it feels to stand in a moment that does not tell you what is in front of you, you won't scream. If you could remember your early days, when you are a baby, when you are a lump of flesh with only the desire for living, only waiting to be helped, you won't scream."

A few of her friends in the neighborhood came forward to support her cause.

Soon she managed to fend the crowd off. But her disturbed mind was unsure about the future of Tyler and Ella. She remembered the man she spotted in the crowd that had a scar and an evil smile. She recalled his dark look, vicious eyes, brown ugly face, and a few missing teeth.

She shivered at the thought of losing Tyler and Ella.

With deep wrinkles on her forehead Analyn had been thinking …. how long she could fight her neighbors, how long the kids would be safe in her custody. Upset human can take many twists and turns. "Give them away for adoption…remember the lady with the glow and her husband….save them…they will be safe …they will live…." She remembered the last words of the old man who brought Tyler and Ella to her house. Unexpectedly the old man's mysterious face flashed in her mind. Quickly she felt happy. She knew what to do. That night she went back to her hidden cabinet in her master bedroom and took out the cloth. She walked back to the room where Tyler and Ella were in

sound sleep. She took out and placed the *'Golden Dome of Magic'*
over the kids.

The *'Golden Dome of Magic'*, what a name! A name that will
captivate anyone. The golden red cloth started to float over the
kids. Immediately the whole house sparked with a blue light
originating from the heaven. It went on for a few seconds and
then subsided. The cloth unfolded on its own around the kids
in the shape of a tent. Then the cloth revealed the map of the
two kingdoms submerged deep beneath the ocean, yet fully
protected from any ocean water. Fourteen palaces were shining
in the background: seven in each side, each lit with a precious
stones sitting in a lake. Sky was shining with the midday sun.
People living their everyday life. Some walking on the roads,
living in their houses. Rivers, meadows, forests everything. A
floating red chakra was beaming with light on the top of a
Temple-Tower made of golden stone. It was named Temple-
Tower of Magellan. Two floating giant black cobras emerging
from the opposite sides of the Temple-Tower were holding the
chakra tightly with their open jaws. Very soon all the magical
images and glow subsided. The cloth became invisible and the
only scene visible was the sleepy faces of Tyler and Ella who were
in deep sleep.

Analyn whispered to her husband, "I don't think they got
any more fever. Look at them, see they appear much better now."

Isaac nodded his head and came forward. He was present
there all along and was stunned to watch such a thing. He tried
to understand what was going on. He extended his hand to
touch the cloth to get a feel.

"No!" Analyn pulled him away quickly, but by then his right
hand faintly came very close to the cloth.

A sudden electric shock almost knocked him out and
cauterized his hand. He was going to scream. Analyn came
running, took his hands and prayed as she whispered something
into his ears. In minutes, Isaac felt better, his wound had healed.
Then Analyn leaned forward and moved the invisible cloth

with her hands to check if Tyler and Ella had any fever. She felt comfortable to know their body temperatures were getting normal. In the next room her three children were in sound sleep.

In a happy mood, Analyn went to bed with her husband.

Early next morning, Analyn took out the cloth, folded it and kept it back in her hiding place. She went down and opened the front door. She found a hole next to the doorknob as if something had chewed up the doorknob. A heap of dead spiders was lying in front of her door.

Two little girls were playing on the street. One of them turned and said to Analyn, "dead spiders are everywhere, not just here. They came to every house. That black line is the line of dead spiders. We went up the hills and saw it went all the way up the hills to the top of the mountain!"

The girls ran back to their house to play with other kids.

Analyn was stunned. She just smiled at the girl and said, "thank you!" She came inside and checked every corner if there were any dead or alive spiders hanging around in her house.

"What are you doing?" Isaac asked out of impatience.

"Nothing to worry." Analyn just kissed him and smiled. She felt safe in his arms.

The next day was uneventful. The weather improved. The sun was shining. Analyn and Isaac were relieved not to see any unwelcome guests moving around the neighborhood. They felt better and better as no one was coming to take away the kids either.

That evening after the dinner Analyn was chatting with Isaac. The kids already went to bed. Tyler and Ella got little better and were sleeping comfortably under the protection of the magical cloth.

"I can never let them go. They are mine. My blood. My own sister's kids." Analyn was saying.

"I agree. Why should we? With that magical cloth around, they are fully protected. Nothing can ever happen to them. I mean nothing." Isaac firmly said. "Those people must be some sort of whiz."

He had a suspenseful smile on his face.

"Maybe we can have that cloth for our own protection too. No one can ever touch us. Don't you see? I'm sure those scumbags stole the cloth from somewhere. They just lied to you." He snarled.

"No, I don't think so." Those people, whoever they are, didn't lie. I know it all. My past. All of it. This cloth is a magical cloth with magical powers. And it is not a stolen cloth either."

"Well then. What are you going to do?" Just give your kids away for nothing. They are treasure. We can get rich if we can hold on to them. Don't you think? We can even sell them to the dark master!!" Isaac whispered at her ears.

"Would you stop? I am not thinking that. I just can't let them go. I love them too much already. They remind me of my parents, my sister…everything." Their conversation continued for some time. The night got deeper and darker. Shortly fell asleep.

In the distant mountain, the night started differently. A black jelly like substance started oozing out of the mouth of the mountain. The jelly flew down to Analyn's doorstep. Many deadly looking huge spiders started erupting from the black jelly. Through the small hole, the jelly seeped into the house. A one-eyed man emerged from the jelly and so did many ugly looking spiders. The spiders moved across the house in different directions. The one-eyed man had deep dark scar of the devil Scorpion King Sculptor imprinted on his cheeks and a tattoo of the devil master on the forehead.

With a knife flashing in his hands, the one-eyed man first unlocked the front gate in silence. Then he sneaked into each bedroom one by one searching for the kids: Tyler and Ella. Finally, he came in front of the dimly lit room partly closed. He pushed the door and slowly moved in. His eyes were glowing in rage and anger.

"And there they are!" His creepy smile brought out all his hatred, anger, and rage.

"Take them and bring them to me, but don't you ever hurt them. I need them alive." He heard a creepy voice coming out of a dark dancing glowing face over the knife he was carrying. It was dark master talking to him. The image disappeared.

He took his knife and moved forward. He did not see any barricade. The kids were clearly visible.

In one slice, he wanted to finish them. But he resisted and kept his knife away in the holder. He paced forward. He was in-front of the kids directly looking at their innocent faces.

He took out his hold-all and kept it on the floor. Leaning against the bed he decided to slowly pick up the kids one by one without disturbing their sleep or making much of a noise. With a glowing red face, he moved to pick them up.

But the moment his hands touched the invisible cloth, an electric shock made him paralyzed. His body was caught in fire. The one-eyed man screamed in fear and jumped from one room to another before he could find his way out to come down the stairs and running out of the house. The kids in the next room all woke up and so did Analyn and Isaac. But by then the man was gone. A body in fire was sprinting to the top of the mountain as his scream could be heard from miles. A stream of deadly spiders was following him covering his hands, face, and body, burning alive and dropping dead as the man was running for his life. Most of the neighborhood woke up and came to the streets to watch the scene.

Analyn gazed up to the dark sky. A cloud was covering the half moon. A gentle breeze was blowing. A blue-gold macaw flew by the house and sat on the tree. It was holding a large dead spider in its beak. She nodded her head and appeared disturbed. She was not aware someone was watching over the kids. Soon she walked back into the house.

Suddenly the gentle breeze died out, and a wind started to gain strength on the hilltop across her house. Analyn stopped and glanced to the mountain. The wind gained more strength, it turned almost into a twister, moving down the hills and came all the way up to her door front. It stopped there for a few seconds, sucked out all the deadly venomous spiders hovering in deep dark corners of her house, then turned back toward the ocean and took all the spiders with it.

No one noticed, far on the top of the hill, the one-eyed limping man was trying to escape to get to a boat anchored on the river. As his charring body was slowly giving up and the half moon was rising over the top of the hill, he was losing his strength, his body was becoming weaker and weaker. A giant spider was sucking out all the blood out of his body. It was about to take him down. In a few minutes it consumed the entire body of the one-eyed man. But the spider could not move much further after its meal. In that cold night under the dimly moon light, the massive spider fell dead on the ground. Soon, the spider was consumed up by bullet ants.

Little Tyler and Ella heard nothing. They slept blissfully inside their magical cloth all through the night undisturbed.

CHAPTER V

New life in Eridenious

The next day was uneventful. The weather improved. The sun was up but sometime hiding behind the clouds. With drizzling, it was windy and chilly. Tyler and Ella's condition further deteriorated.

Linda and Jay were back in the area and heard the shocking news of a spider attack on some houses. The news alarmed them.

One morning, they decided to visit the area. As they came out of their car and approached the neighborhood, a group of kids ran after them, as if they were expecting them.

"It's them." A girl whispered at her friend.

"Which one?" The boy reacted.

"They are doctors. My mom talked to them the other day in Berenices. They also went to Canopus., she told me." The girl said with a confirming tone.

Jay and Linda joined their team and dispersed around the neighborhood bringing stockpiles of PPEs, food, water, and medicine door to door.

Linda and Jay were checking on people's health and safety. Finally, they went inside to check on the old man living in a house just opposite to Analyn's home.

"Our cousins are running high fever again." Borealis complained who was following them all along.

"We'll be there soon honey. Give us a minute." Linda said. Jay took the temperature of the old man. After administering an injection and providing the instructions to his assistant with all the details they moved to the next house.

Tyler and Ella were coughing again, sick and feeble. Sleeping over a bed under a dirty bedspread they appeared helpless and vulnerable. Analyn and Isaac were sitting next to the kids. Not far from them were sitting a group of people on a shaded patio outside in that gloomy morning. They were having an argument. None of them paid much attention to the kids in the house.

"Mom, mom, the doctors are coming." Borealis came down running to report to Analyn.

Analyn stood up. Isaac turned toward the road.

Cosmos came running behind them. "Mom, Tyler got high fever. We need to take him to a doctor. Mom!" She and her sister Azalea were crying as they were following Borealis everywhere.

"Yes, I am getting worried too honey! Please calm down."

Analyn sat down again next to Tyler and Ella, felt their temperature, hugged, and kissed their cheeks. She offered them some milk. The kids were little awake now and took a sip one by one.

"You two need some medicine. Doctor will be here any minute. Try to stay awake." She said thoughtfully and started to pat their back.

"Now Azalea, Cosmos and Borealis, you guys please try not to disturb them. Go and play with your friends, would you? They need rest!" Analyn finished her sentence as she gave a serious look at Azalea, Cosmos and Borealis with some anticipation. A look that made them cautious and vigilant at the same time.

"Who are they mom?" Azalea asked, she was now pointing at the people getting down from the truck to distribute aids.

"They are here to help us. They want to save us from famine

and disease. Don't disturb them. Let them do their work. We all need their help." Analyn explained in a lucid voice while looking at the distribution. She exchanged looks with Isaac.

"They are here to eradicate the disease. People are dying helplessly. Nobody knows who the next victim would be!" Isaac commented in a grave voice. He stared at the kids and reminded them: "Stay out of trouble. Would you?"

Borealis, Azalea and Cosmos nodded their heads and ran away.

"Go and play with your friends. But don't go too far!" The mom screamed behind them. The mother repeated with anxiety before turning to Tyler and Ella.

"I'm getting worried about them." She spoke with a concern on her face. A face that had both the beauty of a mother and the pain and suffering of a loving aunt.

"We need to ask them if they got any doctor." Isaac replied.

Borealis ran away with his friends to another adjacent hilly area. The little girl Azalea ran in another direction with her sister Cosmos, but soon Azalea came back to the house.

"I want to be with Tyler and Ella." She said.

"Me too." Cosmos was standing behind her.

They sat down next to her mom.

"Ok, you can stay here. We will go to get some medicines." Analyn and her husband moved out. After discussing with their friends, she and Isaac approached Linda and Jay who were now moving to visit the next house on the opposite side of the street.

"Would you mind checking our two kids who are very sick?" Isaac approached.

"Our kids got high fever and don't look that good. Please come and give them some medication. They are weak, sick, and cranky." Analyn said.

"We don't know what to do. They are not eating anything… got bad cough. It is almost five days now." Analyn was worried. Her explanation in tearful eyes only made it more obvious how much she needed their help. She was talking while looking at the lighted pins that were shining on their chests. The heart-shaped red fiery emblems had a golden star in the background and a sitting white horse with spread out wings flying over a vast blue ocean. It was the official pin used by Linda and Jay. They created it themselves and the aid group decided to adopt it. Even in that stage, she had a faint smile attached to her face once her eyes caught the attention of the emblem.

"Sure, we will be right there.... Let me grab a few medicines and some essential things." Comforted Jay who was listening to their stories very calmly all along. "Please go and stay with the kids. We'll be there in a minute."

Jay became concerned and immediately instructed Linda and her associate to grab a few things from the truck. They rushed toward the house where Tyler and Ella had been asleep. A big crowd followed them.

Jay looked at the house. A dome shaped house made of brick. A few paintings were hanging from the walls. A nearby kitchen had a kettle and some pans on the oven. The mostly empty pantry filled with a few breads and drinks was visible. The signature of poverty was apparent everywhere.

Jay and Linda sat down on the chair next to the kids. Linda took Tyler and Ella's temperature. She showed the readings to Jay.

"He is running very high fever." remarked Jay. "She too!"

"It's pretty high!" Linda stared at Analyn and Isaac.

"Not sure if they are going to make it!" Analyn appeared devastated as she stretched her hands at Isaac. She was shaking her head and became nervous. Isaac took her in his arms and made her sit on a chair next to them as she started to weep.

Moments later, she turned toward Jay and Linda, "I just got them a few days ago. I beg you, please save them. The poor babies lost their parents. Give them the much-needed medicine. They are my sister's kids! Please treat them as your own. PLEASE!!!!"

"We will do everything we can. We think we can save them.

Be patient. Let's bring down their fever. Please arrange for some heated water, we need to give them a lukewarm bath." Jay said.

In the meantime, Tyler and Ella were waking up. They appeared weak.

"How are you feeling? You guys must be hungry?" Linda asked with a sweet smile on her face.

"Tyler stared at her but didn't say anything.

"Ella replied in a prattle.

Analyn ran toward the kitchen. A few of her friends were there. By then they have started heating up some water.

Analyn and two more ladies came over to help the kids getting a lukewarm bath, changing their clothes, and to change the bed spread.

Linda retook their temperature. She nodded her head while sharing the information that the fever went down. The kids started moving again, looked better.

Azalea ran toward the kitchen. She returned with a basket full of bread. She offered them the breads. With help from their aunt, Tyler and Ella sat up for eating the bread.

"It is better to take this medicine with some food, instead of having in an empty stomach." explained Jay.

Jay gave them some medicine with the milk.

"The fever should come down in a few minutes. But the temperature needs to be watched throughout the night. We will check on the few other patients and be back again." Finished Jay.

After spending some more time with the kids, he and Linda walked out of the house and went to see the next patient. Isaac and Analyn stayed with the kids. Rest of the crowd walked back to their group and rejoined their debates.

The adults were busy in their own conversations. Some were watching the distribution of aids. Kids were having fun, chasing each other, falling, and screaming. Their parents came to their rescue when needed.

"I love these two kids. Wish they are mine." Remarked Linda.

They just finished with another patient and were on their way to Analyn's house.

"It would be nice to have them as our own. They are beautiful," noted Jay. "It would be wonderful if we could adopt them. They are so innocent, so little and fragile…. let's hope they get better soon….." Jay paused.

"I'm going to ask them if we could adopt them. We can at least ask them Jay! You never know." Linda whispered to Jay's ears for his approval while looking around.

"Not now. It is too early to discuss that. Please wait. Let's take care of the kids first, so that we don't lose them. It is a bad virus. We need to do everything. Can't take any chances." Jay remarked.

They walked back to the house at a slow pace. Linda noticed Analyn and her husband were sitting in the chairs while talking to Tyler and Ella.

"May we check them again?" Asked Jay.

"Of course! Please do whatever you need to. That's why you guys are here, right? Why ask? Just do it. Fine!" Isaac laughed with a cough.

Jay and Linda stared at Isaac and Analyn, nodded their heads and stood there in silence.

"Please do what you think is the best for our kids." Analyn repeated.

Jay nodded his head. He was looking at Linda, "yes, they got bad infection. But soon they will feel better, their fever should come down."

"It is more than an hour. We need to check their temperature now." Linda remarked.

Jay went back to the seat near Tyler and Ella while Linda took their temperature. Analyn and Isaac followed.

Jay checked the kids one by one. He gave them some more medication.

"All I am trying to do is to bring their fever down." He remarked. "Now they look better. Soon they will be okay."

Linda gave each a bottle of juice to drink and stayed with the kids while Jay went up to Analyn and Isaac.

"You guys are marvelous people!" Jay continued. "Really sorry to see you all suffering so much. But we still need to know a few more details. It is necessary for our database. We must register the details of the family history and background of these two kids. If you could please tell us where they came from, who their parents were, and how they got here that would be a big help."

After a few more minutes, Linda and Jay left the house with many more information about Tyler and Ella in a happy mood. Tyler and Ella's condition improved. The fever went down.

Linda reminded Analyn and Isaac again for taking the temperature throughout the night. She also asked them to get to the nearby camp if there was any urgency. Their aid organization had already set up a few huge camps in the area.

Jay and Linda checked on Tyler and Ella regularly every morning. A few more days passed. Jay and Linda started their round at the usual time. After finishing with some emergency patients, they came over to Analyn's house.

"How are the kids?" Linda asked.

"They are getting better. We think they will be fine. No fever and they are eating and sleeping well."

Excellent news!" Said Jay. "May we?"

"Sure, please come in." Analyn replied politely.

Linda approached the kids. Took their temperature and noted down on her chart.

Jay checked the kids, took their pulse readings, and glanced at the chart. "No temperature at all. They look excellent. Soon they will be alright."

Borealis, Azalea and Cosmos all brought in some more bread, and juice. Tyler and Ella were hungry. They were awake and ate some. Soon they fell asleep.

Linda and Jay came out of the house.

"I'm not sure how to thank you. You saved our kids." Analyn said cheerfully. Isaac was also smiling.

Not far from there, some kids had been chasing each other over the ownership of a statue. One little girl named Sia found the statue in the Red Eye Bay while watching and chasing fish. The red colored water of the bay was the reason behind such a name. Nobody knew how deep the bay was, but many old artifacts showed up on its shore. People thought Red Eye Bay can even hear. It can see their past, their present, and the future. If one prayed hard enough, especially on New Year's Eve, the dream could be fulfilled.

Sia brought her new discovery to share with her friends and to get some credit explaining where and how she found it.

While she had been describing her piece, another boy Corvus immediately demanded the statue as his own and a fight broke out. Corvus, abruptly snatched the statue and started to run. Sia started crying. All the kids chased after Corvus to stop him.

The little statue was of a saddled man on a galloping horse. It was made of beautiful black metal. The black galloping horse appeared real with wings spread out. The horseman wrapped in a black cloak had his head covered with a red striped hat.

While this had been happening, Linda, Jay, Analyn and Isaac all paced toward another part near the ocean not very far from the crowd.

"I'm sorry to ask you this question. We are looking for adopting kids." Linda paused and breathed heavily. "We don't have any of our own. Please forgive us, but do you guys wish to keep and raise these kids Tyler and Ella?" Linda asked.

Analyn was not looking at her. Her eyes were stuck on the emblem that Linda was wearing. Then she turned with an impolite look with a question in her face.

"I'm sorry, but we really like them." Jay said with conviction. Linda had tears in her eyes, she took a pause and nodded.

Isaac didn't answer. He turned at them with a stern facial expression and a sad absolute blank face. At a slow pace Analyn walked to the bench, sat, and broke down. She began to weep. Isaac took her into his arms before she completely lost her control.

In a few minutes, Analyn stopped and began to say something while pointing at the kids. Isaac sat down next to her, kept his arm around her while consoling her.

"You already know. I have nothing to say. They are orphans. Their parents died in an unknown fever. Not even a week ago. Argo-Navis got completely devastated by the pandemic. The people from Argo-Navis brought them here." Analyn paused with exasperation. Her sobbing was prominent.

A local man named Pinwheel, in his late sixties, with wrinkled forehead, and a roughly look was watching them from a distance. He made his way through the crowd. He came forward from the babble. No one noticed him and were even unaware he was there. He was sitting quietly in the crowd.

"What do you want, how dare you bring tears to our dear Analyn's eyes?" The old man asked, with his face straight up and a rough look at Jay and Linda. He was sick but was still capable of taking control of the situation.

"Pinwheel, we are talking. Please excuse us!" Clearly upset Analyn took the old man aside and whispered something at his ears. She then signaled and requested him to keep quiet.

"We are here to distribute medication and aids. Medicines save lives." Linda exasperated.

The old man glanced at Linda and James in disbelief. But gradually he moved away toward the house and walked to the bedside of Tyler and Ella.

You don't have to take a decision now. Take your time to think if you would like us to adopt them." Jay said with a sharp glance.

Analyn gave them a silent look. She didn't say anything. She glanced at the emblem Linda and Jay were wearing. Isaac glanced at Jay, his dress, and his lighted emblem. For a few moments he was silent. He pondered and then said, "Wait here. We'll be right back."

Isaac gave some instructions to Pinwheel and another woman nearby to prepare lunch for everyone and watch Tyler and Ella. He and Analyn came out of the house.

"Please follow us." Isaac said to Jay and Linda.

They started walking back to another empty house sitting at their backyard at a distance.

Jay and Linda exchanged looks. They followed Isaac and Analyn at a slow pace. Isaac and Analyn walked past another crowd standing nearby. The people stared at them with suspicious looks. They had strange outfits, with their bodies fully covered in black cloaks. On their forehead was visible the tattoo of a black serpent.

They passed across the meadows, went through a tiny passage, crossed another field full of bushes and trees to get to the house.

Isaac pushed the door. The door opened. A shaking and a streaking sound came out. They went inside and sat down on two chairs across an old table. Few old chairs were scattered across the room.

While all these had been happening, the boy Corvus, who grabbed the statue from the little girl could not run any further. He got surrounded by everyone. When he found there was no escape, he threw the statue high into the air with full force toward a nearby lake. Suddenly they realized two wings were coming out of the small statue. It started to flip its wings. The statue flew higher and higher. It crisscrossed the sky a few times, went high above into the clouds and came rolling down. It continued the descent to the hilly area, flew overhead and approached the house where Tyler and Ella were asleep. It flipped its wings, made its way inside the house through the opening of the front door. The flying statue circled around a few times across the rooms and dropped on the bedside where Ella and Tyler were asleep. The noise woke up Tyler and Ella.

Pinwheel and the other lady were busy in the kitchen. They were unaware of any of this.

The boys and girls were screaming while coming down the hills, following the flying statue and came in front of the house.

Tyler and Ella were looking at the small statue. Tyler stretched his hand to grab the statue. Unexpectedly the statue came to life. The horseman took out the cap and saluted Ella and Tyler. In a human voice he said, "Oh, Chosen Ones. Glad to see you again. It has been a long time. How many years? The horseman scratched his head. "I don't remember. But please do not hurt me. I am your friend, not an enemy. You remember. Bernard. My name is Barnard. The guy with magical powers. I can start a fire, make people disappear or create illusion. Please save me from these kids. Give me shelter, protect me, save me. I am a fighter. I fought with you side by side, for the Prince Anish. In the forbidden kingdom. The Shadow Kingdom and The Land of Nines. I will always protect you and our Prince. Now if you touch my head and use your power to absorb me into your shadow. You need me, call out my name "Bernard", three times. I'm Bernard. I will be there for you. Now please touch my head."

Ella and Tyler were too young and didn't understand what was going on. Neither did they realize or know what to say. They sat up on their bed and simply stared at the small horseman statue saddled on horseback in surprise.

"Please! They are coming." The little horseman insisted. "Can't you recognize me? You two are the chosen ones! Remember? I am your friend Barnard. Don't you remember me? I know, you are too young to understand." He jerked his head a few times in anger! "I am safe with you. Please touch my head and save my life! Please!"

Ella and Tyler were awestruck for a few moments. They did not realize what to do. Tyler glanced at his sister and then softly touched the head of the little statue. Ella followed. Right in front of their eyes, the saddled horseman turned into a puff of white smoke. From the smoke a human face came out and a voice rolled out softly: "I'm Bernard. I know, you two are young and might not remember. But I will give you this gift. As you grow up, there will be many things that you will forget. But you will remember this. You will remember and you will remember everything of this day. Remember! You two are the chosen ones! Call out my name three times when you need me. And now you will handle this situation by saying what I want you to say." The smoke came rolling down to Tyler and Ella and then disappeared in their bodies.

The kids ran down the hill screaming and soon arrived in the house.

"Where is it?" The big boy Corvus enquired angrily looking at Tyler and Ella.

Tyler and Ella stared at them. Then they gazed at their body. A rolling smoke came out to their ears: "We don't know. We were asleep. We just woke up hearing a noise." Tyler jabbered.

"Give it back!" alleged the boy! As he approached Tyler and Ella. He grabbed his shirt and started pulling.

"You hid it." Screamed another girl.

"Search them! Search everywhere" another boy screamed.

"Give it back! Give it back!" A few others screamed again.

The older kid shouted in anger, "check under the bed. All their pockets." He removed the bedspread and the comforter out of their bed and searched under their pillows. The other kids were looking everywhere in the house. Some rolled under the bed. But they could find nothing.

"What are you guys doing here? They are sick. Leave them alone." Pinwheel came and shouted at the kids.

The kids left unhappy.

Without understanding much what was going on, Tyler and Ella went back to sleep.

In the meantime, Linda and Jay reached in front of the other house. They knocked and pushed the door. The door was open.

"Excuse us, may we come in please?" Jay politely asked.

Isaac replied in a rough voice, "Yeah, sure come in. It's open!"

Linda and Jay hesitated a bit and then walked into the house. They stood across the table from Analyn and Isaac.

The huge two-story house was full of strange items. They were in the living room by the kitchen. Another door connected the area through a hallway to the rest of the house. A few weapons: daggers, axes, rifles, spades, and swords were hanging from the walls across them. A large picture of a hunter was on display from the wall.

"That's my father." Said Isaac. "The man with the moon. He went out with two of his close friends in each full moon for deer hunting. He did that for thirty years, and never had any problem. Then last year, he went out with his friends and did not return. Next day, the three horses came back with their corpses. All had been hunted down by black spiders of the Scorpion King Sculptor, the Dark King. Parts of their body was missing." Isaac stopped.

"I know, it is a sad story. Just wanted to share with you." Isaac stood up and went outside to suppress his tears.

At the kitchen, a kettle was hissing on the stove. Another woman was visible. She was getting some hot drinks ready. The kitchen cabinets had eggs, breadbaskets, fruit baskets, wines, some pans, and dishes. The few pale discolored armchairs and the huge mahogany wooden table were telling the fading story of a family once rich and famous.

Jay and Linda were waiting to be seated.

Isaac came back from the kitchen, looked at them, and said jaggedly, "please take a seat."

Analyn began in a docile tone.

"We know why you are here, with the aid group, distributing necessary items, food, medicine, clothes, PPEs …everything that we need badly. You are trying to eradicate the disease and famine that is sweeping across this land. We trust you and thank you from our heart." Analyn detailed with a somber smile. A smile that still had pain in it, a smile that carried the look of a mother worried of losing her children, a smile that only she knew how to paint.

"We know why you guys are here!" Isaac said with bitterness. He had tears in his eyes. To withhold his tears, he stood up again and went to the other side of the room. He stood beside the window and gazed outside to the huge ocean across the meadows.

"Our organization can adopt any children that have nowhere to go."

"Thank you!" Analyn's white teeth with a cute smile was visible. She didn't even try to hide her tears this time. "But we prefer individual people, rather than any organization."

"We are just curious," Linda continued, "if you guys have any plans for kids let us know. We are not here to take them away from you or anything. We are here to only help if you need it. Yes, it is true, we do not have any children of our own. But still….." Linda humbly finished.

"Of course, we got plans for Tyler and Ella." Isaac erupted with a thunder from the other side of the room as he was walking back.

"After their recent loss of parents, the people from Argo-Navis brought them here and quickly shuffled out of the door. We have been taking care of them since. But why? Why do ask all these?" It was clear that Isaac was not willing in letting the kids go anywhere.

Analyn was quiet. Tears were pouring down her eyes. She tried to withhold her tears, "I love them as much as you do Isaac, if not more! They are my own sister's kids. But it is all about their safety and wellbeing…." She finished her sentence with a concern.

"They are completely safe here, what are you talking about?" Isaac questioned.

"We don't know that! We don't even know if we have enough for ourselves Isaac! Can't you see?"

Linda and Jay listened quietly. They just stood there with desperation and love although they were not expecting such comments.

Linda came forward. "We are here to help. No worries. Sorry if we hurt your feelings." She glanced at Isaac and counselled.

Isaac was quiet. With a vacuum look he was watching the crowd. It was hard to guess what had been going through his mind. But he had a vivid expression of dissatisfaction. He took out a cigar and lit it.

Analyn was sitting silently. She was deliberating in her mind if these people were trustworthy.

Finally, Analyn stood up with a hesitation painted on her face.

She was staring repeatedly at Linda. In fact, she was looking at the lighted emblem attached to her chest.

Then Analyn commented, 'nice badge!"

Linda and Jay gazed at each other.

Linda smiled, "yes, these are our official emblems: called 'DREAM FROM THE STARS'." She took out the lighted badge and kept it on the table. Then she began to explain, "the light depicts the hope and service that we bring to people. The redness indicates our service to the disaster areas. The ocean indicates the fluid nature of human lives. The wave tells the wavy nature of human minds. The lamp that is lit at the center depicts the lamp of love that we all have in our heart for the humanity. The star that beholds the lamp in the middle indicates we can prevail, and the horse with wings specify that we can reach for the stars when we have wind under our wings."

"I love it! Awesome!" smiled Analyn. "May I touch it?" Her hesitation was obvious.

"Sure, I can offer you one. Linda took out one lighted badge from her bag and gave it to Analyn.

Happy Analyn took it in her hands. It lit up immediately. She could see the white horse was flapping its wings over a ocean under a starlit sky. She was filled with joy. Her face lit up in beauty.

At a slow pace, she walked toward Isaac. Isaac was quietly thinking. He was looking across the distant mountains. Analyn stood beside him and showed the badge. A smile lit up his face. Analyn noticed, Isaac was still not convinced.

There was a brief silence, they had been chatting in a low voice.

Linda came close to Jay and whispered "Maybe we should leave. They went through a lot. It is getting too much for them to bear." Their discussion continued.

Linda turned back at Analyn and Isaac. As she was going to say something Isaac and Analyn walked back to the table.

"We understand how difficult it is. Disease, famine, scarcity of food, water.!" Jay intervened. He was getting the impression that it might not be that easy to get the children's custody.

"We will be kind to them just like you are! And our organization have helped many foster parents on their adoption. But after all it is your decision." Linda stated.

Then there was a brief silence.

"They will have good food, good education, and a home." Linda took the silence as a "yes" and continued her monologue. "We are ready to do anything and everything to save your family and eradicate all the disease from this area." She continued, "We will make sure you all are safe!"

Jay had to pat Linda to bring her back to her senses. He knew how much Linda wanted kids of her own, and why she was becoming emotional.

Isaac nodded his head but didn't say a word or showed no expression. Finally, he and Analyn took their seats.

The last few sentences of the old man who brought the kids in the carriage was echoing in Analyn's ears..…. 'Protect them..…. send them far and away…give away for adoption ……that is the way…remember the lady with the glow … her husband by her side. …the kids will be safe. They are here for a purpose... to fulfill a prophecy.... save them ..... they will be safe ...they will live......'

"Take them with you as your own. But please bring them here once or twice a year." Analyn took the hands of Linda and started to kiss. and cry. "Please forgive me for being emotional, it is hard for me!" Tears were pouring out of her eyes.

"I don't want to let them go. But I want them to live. Their lives are at danger. Maybe they will be safe with you."

Linda was getting emotional, she took Analyn's hands, "we will make sure they are fully protected. They will be comfortable and have a home."

"And of course, we will try to visit you once or twice a year." Jay persisted.

"At least, twice." Linda looked at Isaac and Analyn straight in their eyes and repeated, "twice."

Analyn took a glimpse at Isaac, for an answer or a comment. But Isaac stood still with a stern look on his face and no expression.

"We will be back next week. Hopefully, the kids will get much better by then. We will finish up the process and take their custody." Jay reminded. He understood it would be risky to move the kids at their current situation.

Isaac stared at Analyn with a harsh expression. He gave a concerned look at Linda and Jay. Upset Isaac walked out of the house in a hurry to hold back his tears. He was getting emotional again.

Linda and Jay picked up their bags and went back to their trucks. Analyn rushed toward Isaac to calm him down. She grabbed Isaac's hand and turned back to the house where Tyler and Ella were still asleep. Then they heard something.

A huge crowd gathered in front of another house. An old lady with lots of pain was groaning at the porch. A large scab on her right leg was noticeable. A few flies were buzzing around her wound barely covered with a soiled linen. Her hands were in constant move to drive them out! The red and yellow scab had fresh blood oozing out and was making her dress red and wet. The situation was too difficult to even look at. With her every move, she made it worse as she pushed her leg around to get away from the flies. Everyone noticed her situation, but no one was willing to come forward to help her.

"We need to do something!" Analyn shouted. They approached the lady to investigate. She turned at Isaac and screamed, "don't just stand there! Please go! Rush and get that doctor over here now!"

Jay and Linda had returned to the truck and were leaving. After hearing Isaac's story, they hurried back to the crowd.

"This can lead to the amputation of her whole leg." Linda leaned over and commented at Jay in a low voice.

Jay sat down next to the old lady, took her hands, and checked her pulse. He checked her eyes and said softly, "Maybe not. Please don't jump into conclusion so quickly. She will be fine!"

It was hard to know if the old lady had heard him. With her eyes closed, she was dozing. Waking up in between her naps, she was moving her hands and legs to get away from flies.

Jay observed the scab for some time and explained, "it is not as bad as it looks."

With a few taps, he woke her up and asked, "What's your name?" I'm a doctor. I'll take care of your wound. No worries." He had a reinforcing smile on his face.

The old lady gazed at him with a blank look and disbelief.

Jay repeated, "I'm Jay, a doctor. Do you hear me? I'm a doctor. What is your name?"

"My name is Eliana." The feeble voice drifted away in high winds. She stared at Jay with a sad smile. A few drops of tears rolled down her cheeks. At a distance, the sudden raindrops were touching on the drifting shadows of sunlight before immersing into the vast ocean.

"Eliana, I need to clean your wound very soon. I will give you medicines." Jay commented while sitting down next to her.

With a sad smile the lady stared at her. Her blank look pierced through the minds of Jay and Linda. The history of poverty and malnutrition for centuries was reflecting in her eyes.

"I need some help here. Need privacy to check the wound. It would be great if you could take Eliana inside." Jay glanced at everybody including Linda for affirmation.

No one moved.

Linda stood up and repeated, "please take her inside. We need to clean the wound immediately and apply medicine with dressing. PLEASE!" She was holding a tube of antibiotic cream in her hand.

A discussion started. Four people from the crowd came forward. They carried Eliana into the house and laid her down on a bed. Jay and Linda followed.

After entering the house, Jay sat on a chair next to her. He took the briefcase from Linda. From his briefcase Jay took out clean towels, bandages, and syringes. He put down the large towel on the table. Soon they were ready for an operation.

In the meantime, the ladies of the house came forward.

"If you need any help, we are here." One of them said softly.

"That would be great. Yes, we do. Would you mind boiling some water and bring it to me?"

"See if you can do it quickly."

"Oh, sure." Answered the lady with a big smile and curious eyes.

Soon two big bowls of boiled water came.

Jay cleaned her wound, gave her medications and two injections.

Eliana was in pain. Yet she did not scream. She was awake all through. Then she fell asleep while resting on the bed.

"Please ask her to be careful not to hurt herself. Her wound will heal completely." Jay finished. His eyes were fixed on Analyn and Isaac.

One old man came out of the back of the crowd and

approached Linda. It was the same man who yelled at Jay and Linda in the morning.

"I want to thank you! Sorry, I misjudged you. Please forgive me!" The old man tried to bury his tears. "She is my wife. Please save her leg........" He could not finish his sentence.

"Of course! Everything is fine! I'm here. Don't worry!" remarked Jay persuasively.

"One thing! Please ask her to take this tablet for her pain. And ask her to be careful and to protect this area. No shower for a couple of days. Dress the wound three times per week with antibiotics." Linda left some dressings, antibiotics and other medications on the table and explained everything to that young lady while others continued watching them.

"We will be in the area for next few weeks. Please let us know how she feels or if she needs any more help." Jay commented and left with Linda. The old lady was asleep. A moaning sound was coming out of her mouth.

"How are you all doing?" Linda stopped and asked a group of frail boys and girls when she was walking back to her truck.

One of the girls replied with a vacant look at Linda. Her body was shaking. "We are very hungry. Did not eat for many days. Do you have any food?" She uttered with difficulty.

Linda ran back to her truck and got some fresh sandwiches for her. Kids across noticed and within a few minutes Linda found herself circled by an army of young and old hungry people. Their desperate appearance and feeble look brought tears to Linda's eyes. Many of them had little amount of clothing.

Linda did not get frustrated, rather she signaled her other colleagues standing nearby. A full truck load of food, clothes, pillows, comforters, candles, and many other everyday necessities got distributed that day in that area.

"You guys are great," Isaac laughed. "Sorry I misjudged you."

"They will be safe and have a new life at your place. We will miss them. But it is good for them. We hope you bring them around more often to visit their families here, this is their roots."

Analyn was sad. But she was happy for the kids. Borealis, Azalea and Cosmos, all were weeping as they were hugging Tyler and Ella again and again to say goodbye.

Tyler was sad but Ella was too young to understand they were leaving behind their homeland, their uncle and aunt, their families, and friends. They had no idea where they were heading to. With sobbing faces, they followed Linda and Jay. Tyler was missing his father. Ella was crying and was stretching her hands toward Analyn: she was missing her mom.

Linda and Jay felt sad to take the kids away. But everyone understood the kids would be better off with them.

Jay and Linda adopted Tyler and Ella and returned to Eridanious. Analyn did not forget to hand over the magical cloth or share her power to protect the kids.

"Spread it over them each night. They will be invisible. A tent will form around them that will look like a kingdom of its own and shield them. You will see. It belongs to them. In time they will ask you for it."

Back in Eridanious Linda and Jay were raising Tyler and Ella as their own. Each night after the kids fell asleep, Linda did not forget to spread over the magical cloth over them. Jay was amazed to see such a floating magical kingdom protecting the kids all night. He had the miserable experience just like Isaac when he touched the magical cloth. But Linda was happy with the magical cloth since she had no problem to check on the kids.

CHAPTER VI

And it began

In the new surroundings Tyler and Ella grew up quickly. As time went by, Eridanious became their new homeland. From their early age, Tyler and Ella showed aptitude in martial arts. Linda and Jay were shocked when they found Tyler walking with ease over a rope high above the ground. On another occasion, Linda noticed Ella jumping around from one treetop into another with ease.

"Why don't we give them some training in such skills?" Jay was talking to Linda.

"Very good idea. Indeed, I was thinking on the same line. They have several natural abilities. It might come to their advantage someday."

"I feel like they are born to be fighters. Don't ask me how I know this, but somehow, I do." Said Jay.

Tyler and Ella began their training. One of the best gurus Khedrup Tenzin from far east was hired. The martial arts training included getting trained in almost every weapon such as fencing, shooting and archery. Khedrup decided to teach them each skill for many hours. He wanted to make sure they had mastered them.

Their first training session started. It was on developing concentration.

"Sit down with your spine straight in the lotus position of padmasana. Concentrate on your chakras. Let your kundalini travel from Muladhara to Sahasradhara chakra."

Ella and Tyler sat down in the lotus position. With eyes closed, they started meditation.

The voice of Khedrup came out like a music of commitment from a distance, "Clean your thoughts, beseech the divinity, and behold. See the unseen. Hold onto your inner strength, the energy that makes you real. Clear your mind, let light that beholds you open the space of infinite freedom."

"But how do I master something that I do not even understand?" asked Ella.

"Work your way up from your base, the root chakra: The Muladhara to the Sahasradhara….let the energy be revealed in front of you, let it unfold."

The training on concentration continued for months. They stayed in lotus position for hours, sometime for days without any food or water.

The Guru seated in front of them was floating high in the air in padmasana. He said, "let your mind control your destiny, let the energy of the universe awaken in your soul. Control your mind, focus, and behold. You are creating your own destiny. As your energy hits your passion and gets united with your soul, the aura of your chakradhar will unfold and reveal."

Days, weeks, months, and years went by. Then one day, their inner energy was divulged to themselves. A golden flood of light flooded their body, mind, and spirit. In that illuminating experience, ecstasy of joy and liberation were now within their grip.

"You have attained the state of mental liberation. Your Kundalini Siddha Yoga has been completed." Guru announced. "Now your physical training will start. Without mind control, any physical training is insignificant. It does more harm, than good."

The next phase started. The Guru emphasized on the

development of the physical strength. He trained them in every weapon: Rapier, hammer, war flail, sword, longsword, bow and arrow, spear, axe, pike, staff, club, flanged mace, morning star and javelin. Their swiftness, strength, and their breathing pattern all were being tested. He led them to their extremes and pushed them over the edge. Jumping from the top of the mountain, or diving deep below into the blue ocean, or fetching the blue pearl from the hidden submerged cave in the ocean and place it on the third eye of the two deities sitting in that cave, in each of these tests they were successful. Guru asked them to cross miles after miles over the fuming ocean in small boats. Sometime they had to reach a distant island by stepping or jumping on floating small leaves or woods. Once they had to enter a dark cave, fight wild animals, and kill the infamous black Jaguar Apepa who was praying on pets or small children living at the foothills. Although Tyler was the first one to reach the island, Ella easily killed the Jaguar Apepa with a single shot of her arrow piercing through the middle of its eyes.

Their final week for taking their test came. They were allowed to take only three things along with a map:

A weapon of their choice
a bottle of water
an animal to ride
a bottle of gasoline to start a fire
a dog as a companion.

"Pick any three at your choice. Enter the forest and reach the lake. You will be instructed about your next step once you reach the lake." Guru told them.

Ella picked up her javelin, took the bottle of water and the dog. Tyler took the axe, the horse to ride and the bottle of gasoline.

So, it began……

Early in the morning, two horsemen took them to the exact opposite sides of the forest and dropped them off.

"It is 5:00 A.M. now. The Sun is rising. Follow your map and reach the lake. Come back to this exact spot tomorrow by noon. The next set of instruction will come to you in due course." The horsemen left.

Tyler and Ella entered the deep cavernous rainforest through the tiny, muddy, and slippery dark deep passages.

The vast and dense rainforest covered an area of more than one hundred square miles with poisonous snakes and wild animals. To get to the center point and the lake was not easy.

Ella spotted a leopard waiting to attack a deer. She was careful not to be on its way. As she took a turn, she faced a peacock. She moved forward and came to a circle of canopy of trees. It was filled with many types of colorful birds. She ran at high speed to reach a canyon. But she lost a pair of her shoes. Her leg got buckled into a root, the pair came off and one of the pair flew and fell into the deep canyon. Naturally, she was bare foot.

Ella took a tiny path looking at her map. Soon she came across a series of open-ended dark cavern sitting under the mountain of quartzite rocks and bluffs.

"It is going to be interesting. Right Finn? Let's move through the caves quickly." Ella talked to her dog.

With her bloody feet Ella moved fast. The caves were completely deserted; bats were flying right over her nose. The leopards, and hyenas came out of hidings and followed her bloody trail. She managed to use the long roots hanging from the trees as ropeway to traverse a huge amount of distance, while her dog was running behind.

Ultimately, she came in front of a river. The apparently peaceful river made her happy. But just before diving into the river, she spotted something. It was the head of a crocodile.

Ella spotted many more crocodiles. All were sitting calmly hidden in riverbed and enjoying the warmth of the rising sun.

With little time to think, Ella decided to run. At an enormous speed, she crossed the river with steps on the rocks rising above riverbed or taking long jumps on the heads of the crocodiles. Her dog Finn followed her and made it through. Although Finn almost got swallowed and lost part of its tail on its way when it got distracted looking at a large fish jumping above the water. One of the crocs observed and came all the way through, but barely missed them.

Very soon they found themselves on the other side of the river. Ella reached the lake with her dog at noon. She noticed a Jaguar was taking a nap at the distant corner of the hilltop. The tail of one of the cobras was hanging from the cave nearby.

Finn was getting hungry. This time it was successful to catch a large fish that jumped out of the water in the lake. Finn carried the fish to a side and had a good meal. Ripples were visible over the blue water and then it subsided.

Ella found many fruits and vegetables with fresh water of the lake to quench her thirst. She decided to wait for Tyler. She climbed a tree and sat down on a branch.

Tyler had a terrific start. On horseback he travelled a long distance in an hour. While crossing the river he had no trouble. This part of the river had no crocs.

It was close to lunch time. He caught and killed a large fish, started a fire, roasted, and had a good meal. The running water from the river quenched his thirst. He climbed to the top of a tree, rested for a few minutes, and soon started.

While waiting Ella fell asleep. When she woke up, she was feeling pain in her neck and her chest. Something was trying to squeeze her. She opened her eyes, found a mammoth python was trying to squeeze her to death. Her hands were becoming numb due to lack of blood flow. Suddenly she heard a sharp stab on the back of the snake. The snake got hurt and loosened its grip.

It was Tyler. Soon the dead python was lying on the ground.

"Dead be the cobras.
jewels be the keys."

A voice from the heaven came in. Tyler and Ella looked up and noticed a talking red-blue, scarlet macaw with purple tail. It was holding a piece of paper on its beak. The bird slowly flew in toward them and presented the paper.

"Deep in the lake,
Sits a temple
Ask the Dolphins
Collect weapon using keys"

The two black cobras were awake and slowly came out. As they were emerging out of the caves, Tyler and Ella could see the amazing blue golden light coming out of the jewels sitting on the crowns of their heads.

The snakes jumped into the lake, as they were talking.

"Came for our jewels? Two more humans." One of the cobras uttered in a grave voice.

"Soon you will be our meal. I'm hungry." Spoke the other one looking at Tyler and Ella.

Slowly the cobras crawled out of the lake and started to chase them coming in from opposite sides. Tyler was riding his horse holding his axe and Ella was hanging from a treetop looking for the right opportunity to throw her javelin.

A strong hissing sound came in. Tyler barely avoided the cruel bite of one of the cobras but watched with horror how his horse fought against those huge serpents. The horse jumped high in the sky and came down hard on the cobras to smack them. One of the cobras was injured.

But before long, the other black cobra flew and jumped on the black horse. The horse leaped and started to scream in pain. White foams began to form in its mouth. The horse fell to the ground and died instantly.

Tyler and Ella did not give up. Tyler flew with his sword to the back of one of the cobras. From there, Tyler made his way through to its neck and while standing there he chopped its head off.

The snake fell dead to the ground. Tyler did not forget to pick up the jewel just in time. The other cobra that was injured was watching from a distance and it did not want to give up.

With angry fangs out, it jumped with full strength to bite off Tyler's head. Ella's javelin pierced through its chest as she came down from a tree branch right at that moment. The dead cobra fell on the ground next to the lake. They got the second jewel from its head.

The setting sun was leaving behind a rosy sky spotted with crimson. The animals were coming out of the forest to drink the water. They were approaching the lake slowly. Many were quenching their thirst after days. It was a scene of rejoice. The animals sat down on the side of the lake with a mode of salute for Ella and Tyler.

> *"Today is the day,*
> *now is the time.*
> *Chosen ones are here*
> *Prince is waiting."*

A roaring voice came down from the heaven.

Tyler and Ella turned around. It was the Scarlet Macaw. Still sitting on a branch.

"We need to dive in." Tyler said.

"First you dive. I will follow." Ella said.

They walked to the side to take a dive.

Suddenly the water in front of them started to swell.

A huge dolphin came to surface and spluttered water on them.

"Dolphin as the swimmer." Both repeated. "Let's go."

Tyler and Ella jumped on the back of the dolphin. It took a

deep dive. The dolphin swam miles after miles through under water ocean caves in seconds. In minutes they found themselves in front of a huge, submerged building. At the gate of the building a lion was sitting. Its eyes were glittering with red light.

Tyler and Ella placed their jewels into its eyes. The darkness was gone. A flood of light emerged from every corner, and they understood it was a place for prayer. Slowly the gate started to open. As they came off the dolphin and walked into the prayer hall, they were amazed to see none of the rooms in the temple had any watermark. It was sitting under the lake, yet no water was touching or getting inside. Also, they had no problem to breath normally.

Tyler and Ella went from room to room in search of their weapons. Every room was empty. Many types of sentences were inscribed all over the temple walls. At the very end of the hallway there was another room. They pushed the door. A small room, in the middle was sitting a chest.

"May be this has it." Tyler said.

Coco pushed open the door. Inside the chest were sitting two long unopened parcels with seals from the crown. Tyler and Ella picked up the parcels and came out of the temple. The parcels were flashing with blue golden lights. As they were leaving, the gates of the temple started shutting down on its own.

The lights became dim, and a voice reverberated from the mouth of the lion:

'Prince will rise
Meek shall be gone
Mighty be thy heart
Chosen are the one
Bravery is thy power
Wisdom is thy soul
Use thy weapon
Truth is thy goal'

Tyler and Ella were back on the dolphin and soon they came out of the lake. They had to walk all night to get to the starting points. But this time, they were riding two elephants and reached there in time.

On Tyler's twelfth birthday the two siblings were in for a big surprise. Their teacher divulged the secret in front of the guests: "Today they will show some of their skills in fencing and archery."

Everyone was keen to know what these two kids were capable of. Ella and Tyler approached each other with their swords. Their foot work, their focus, and concentration were evident. Soon with their skills, speed, attack, and action, they hypnotized the crowd. Tyler and Ella were of equal skill. But at the end with a single blow Tyler was able to break into Ella's guard and won the match.

Next item was archery. Targets were visible at a distance. The two concentrated and began shooting arrows at the targets. Within a few minutes, it was obvious Ella was clearly the winner. Tyler was awfully close, but he could never beat Ella. Targets were moved further and further. Even at 500 feet, then to 800 feet, and finally to 1200 feet. Ella could strike her targets with precision and accuracy, but Tyler fell short of a few millimeters. The show ended with an applause!

Next the guru asked them to sit in two separate chairs. At a distance on two different tables the two parcels were visible.

"Connect with your Kundalini. Reach out to your soul to find out who you are. Concentrate on those parcels and think of the weapons they might hold. Use your power to get your weapon of choice. If you can rightfully identify the weapon and can connect with it, the parcel will open, the weapon will fly at you. Catch it in time. If you miss, it might kill you or knock you out. Now concentrate."

They sat on two separate chairs with closed eyes and began their meditation. The viewers were at a complete stillness.

For some time, nothing happened. There was a pin drop

silence in the court room. With closed eyes, Tyler and Ella were in deep meditation.

Then, abruptly one of the parcels started to fly in the air as it progressed toward Ella. The other parcel remained on the table, did not move. Then from the parcel emerged a diamond gilded bow with an arrow and a diamond gilded quiver. Seated Ella flew, caught the bow and the arrow that came flying at her in high speed. The quiver went behind her back and attached its straps to her body. Ella went back to her seat. Then there was silence.

Tyler was not aware of any of this, did not move, was still seated in meditation. Then a gold plated, diamond engraved long sword slowly emerged from the other parcel. It flew toward Tyler at lightning speed. Tyler caught it just in time. The holster came flying, went straight to his waist and strapped itself.

The crowd cheered in delight.

"You are now ready to face the world. These weapons are not just any weapon. They come with enormous powers. They will be your honor, your protector, shield, and your guardian. Even if you lose them, they will come back to you when you call them up. They will be the guards of your faith, honor, brevity, and integrity." The Guru blessed them presenting both with the golden medals of honor.

Tyler and Ella bowed and accepted their rewards with humility.

"You will never lose a fight when you use them with good intention. As you take an arrow and point it to your enemy or draw your sword and thrust it into your opponent, your enemy will be defeated. Remember, from this day, you two can never be defeated by anyone in this galaxy in a direct fight. You will only lose when you choose to do so."

The following winter, a circus came to the town. Linda, and Jay took the kids to watch the show. The ringmaster introduced his stuntman with an exceptional ability.

"Here is our man of blades: Marakinon." The circus manager

came to the dais and started introducing his swordsman, "with his sword he can slice anything animate or inanimate, living, or non-living. I found him as a boy on the bank of river Pompeios. Gave him proper training and now here he is. Currently there is no match for him in this part of the world."

The swordsman demonstrated his skills in fencing defeating everyone. Next, he openly challenged anyone present in the crowd to come forward to fight him. He reiterated, 'No worries, my sword will only touch your sword, not your body. I will do you no harm. Come and face me if you've got the courage!"

Tyler stood up. He accepted the challenge. Linda and Jay exchanged looks. Linda whispered to Ella, "Is he crazy?"

"I don't think so! He can beat him, I know it!" Ella's solid answer. She was sure Tyler could win.

People watched, and to everyone's surprise, Tyler took a huge vault and made it to the dais. The manager threw over a sword, a long double aged sword. "Take this. This is Horathion's sword. The previous swordsman who was defeated in a fight by Marakinon. He lost his head before he knew. It was not a fight, just an accident." The manager laughed again.

Tyler looked straight at the eyes of the Marakinon. He found the glimpse of wrath and cruelty. Marakinon's laugh would make anyone uneasy.

"Come on. I am here just for fun. No worries. I will not touch you. You'll see." Marakinon shouted.

The fight started. Tyler's sword sparked in the air. The fencing continued. Tyler flew in the air, came down from above and defeated the swordsman who lost his sword and was now at Tyler's mercy. Again, Tyler defeated the guy with his speed, technique, and strength. He was the winner.

Time passed. Tyler and Ella came to Canopus once or twice every year. Last summer they visited Canopus with their parents and had lots of fun. They roamed around the villages with their cousins in their pick-up truck. They went fishing in the river on a boat, played card games with Azalea, Borealis and Cosmos.

The warm and welcoming cousins and great uncle and aunt greeted them with love.

On their way back, Tyler and Ella even had a chance to visit Argo-Navis. The abandoned house was still standing like an old man gazing across the vast farmland. Most of the people either had died or left. It was a deserted village.

Everything had been looted, parts of the house was falling apart. Spider webs were all over the place. Snakes had been hiding beneath the tiles in the cracks on the floor. A few of their parents' old pictures and memorabilia were scattered across the house. Tyler's small rifle was still hanging on the wall. So were their pictures with their parents and their grandparents' photos. They picked up most of the memorabilia. In a nutshell, they had a mixed memory about their past Canopus visits.

Almost another year had passed since then.

Recently news broke out about pandemic spreading across Canopus. The town had been hard-hit with people dying every day.

Hearing the news, Tyler and Ella instantly wanted to visit Canopus.

"Let them go. Provide them a guide this time. I need a break." Smiled Linda. She was still recovering from her twisted ankle from the fall during her yoga lesson.

"Are you sure? Do you think they would be able to manage by themselves? It might be too risky. Someone needs to go with them." Insisted Jay. "Think Linda!"

Finally, it was decided Linda and Jay will go with the kids. The date got fixed. That morning, Linda was packing her last-minute stuff and tipped over with a wrong step. Jay had to take her to emergency to get a cast. The trip got cancelled.

"I think they can go with Ryan. I trust him as a guide. Please ask him if he could go. Can't he?" Linda glanced at Jay for his approval lying on her bed. "Why wait?"

After a brief discussion with Tyler and Ella, Jay and Linda agreed to send them to Canopus with their family friend Ryan as the guide. A family man Ryan Major was also an employee looking after their ranch.

More than two weeks had passed since the kids had gone to visit their aunt.

"This house feels so empty. I wish the kids were here." Linda glanced at Jay while pouring herself a drink.

"Oh, yes! It really feels strange. Doesn't it? I am starting to worry why I haven't heard back yet." She continued with questions in her eyes fixed on Jay.

Jay agreed and nodded his head. "I think they might be visiting all their old friends...they even went to Argo-Navis."

"Have they decided to spend a few more days with their uncle and aunt?" Linda questioned. "How come we have not heard back from Ryan yet. He could have called or sent a message at the very least?" She enquired in a grimly face.

"I tried to get in touch with Ryan. But no call is going through. Don't know why! The last time I talked to Ryan, they were on their way to catch the ship." Jay said thoughtfully.

The conversation continued until they fell asleep.

Not far from Linda's house, in the middle of the Ocean in this peninsula in the Draco island, within the murky forest of Eridanious in Red Eye Valley, another woman Amber BlackRock woke up startled from her afternoon nap. Her husband Ian BlackRock hurriedly walked into the room and asked, "Amber, honey! Are you alright?"

"I'm fine! Just a strange dream!" She replied. Ian sat down next to her.

Amber paused for a while and said, "Let me tell you honey something about a dream, a peculiar dream that I had one night. Since that night, I am having the same dream again and again, not sure why.

"Just dream Amber, it can happen. Happens to everybody. We all sometime see the same dream!" Ian said with a smile.

"Yes, I know. But this one is different. It is about a Prince, as if my own son talks to me in my dream. I see a Prince walking with me and taking me from palace to palace, sometime on the beach, holding my hand tightly and talking to me. I see myself in past lives and even in my future lives while I am standing next to a prince. A tall handsome prince is talking to me. He calls me as mother. He hugs me, takes me for horse rides, and walks with me from room to room in a land of palaces."

Saying this much, Amber was breathing heavily. It was like she was drawn more and more deeply into her dreams. She closed her eyes tightly and opened them again and started telling, "I just saw him growing up in front of me and becoming a strong man. A few minutes later, I couldn't see him anymore. He was gone. My sleep got disturbed, and I woke up sweating." Amber stopped.

Amber was sweating and breathing heavily.

"It is just a dream honey. It is alright." Ian said patiently. "Let's go to the veranda and watch the waves in the ocean."

The villa was sitting in a valley, known as Red Eye valley, The BlackRock couple lived in this two-story huge chalet, *Rising Villa.*

The BlackRocks had moved into the villa a few years prior. It was an ideal place to start a family for the young couple. With its large and spacious design and panoramic ocean view from the master bedroom the villa was relaxing. The sun shone vibrantly over the tropical trees. The colorful flowers added extra beauty to the home. The BlackRocks spent many of their evenings in the backyard or on the balcony watching the sunset and listening to the waves.

Ian, a tall, well-framed person had a huge mustache. He was a construction engineer employed in a local company. Ian loved his wife more than his life. He was always willing to spend time with her. But it was difficult. The phone service was not great around the area. Ian was away busy at work. Rarely could he reach his wife over the phone. He was not aware about what had been happening back in the house.

Serious about his work, Ian showed up at work on time

loyally each day at eight o'clock and left for home five in the evening. It took him about ten to fifteen minutes to drive his jeep down to his office from his home.

The regular and comfortable lives of the BlackRocks had few surprises. A long time ago, Ian's grandfather (BlackRocks claim their great-great-grandfather was nominated for knighthood, but before he could be honored, he died in a battle) traveled to the area near Argo Navis and settled there for some time. According to the BlackRock family legend, Ian was just five years old when his parents, Hoover and Asia, moved. Fifteen years later, his parents moved to Eridanious where Hoover, his father, a pious man, took a job as a carpenter. The parents liked the place and decided to settle down there. This is where Ian, met a woman, named Amber whom he fell in love with and later married.

Ian's father and mother liked and learned the local language and culture. His parents developed interest in the area and got involved in the community. They frequently visited the Temple, where everyone came and practiced their own faith. People from near and far came to visit the Temple-Tower and the community began to grow. First a few people came. For everyday livelihood they depended on each other. Then as their number grew, the businesses were booming. Initially a few stalls popped up to deliver the daily necessities. The food stalls turned into regular stores. They were full and stocked to the brim. There could be found a few clothing stores and furniture shops. As more people came, a booming bazar began to thrive in that community.

Within a few years; post-office, banks and other community offices got established. The laid-back community changed, and a new bustling municipality replaced the old peaceful village.

The old villa, where the BlackRocks lived, was hidden on the edge of a dark but peaceful forest facing the ocean. However, it was not too far from the Temple-Tower of Magellan. People did not know how old the tower was or where it started. The only thing they knew was it had a root at the base of the ocean.

In recent past, Amber had been spending much of her time just watching television or visiting friends' houses. She took advantage of playing with the children of her neighbor Rumelia or her cousin Linda Demarest. When Linda and Jay had adopted the two beautiful children, Tyler, and Ella, she and her husband became extremely happy.

These two kids were Amber and Ian's favorite. A jovial beautiful woman, with a wonderful smile, Amber was always kind to Tyler and Ella. Due to her caring nature, she always made everyone happy. She was willing to help people any way she could. She worked with the high school students on their homework, took them for swimming or a ride. She spent time with them, discussing books, talking about their adventures, sports, or games.

Through all these activities, Amber was busy. Very often she forgot that she was getting close to her thirties. Being with the kids, she got lots of energy and motivation. She felt much younger while spending time with them.

The couple had a happy life. On weekends, when the families had free time, the two families went out together for a boat ride exploring the ocean, for scuba diving, or for hiking.

Recently, after their birthdays, Tyler and Ella went to visit their aunt in Canopus. Everyone in Red Eye valley had been eagerly waiting for their return after the news broke out about the recent loss of a cruise ship that boarded for Eridanious from Canopus.

CHAPTER VII

Waking up to a strange land

It was a dark silent room. Nice and soft mellow wind was moving with a strange, wild vibration. The long night was over. The ferocious ocean was becoming peaceful outside. Seagulls were flying. The dark, deep forest leaning beside the ocean that was murky and scary a few hours ago was now calm. As if nothing had ever happened. But on scanning, one could see the devastation. With uprooted trees, damaged boats, parts of shipwrecks piled up all over the shore, a picture of ruin and destruction was prominent.

Many rescue teams were now hovering over the ocean in search of survivors. They had no idea they were floating right on the top of a magical sunken Shadow Kingdom of Forbidden Palaces.

Tyler and Ella had new clothes. Not only they got a full few hours' rest, but they had royal outfits now. Tyler might have tried to retrace his legs while turning. So was Ella. Ella by now turned and twisted a few times and got into a cozy position. A strange noise was coming out through Tyler's mouth. There was no mark of injury on his body.

Time passed. A soft classical music was gaining strength from a distance filling the air.

Tyler and Ella were waking up. Their heads were spinning

with no strength left in their body to sit up or move. A vivid dream haunted Tyler -a flashback of memories from last night.

Their bodies regained strength, texture, and shape.

The first person to wake up was Ella. Tired and exhausted she was coughing. For a while she was not aware where she was. Her first thought was about last night's episode. Still shaking in the reflection of the soreness, she did not feel like opening her eyes. Keeping her eyes closed Ella placed her hands carefully on her head to see how it felt. The excruciating pain left her head pounding was now gone. She could not believe it! Ella jerked open her eyes. In that early morning faint light was coming through the windows. Ella could not see things clearly. But even in that partly lit room what she could witness made her speechless.

A golden dome of a palace was revealing its beauty as she was looking up lying on the floor. This was one of the most exquisitely decorated room she had ever seen. The white walls were carved with gold and silver. The furniture had been specially selected and matched according to the design of the room. Sculptures had been sitting on the pedestals in the huge room.

"Where am I?" She was coughing. Some water came out of her mouth.

Ella tried to get up. Fatigued, and without any strength she fell on the floor and passed out.

A long bright red strange looking creature slipped into the dark room through the tiny opening under the door. It had a large open mouth with sharp teeth, small torso, a droopy red stripped nose, four legs and a brown tail. It was searching for something.

The creature advanced quietly and sat on the floor at a distance. It came close to Tyler and Ella, gazed at them for a few seconds. A strange smile appeared on its face.

It began scratching the ground under the table at a corner. With its long legs and paws lined with sharp nails it dug up a hole quickly. In minutes, a deep gap was visible. The creature slipped into the gap and buried its body. Only the two black-red eyes sitting on the top of its nose could be seen. Due to complete camouflage, no one would notice anything.

After a while, Tyler was waking up. His fingers were moving. Tyler began to think what happened to them. He slowly opened his eyes a bit. As he turned his head, he was much happy to find his sister in the same room on the floor not far from him. Events ignited through his mind like lightning. In a few moments, he could remember how their cruise ship was trapped in the devastating cyclone and sank in the middle of the ocean, how they took the lifeboats and were then almost thrown out of the vessel, how a whirlpool sucked their boat and they almost drowned, how his body turned into a tiny sphere-like ball …..the way he got transferred into this room along with a chair or a throne.

Ella was coughing in her sleep. Some foamy water came out of her mouth again. Tyler feebly looked at her. He pulled his strength together to move. He stretched his hands toward Ella!

Nothing was registering in his brain.

Tyler stood up and glanced at his sister.

"I had the weirdest dream ever . . . jumping off the ship. Then the ship started to sink in front of our eyes. We had been floating in the ocean for hours while being thrown here and there…then a piece of debris arrived, it looked like a chair and—" Ella was waking up..she lingered….

Tyler turned at Ella and paused. She turned her head toward him.

"I don't think it was a dream Ella." Tyler said.

"What do you mean?" Ella questioned as she slowly stood up.

"Come on! Did you lose your memory completely? Think Ella. Look around." Tyler said.

There was a brief silence. Ella glanced across the room. It was hard to figure out their surroundings. The room was dark, with little light. It appeared creepy.

"Uh, yeah, I'm not sure where I am right now. But if that's what has happened to us in real life, we would be dead, right?" Emphasized Ella as she was trying hard to remember last night's tale and as if it were the most obvious thing in the world.

As Ella tried hard to remember more and more. The memories from the last night were coming back to her as she was standing up.

"Where are we?" Ella finally asked.

"Did you know what happened last night?" asked Tyler. "Dad told us to be always ready for surprises."

"No, not really, I remember getting knocked out right after our fight about a chair," said Ella. She stared at Tyler for a response with a thoughtful inquisitive face.

Tyler remembered what his father told him once when he was young and crying for not scoring a goal in the soccer game. He could see himself running in full speed from the right wing and getting into the penalty box to score the goal. But he missed! He missed and felt devastated.

His father took him close, "no matter what, always be strong my son! In life, there are almost always surprises."

"So, what happened?" Tyler asked after a long period of silence. "Well, continue!"

"We jumped out of the ship on lifeboats. Then we drifted in the ocean until a series of unfortunate events unfolded. Our boat was smashed into pieces. We found the wooden chair that got us here maybe?" Ella said.

"So, you understand: a strange force brought us into this room. Right?" Asked Tyler.

"Yes. I don't know exactly how."

"It was a surreal bizarre experience almost like a dream. You might have not seen or felt it since you were almost unconscious. But I have seen it all with my own eyes." Tyler responded.

"We will have plenty of time to think about what happened. First, we need to go home." Ella commented.

There was a brief silence. Then suddenly she asked: "What happened to the chair—I mean, the throne?"

Tyler turned at the chair in the corner and pointed. "That's it. We had been riding this mysterious piece of wood a few hours ago." Finished Tyler in a mystical tone.

Ella stared at Tyler deeply. Her voice was ponderous. Her face had a mark of anxiety. Deep inside, she was feeling afraid for a moment. Then it was gone. As if she was thinking Tyler was crazy, while listening to his remarks. She didn't notice any wet throne in the room or any water on the floor.

She glanced at the old chair in the corner; it seemed like a palatial chair. There was no room to confuse it with a throne.

"It looks different. It can't be." she quizzed in a firm voice.

"That's the throne" reiterated Tyler, shrugging his shoulders.

"Well, it appears new, not old. The throne from last night was old," said Ella.

"How would you know? You must have been unconscious the whole time while we are travelling to this unknown land. You could not even know what was going on! The throne made a copy of itself; one carried me, and the other must have carried you I think." said Tyler. "So how would you know if it was an old throne or a new one or not a throne at all?" asked Tyler with his eyebrows raised.

"I don't know, okay? It just does not make sense," said Ella, not finding anything else to say. She was clearly getting frustrated with the arguments.

"But how would you know? What you are saying does not make any sense either. . ."

As Ella and Tyler were arguing about the throne, the creature on the floor was watching and listening to them. It blinked twice. A golden blue light started to flash in the ceiling. An music could be heard playing in the nearby room. A faint sound of vibration came out of the ground.

A strange thing was about to happen. The chair from the corner came forward. The other chair popped out of it and plopped itself next to the first chair. The chairs stood side by side for a few moments.

Suddenly, the chairs began to change their colors. They slowly turned into golden thrones with regal seats in the middle crafted with jewels to lit up the majestic room. Two golden serpents were visible wrapping the handles of the thrones.

Ella and Tyler lost their words. In front of them stood two thrones made of gold and jewels, exactly like what they had seen last night. Gradually the thrones merged back together to become one. The color faded. The chair went back to its original stature and slid into the corner. The background music and the vibrations faded away, then it was all silent again.

Witnessing what had just taken place, Tyler and Ella interrupted their conversation and moved aside.

Tyler and Ella were at a loss for words.

"What happened to the throne?"

"Um, an optical illusion!" Tyler suggested.

"An optical illusion? Really, Tyler?" said Ella, sarcastically.

"Well, what do you think just happened?" Tyler retorted.

"I don't know, don't want to think about it right now. We don't know where we are. We are here trapped inside a dark room, don't even know how to get out of here and go home!"

Ella appeared tired; she sat down on the floor, fell silent. Tyler sat down next to her and shook his head, a small grin appearing on his lips.

Moments later, Tyler could smell something in the air. A wonderful fragrance of fresh flowers was circulating into the room from somewhere. Soft beautiful music began in the background again. He felt he was losing his mind. Tyler tried to stand up. It was difficult.

He glanced around the room and was impressed to find out they were sitting over the carpet of an extravagant decoration. The area was full of paintings, fine porcelain and chandeliers dripping with crystals.

Tyler sat down near Ella. He whispered: *"This seems like a room in a palace!"* thinking back about some of the pictures he had seen in a book before.

"What on earth is happening?" He tried to wake up his sister. She appeared relaxed like a baby lying down on the floor. In that half-lit room, Tyler was yet to learn he was on the floor inside a well-ornamented room that could captivate anyone's mind. There were intricate-carved stone statues engraved with gold, diamond, and other exotic jewels and carved armors, all reflecting light. The ceiling was decorated with the finest beautiful images of green forests, land, and blue oceans.

Outside the glass wall, Tyler watched. Light was now glittering in the ocean. "It must be morning now," he thought. Sea turtles were swimming by. He could recognize some of the fish outside the window. Tyler smiled; he was getting back his spirit.

"We need to get out of here. We need to find a way." Tyler repeated. He glanced at Ella and murmured.

Ella moved a bit, traced her legs. But didn't answer anything.

Tyler gazed at the throne and couldn't stop thinking about it.

"Strange, Tyler reasoned while scratching his head. "It can't be the same throne," Tyler muttered, he stretched but just could not move his legs. A pain all over his body made him almost numb. Tyler was writhing in pain. With closed eyes, he tried hard to concentrate, regained some balance, and pulled himself up.

Tyler stood up while gaining his balance against the wall. He walked at a slow pace to the window with his shaky legs. He was happy to discover a door at a distant corner. Tyler was thrilled!

"Finally! We might be able to get out of here!" he spoke to himself as he was pressing against the door.

He pushed hard. It didn't budge! He pressed harder, but it didn't open. Nothing happened. He felt quite disappointed and gazed around.

Upset Tyler was trying to find a way to get out of that place through the glass window.

The outside courtyard was neat and clean, the roads were

clear. It was early morning, not many people were around. Only a few guardsmen were visible on the palace gate. Several palaces with gardens, roads, courtyards were scattered around the landscape. In that foggy gloomy morning, Tyler hardly realized what kind of place it was.

Tyler paced toward the chair. The more he moved toward it, his legs felt heavy. Tyler managed to come close and lean against the chair. He said something in an unclear voice before he leaned against the chair to take rest. Tyler felt a bit relaxed, closed his eyes, and lay down on the floor. Before he knew it, he was floating in the air next to one of the chairs.

With his mouth little open and one of his legs dangling on the floor, Tyler was floating yet sleeping blissfully.

As Tyler fell asleep, the two chairs turned back into two different thrones and began to expand. In minutes one fully accommodated Tyler. The other one moved close to Ella, made her float, and moved her into it.

A pair of eyes were scrutinizing their movements all this time. Tyler and Ella were sleeping comfortably on the mystical throne and its replica, the throne of an old emperor which was the source of a force field and was extremely powerful. They were unaware the throne had many powers. The most interesting one it could read someone's mind.

Ella woke up again. She slowly stood up and began to walk around the room.

Tyler was about to open his eyes. Before saying anything more, Tyler got startled by his sister's scream.

"Chill down! Are you crazy? Do you know where we are?" shouted Tyler.

Tyler turned toward Ella. Ella was staring at a framed royal portrait hanging on the wall. The painting had a fountain sitting in the middle of a garden. The more Ella gazed at it, the more the fountain appeared real. She felt engrossed and moved closer to the picture. As she stretched her hands to touch the painting, unexpectedly, something strange happened. A stream of water came out of the mouth of the fountain, made her hands wet as it was falling on the floor. But the floor was not getting wet. The water disappeared as it hit the floor. As if something was absorbing the water. She touched the floor to check if it was real, and noticed her hands were wet but the floor was dry. She was not aware that a pair of eyes were blinking as she was trying to touch the painting.

"What the heck!" she screamed "What's going on?" Ella shouted in a voice of surprise.

She moved her hands away from the fountain. Slowly the fountain of water disappeared, and the painting regained its normal appearance. There was no trace of water anywhere. But she felt a pool toward the painting.

Tyler turned at Ella and came to check out the painting. He glanced at Ella, stared at their reflections on the mirror hanging in the opposite wall only to discover they appeared different. Brand new dresses with suitable outfit, they looked royal. Their dresses were sparkling with expensive jewels. Golden jeweled necklaces hanging from their neck were bringing extra glory to their dresses. They had a new hairstyle and even a new pair of shoes on their feet.

He also noticed the old palatial chair they had seen before.

Ella noticed the scared face of Tyler. She simply smiled and sat down on one of the chairs.

Tyler noticed her smile, came to her, and said, "I don't know, but just to be safe, don't touch anything else right now, okay?" His tone revealed his concern.

"Well, this place is downright creepy. I mean when have you ever seen a painting pouring out water? It does not make any sense! Does it?" It was evident from her voice Ella was now freaking out.

Tyler turned at the picture and then became engrossed. He moved forward and touched the painting, but nothing happened. No water came out. The picture was just a picture. No trace of water could be found anywhere on the floor. The pair of eyes from the floor stopped blinking and nodded its head out of frustration during this time when Tyler was trying.

"Why isn't it working?" Tyler inquired.

"Didn't you just say, and I quote, 'But just to be safe, don't touch anything right now, okay?'" said Ella as she was leaning against the wall. "Yet here you are, touching the crazy painting."

"Well, I just wanted to try it," said Tyler sheepishly. "Anyway, why isn't it working for me?" he asked.

"I don't know. Why ask me?" said Ella.

"It does not make sense! Why don't you come back and try it?" replied Tyler.

Ella walked back and touched the picture. It regained its lively beauty. The fountain was back pouring water. Tyler was amazed. Ella was happy but calm, as if nothing had happened. She was not restless anymore, more composed, and fearless. She leaned toward the painting. Then suddenly she got pulled inside the picture and disappeared.

Ella was in a time travel and moving fast through her past. She found herself sitting in a garden and having a conversation. She could not see the person's face, but from the voice, she understood, it must be a woman. Ripple of fountains took her by surprise. The moon was up, gentle breeze was blowing, the guards were waiting at a distance…. evening sunlight was reflecting on the water fountain, flowerbeds, trees, leaves…. The scene was magnificent.

"You came back! Good news. The Prince has been waiting for you! all these years. Only you and Tyler can wake him up. You know the golden words that will wake him up. Words you need to tell in his ears. It all will come back to you when you see him again. But only him. Do not reveal any of these words or sentences to anyone, not even to his mother….the Queen Eleonora Elenira. Remember ….only him….remember only him. ….Remember and behold ……. The time is coming."

A grave alarming voice was echoing the words as she was watching herself in the garden and yet moving at a lightning speed through the space. Her travel ended abruptly, and she came out of the picture just like a spark and was thrown back into the room. The whole episode happened within a few moments.

"What happened? Where did you go?" Tyler asked.

"I don't know. I just had a time travel. But not exactly sure what its all about. Exasperated Ella sat down on the chair again.

No one noticed, a pair of eyes from the floor began to blink with a smile on its face. Tyler was thinking and trying to understand why his little sister had become so calm suddenly while he was feeling crazy.

"How come you look so composed and happy, whereas I feel so upset to be here?" Tyler cried at his sister. His voice was cynical.

"Perhaps because you're like scared of everything!" she said.

"I am not!" he squeaked.

"Uh, kind of," said Ella while smirking.

"Thanks for the boost of confidence. It really helps." said Tyler sarcastically.

Ella groaned and said, "I'm sorry. It's just like I said before. I'm really freaked out being here just like you. But I also feel a connection… strange….I can't explain it." She continued, "Our ship crashed, we were stuck in the middle of the ocean, and now we're in an underwater palace, walking and breathing normally, not sure how it is even possible?"

"Exactly that is what my question is. How is it possible? Maybe they have a secret source of cyanobacteria or phytoplankton somewhere that gives a continuous supply of oxygen to keep them alive?"

"Maybe. I don't know. and I don't even know what we are doing here. This whole thing sounds so strange and bizarre, and I guess my way of hiding all these emotions that I'm feeling is to look composed and calm. So, I'm sorry for being mean to you."

"Yah, I'm sorry too. I guess it's just that you're right about me fearing everything. But you know, I could be strong as well...you have seen me before, didn't you?" questioned Tyler.

"That's true bro—"

"No, but in a way, it is true that I feel pretty unsafe and crazy about our situation too." Tyler said while cutting his sister off. "I guess, this whole time I've been so worried about what was going to happen next, and so I've been scared about everything and everyone. I was scared about death, not seeing mom and dad, and how we are going to get out of here," he said. "But the way I think of it, for me, it's easier to be scared than it is to be brave," he finished.

"Perhaps, that's why you're scared," said Ella.

"What?" Tyler asked. He was looking out through the window.

"I won't be surprised if they have a living king or queen here! Someone must be running this place!" Said Ella.

"Look at the surroundings, the wagons, horses, huge fortresses, high walls, guards all around." Said Tyler.

"I had a strange feeling last night when I touched the chair. I mean the throne. I felt good. I don't know why."

"Me too! The same thing happened to me!" Said Tyler.

"I don't know...it is my guess...perhaps, this place is really creepy... this old throne...this underwater hidden palace... everything is kind of not normal...you know what I mean?" Said Ella.

Ella continued, "You said you were awake and noticed everything how we travelled here. Now, could you please tell me how many mysterious things happened in between? You should be used to such things by now!" Ella finished with sarcasm in her voice.

"True. At least, we are alive," Tyler said.

He began, "I'm not joking, you have no clue what we went through or transformed into. We were like two little golf balls glued to a tiny chair or a throne whatever you want to call it!" He was now walking across the room. Tyler made an expression to show his feeling. But Ella was not sold. She was silent with a bizarre facial expression.

"I'm not sure if mom and dad are missing us! But I certainly miss them!" Said Tyler.

"Forget it! Let's not get sentimental now!" Said Ella.

"My arm is not bruised anymore. I believe you are completely healed too." Tyler said to his sister.

They were now thinking how to get out of the room and were helplessly looking for an exit. Tyler walked gently and stood next to a sculpture.

"You know what?" Tyler said. "Look at this! It is a bronze statue of a beautiful woman, saddled on a white horse with flapping wings. Look how she is dressed in armor and staring at the bronze statue of that flower girl right there. From her armored dress and vigilant stance, it is clear she was in the cavalry unit."

"It could be that she was one of the soldiers in the Prince's elite unit? But who knows? Was she up for a battle? I don't know! Probably her horse was suffering from mud fever. Look at the greasy heels of her horse!" Ella said with a concern on her face.

Next to those two statues was sitting another statue of a giant black half-human half-lion ready to jump on its pray. The red eyes of the human lion were glittering.

Curious Tyler moved close to the saddled lady. The moment Tyler touched the statue of the horse, the woman and the horse came to life. The woman blinked at them and asked: "Who are you?".

Tyler and Ella were startled and moved back. "We...... are from Eridanious. But who are you?" Ella hesitated but asked in a commanding tone.

"My name is Ashwini. Thank you for bringing me back to life. I was waiting here to be free for many years. Only the touch of pure souls could have freed me. Your souls have not lost its purity! Thank you!"

"What is the definition of a pure soul?" Ella couldn't stop asking.

"A pure soul is the one that think of others in a loving way, with no harm in mind. The soul that can free others from bondage!" Ashwini answered quickly.

Ashwini stared at them for a few moments, took a deep breath and then whistled to her horse. The horse jumped, gazed around, and stepped forward.

"Not sure if you still remember me. Together we fought side by side to save this kingdom. Do you?"

There was no response. She was frustrated.

Ok, ok, I understand." Ashwini said.

But if you need any help, then call out my name three times when you need my assistance. I might be able to help you. But for now, I must tend to finish something that is long overdue. My husband Bernard must be worried! I am late, late."

"Wait, wait!" Did you just say Bernard?" Ella asked.

"That's what I heard." Said Tyler.

"Is it the same Bernard that we met when we are little?" Ella questioned with a curious smile on her cheek.

""I think we met someone named Bernard! We can get him here right now! But first tell us how you became a statue?"

"That's a long story. I'm not sure if we are talking about the same Bernard. I'll tell you my story some other time. I'm sure we will meet. Now I must leave. This is a magical place with enormous force fields created by a saint. If I stay much longer, I could become statue and lose all my magical power. I must leave."

The horse reared. The window in front of them was about to open wide.

"Wait! Don't go! Please wait a few more seconds!" Screamed Tyler. He didn't delay any further. He and Ella together closed their eyes and called out the name: "Bernard, Bernard, Bernard." In a few seconds, a white smoke began to form around them. It grew bigger and bigger and enveloped the whole room. From the smoke emerged a handsome knight saddled on the top of a Pegasus! Tyler and Ella immediately recognized him. It was Bernard! He was a real man with a knight dress, not a little statue.

The knight came down from the Pegasus. When he found Ella and Tyler, he was extremely delighted.

"I heard your call! I'm here. Now please tell me what I could do for you!" The knight asked. "Thank you for saving my life that day."

"We called on you not for helping us, but to meet someone. Tyler and Ella turned back at Ashwini. By then Ashwini came down to Bernard and began to cry. They were at each other's arms for a few minutes in silence.

Ashwini raised her head, turned back to Ella and Tyler, and said "Thank you! I have been waiting for this moment to meet my husband for almost thousand years! Thank you!"

Tyler smiled, and said, "We met him a long time ago. It is a good thing that we still remembered his name."

Then Ella said, "tell us about this place. Everything that you know."

Ashwini started, "this is a magical place, they call it the Shadow Kingdom and the Land of nines. A Prince has been sleeping here in this Shadow Kingdom and Land of Nines under a spell for many many years.....almost a thousand years now. He got into the spell from a saint. I was a member of the elite royal guards that protected the Queen Eleonora in Ruby palace. When the Prince fell into the spell and became unconscious, most of us fell under the spell and turned into statues, dwarfs, or animals. Only a very few could survive. Anyone tried to run away, met the same fate." She paused.

"Unaware of any of these developments, I was with a friend of mine inside the palace talking to her. That's her. She pointed at the bronze statue of the woman." Ashwini paused. Tears rolled down her cheeks.

Bernard was silent. Hiding his tears, he said, "I was one of those unfortunates that tried to escape. By the time I came to know about the spell, it was already late. I was chasing an assassin who infiltrated into the royal guards. He was sent by the Scorpion King Sculptor with a mission to kill Queen Eleonora and the Prince. I was chasing him on horseback, came close to take him down in the forest. But a storm emerged with heavy winds and rain. The assassin managed to escape.

I turned back, returned to the palace. On my way in, while entering the palace gate, the guards told me. Many of them turned into statues right in front of my eyes.

I was still outside the gate, took my chance and rode my horse and decided to escape by jumping off a cliff with my horse into the ocean. We were trying to go across the water to the distant land. My horse was good at swimming but could not go much further. It lost its mobility. I felt different, my body became heavier and heavier, me and my horse glued together and began to shrink. Soon we fell to the bottom of the ocean. That's all I remember. Eventually our statue was washed ashore. Your friends from that town found me, and you know what happened afterwards." Barnard finished.

The open window started to close. The early sunlight beaming through the window glass was tearing apart the darkness.

"We need to keep going Bernard." warned Ashwini. "Wish we could take you with us. But that would be too risky. Whoever brought you here is already aware of you. He knows you are here, and he must have a plan for you. You two are the chosen ones. Our lives are dedicated to protecting the Prince. We are with you all the way."

"Yes, we are with you all the way. And any time you need us, just call out our names three times." Repeated Bernard.

"Be patient. WELCOR is coming…. the Enigma of six! They must be watching and guiding you all along. Otherwise, I doubt you could make it this far on your own. They will assist you. Now, we must leave!" affirmed Bernard.

Within moments, Bernard and Ashwini saddled their Pegasus.

"Wait! Who are they? The Enigma of Six?" Tyler screamed. But before he finished his sentence, the horses began flapping their wings, flew out of the huge window into the sky.

It took a few seconds for Tyler or Ella to understand what had just happened.

They exchanged looks. Ella ran toward the window. Tyler followed. In that early morning light, as they pulled the drapes, they watched two winged horses flew side by side high in the sky and vanished behind the clouds.

The guards were walking near the gate, but it was hard to understand if any of them has noticed that a man and a woman just flew out of the palace on the back of two winged white stallions.

"Hmm..this is weird. What do we do next?" Questioned Tyler.

"We need to find a way to get out of here?" said Ella. She was standing beside the wide-open railed window behind the drapes from where she could see open balconies and winding staircases of the palace that they were in. The guards were now back in front of every palace.

"Hmm…the whole area should be extremely protected! See these high fortified walls! And look at the large and deep moat all around this palace!" Said Ella.

"I'm sure the same goes for all the palaces. Guardsmen standing in position at each Temple-Tower. Looking over the landscape from all directions. Even with such a defense system, they seem vulnerable. with unwanted visitors almost every day. Not fun!"

"The only access point is through the draw bridge over there. Well, for the visitors who they might be expecting I mean." Tyler held. He came by her side to look at the surrounding of the palace. The huge Sapphire stone sitting at the center of the lake was emitting lights all around.

As they were chatting, Tyler and Ella were searching for an exit. They could not spot anything yet and were feeling miserable and angry.

"Hmmm... notice the beautiful tapestries." Said Tyler.

"Everything exotic and expensive." Said Ella. "Look, a door here." Tyler pushed the door. Nothing happened. In a grim face, he nodded his head out of despair.

"Perhaps we need a key or a magic word to open the door?" suggested Ella.

"Sushh!!! someone is coming this way!" whispered Tyler. He kept one of his eyes on the small hole in the door. Someone was approaching. Must be in a hurry. Whoever it was they could hear the footsteps.

Tyler ran for cover under a table. Ella ran behind the long curtains. The door was opening! They held their breath in suspense and tried not to make any noise!

CHAPTER VIII

The Kingdom of Obsidian:
The Seven Palaces of Fire

Deep under the ocean, far from the Red Eye valley, another man was transported into a room. It was a dark space inside a palace in the *Kingdom of Obsidian: The Palaces of Smokey Quartz also known as Palaces of Fire*. The Kingdom of Obsidian belonged to another King. A Devil Scorpion King Sculptor. Situated deep below the surface of the ocean the kingdom also had seven palaces protected by seven obsidian stones. The obsidian stones: source of light, power, and energy for the kingdom.

The man was King Orion, the same King we met before in ship Adora.

Orion was completely oblivious of where he was. Lying on the floor next to a black throne made of mahogany wood crafted with jewels he was in a deep sleep.

This was a different kind of throne. The throne they were looking at had four legs held in place with gold crafted beautiful stones each wrapped with spotted golden black cobras. The cushion was made of a gold threaded pashmina. The arms and sides of the throne had illustrations of past kings and queens of the Rigororiyan Dynasty. The back support of the throne made of gold had pictures of two cheetahs ready for taking a leap.

The cheetahs were motionless, only their red eyes were blinking sporadically, as they were moving their heads occasionally.

Orion was not aware of any of these. He slowly woke up a bit, looked around, stood up and sat on the throne. His hands were nicely resting on the side. Orion closed his eyes only to fall asleep. Then he woke up again and felt better. The headache was gone, he could think with clarity. Orion sat up on the throne, stood up and stretched his hands upward just to relax a bit.

"Where am I? What happened? Am I alive? Where is Zenithia, my wife?" All kinds of questions flew by his mind.

Early morning light was coming through the window. Morning, a time for a new beginning, a time for waking up. Waking up to a new dream, a hope, a flash of activities. Orion always enjoyed morning. Curious Orion walked across the room, stood next to a window, and pulled the drapes. In that early morning he noticed a highly guarded huge iron gate. Not very far from him. A few guards were taking their rounds. Thick forest was visible surrounding the entire landscape marked with a stem of rivers and lakes. The distant grassland, bushes, meadows, and scattered villages were visible. Blue deep lake stretched across before joining the snow-capped mountains at the horizon. Six other palaces were standing all facing a stone sitting in the lake.

Orion heard a sound, a strange sound. The sound of evil. It was a hissing sound, a sound of fear and dizziness, a sound that wraps our mind. A sound that we can never let go. A sound that pulls people into darkness.

Orion was not aware of this. He could catch the voice, the hissing sound, but did not pay any attention. As Orion took steps across the room, the sound got louder. He moved, then paused. For a moment, he questioned himself, "did I hear anything?" Then he moved again.

Exhausted as he was, he couldn't wait to get out of that place. He was looking for an exit, a door to get out of the room.

Orion turned around at the end of the room. He noticed
the throne. It moved quite a bit to the center. He shook his head
a couple of times. "What am I thinking? I must be mistaken....
something isn't right," he thought. He moved back to the throne
and sat on it.

Orion tried to figure out where he was or what happened.
He was sitting in a room where expensive things had been
displayed everywhere. Chairs made of gold, crafted with jewels,
or black velvet. In that partly lit room, he could smell something
sweet. Scared Orion had a strange feeling in his body. And a
sensation. A sensation that was different. Suddenly, when he
discovered a snake was wrapping around his leg, he jumped out
of fear. The black cobra turned its head and began to eye Orion
with its vicious hissing sound and creepy look. Orion became
numb. His black eyes turned blurred. Fear and anxiety made
him motionless.

The snake was ready to bite. A sword was hanging from the
wall. Orion did not hesitate. He rapidly grabbed it, and in one
swing, cut off the head of the cobra. The snake left him, fell on
the floor. But it was not dead. Two more heads came out of the
torso and chased Orion with fury. The head separated from the
body began flying in the air. With glowing red eyes filled with
fumes it was spitting out poison as it was flying with its stretched
out two wings. Fresh blood dripping from the head spilled over
the floor and on Orion's body. From that blood and smoke, new
snake heads began to form. They all came after Orion. Soon
many fiery snake heads were chasing to capture Orion.

Orion sprinted across the huge room, while screaming and
looking for a door to get out. He snatched a hanging torch off
the wall and lit the curtain by his side. A fire broke out. Scared
by the fire the snakes moved away to the middle of the room
only to come back more aggressively to attack him. Defenseless
Orion looked everywhere in despair. He searched for an exit to
get out of there. Spotting a window high above at a corner, he
jumped on the table. In another try, he caught the broken grill

of the window. One snake flew by his side to bite on his right leg. Blood oozed out of his femur bone. Another one captured his arm. A few snake heads started taking bites of his face, hands, and body. He pulled himself up, broke the glass window hitting it with the sword and jumped outside. He fell twenty feet below on another hard floor and got knocked out. He lay there for a long time.

Finally with a blood-soaked dress, Orion woke up. He was bloody, dizzy and in lot of pain. He was physically and mentally devastated. He should have been home by now, his sweet home. A cozy place filled with love and joy. He missed his wife and children.

Everything around him appeared expensive but dark and gloomy. It might be a palace, he thought. Orion took a deep breath.

A flash of his voyage triggered him. The bar, the oceanfront balcony, his loving wife, the drinks, the poker table at the casino. And then things started to shake and fall. He remembered.

It was his lucky evening. He was winning rounds after rounds. And then there was that power outage. This had to be a dream. It must be. And then what happened to him? What is this place? How did he get here or how did he survive in the first place? Many questions came to his mind simultaneously.

Had he been abandoned by his fellowmen or was thrown out of the ship? Where is he? He tried to remember his past. Slowly the picture of his voyage, the shipwreck, and how he and his wife managed to jump into a lifeboat at the very last minute, all came flashing back. Then it all went dark.

And he missed everybody in that ship.

Possibly when he would wake up tomorrow, everything would be fine, and he would realize he was just daydreaming. He moved his fingers across, touched the walls to get a feel for his home, a feel for his loved ones. The cold walls did not respond. He could hear his heart bit. He became nervous.

Groaning in agony, Orion stood up, drips of bloody sweat

had been collecting on his face, arms, and legs. He stared at his wounds. He looked at the sword he was still holding. The blood-stained sword. He tried to walk back but instead staggered forward to the wall. He felt crazy. He wanted to run away. He sought after the blue sky, the beautiful ocean, the clouds, the mountains, and his family. Yes! The family that he had, he loved most. He dreamed of his lovely wife, her warm touch, her sweet smile, her laugh. He missed everything, everything that he had. He remembered his last angry conversations with his butler. It was nothing big. The poor person asked him if he preferred scotch or red wine on his voyage. Angry Orion replied, "don't you know? I prefer both. Scotch during the day and red wine at night? You idiot!" Angry Orion was now missing his obedient butler. The butler. A good individual. A man who was never upset. Never raised his voice. Only served the Vulcans. Generations after generations. Without any question. The distant ocean was fuming with waves behind the window.

So was Orion.

"No, it's not a dream," he told himself. "I need to get out of here. But how?"

He understood he needed to do something.

The place was amazingly opulent but depressing and deserted. At the center of the landscape, Orion noticed a stone in the middle of the lake. Yes! An enormous gemstone of Black obsidian. Fumes were gushing out of the stone.

He was standing next to a tall tree. A tree with lots of branches. Orion became curious. He started to climb the tree. Once he reached the top, he noticed each of the dark seven palaces was made from obsidian stones of different colors. Orion had interest in geology. He knew how to read stones by its color, crystallinity, and shape. He started to read out loud, 'The Black Obsidian, The Mahogany Obsidian, Snowflake Obsidian, Sheen Obsidian, The Rainbow Obsidian, Apache Tears Obsidian, and Starburst Obsidian." Some kind of energy field must be guarding this place from ocean water." He thought. "Might be created by these stones. And of course, they must have managed how to get oxygen to stay alive! May be growing phytoplankton somewhere?" He murmured.

The lights coming out of the stones were being reflected and then piercing through the sky to light up the entire kingdom. As he was coming down, he noticed smoke above some of the palaces.

"But how could I get back home?" he uttered in a raucous voice. He wanted to ask someone. The huge rooms and their intricate structures, the ceiling, the pillars, the stones, the decorations—everything told him the story of a place that appeared miserable and depressing. The palace in front of him was made from black and grey stone.

"It is much bigger than the palace that I live in." Orion thought. He shook his head. The huge doors were mostly closed.

He walked around and took many turns. He approached another side of the palace. Noticed one of the doors seemed to be open a bit. Orion pushed the door with his full strength. Finally, the door opened. He came out of the room. Entered the courtyard. A gloomy picture emerged all around him. The glittering statues, the roads, the columns, the corridors, the passages—all royal, gorgeous, but none well maintained. He turned at the groves, well-paved canals, and ponds adorning the roadsides. Large bushes, high up trees and a few small forests were visible.

He turned at the corridor. It was completely empty. He could hear a sound coming out of the thick forest at the back. Dogs were roaming around. Insects were flying over a dead animal in the forest. An unpleasant smell made him uneasy. The trees and plants had very few leaves. All the rivers appeared almost dry. Crows were flying picking on dead animals alongside vultures. No other birds were visible. The gardens had few flowers or flowerbeds. The distant waterfall had little water falling and the silence of the whole place made him dizzy. He felt scared.

Orion was in a pensive mood, unsure about his future.

While walking, he felt as if someone pushed him from behind. A sudden jolt made him tense. He whirled around but couldn't see anyone. He felt anxious and panicky.

Orion went in and entered the hallway. Soft whispers made him alert. He moved behind a pillar. He heard pieces of a conversation. But was not sure where it was coming from.

Orion walked away in another direction. He heard the scream of malnourished children. The horrible moaning sounds...he became alarmed and afraid. It was coming out of rooms beneath his floor.

"Something must be wrong." Orion himself was in tremendous physical pain. Yet, he wanted to find out. He came closer to the end of the hallway. He noticed a staircase going down and took the stairs.

Orion came down to a dark passage. The sound was still there. It did not go away. He followed. Followed the sound. Followed with a beating heart. Followed with his sweaty and blood-soaked dress. He wanted to know. He had to.

He passed a series of dark rooms. The rooms were packed. People in shackles were screaming in pain. Guards that were making rounds appeared well-fed, well-dressed.

"You must be lost! A wrong man in a wrong place!" A voice from behind made him alert and afraid.

Orion turned back. He noticed a guard with a long head, big eyes, rough cold face, and big nose. The guard was scrutinizing him head to toe.

"Yes, I'm kind of lost! Not sure how to get out of here." Smiled Orion. A smile that we take advantage of when we lose words. When we are uncertain.

"From your dress I can tell you are not from here. Come with me."

"No, I can't. I don't want to. Who are you anyway?"

"Soon you will know. Come with me, if you want to live."

Orion glanced at the guard and thought for a moment.

"No. I'm not going anywhere."

"You have to."

The guard moved back, took a turn, and came back at him in full force. Orion was ready. The two swords flashed for a few minutes. Then, the guard found himself on the ground, and Orion's sword was pointing at his neck.

"Never follow me again. And never tell anyone that we saw each other." Said Orion.

He left the place and moved ahead. The deserted road was leading him to a strange place. A place of destitute. Hunger, hatred, and poverty was prominent.

Orion was now more cautious. He just wanted to know. Know everything about this place. Strange place. A place he wanted to leave immediately.

He noticed people of every color. They came from different age groups, young, middle, and old. Some of them were exceptionally young children. Weeping women crying over the floor. They lost their husbands. Father screaming over the dead body of his son. A hungry skinny mother breastfeeding her child. A small piece of bread on a plate in front of her was being shared by a rat who decided to visit her.

Now he could see the sobbing beautiful woman in chains.

"Just agree to it. He will make us happy." One skinny man with broken teeth and a gaping wound in his head was talking to her.

"He is the king's chief minister. Only thing he is asking you to say goodbye to your family for now and go to the Land of Nines. Stay there for a few years in disguise. And yes! When the time is right, ...kill the queen." The old man was breathing heavily.

"And being my husband, you ask me to do that? Betray our Prince? And the Queen? Who saved all of us for generations? And leave my kids behind? You are a monster. I'm ashamed I ever married you." She screamed out of desperation.

"Look Valeria, look here." Tears were dropping from the man's face. "See, what they did to me? I don't even carry the blood line of our Prince Anish. But just for saying 'No' they tortured me for months, took away our children and now we are here. Think. They will be back. They will kill us both."

Orion moved forward. Watched guards rounding up and forcing prisoners into their cells.

The guards turned toward him. But they could not spot him. Orion hesitated. Anger was taking him over. He took another turn and found a door. A door to escape from that dungeon.

He stood quietly at a corner. He thought for a while.

"These people need help", he thought. Their sobbing painful look, their hungry thin bodies made him mad. He wanted to scream. Scream out of anger and pain. Scream and scream and scream. But he controlled himself. He had to. He wanted to live. Wanted to go home. Wanted to see his wife and children.

The guards went past him. They did not see him. Orion swiftly moved closer to the cells.

"How did you get here? Who brought you here?"

The people turned at him in vacant looks. Their pale eyes only reflected the evening shadows. No answer came back.

"Are you all from the shipwreck? Did you face the storm?" He questioned.

Again silence. No one answered.

He wanted to go near the people. Talk to them. Ask them questions. Make them free.

"Freedom. That's what they need. Freedom. The most valuable property any human can have. Something very fragile. If lost very hard to earn it back. The Freedom. They need the Freedom." Orion murmured.

The cells were behind doors that were locked from outside. Malnourished young and old people, men, women and children in frail health and tattered clothes were looking at him. Tears were coming out of their eyes. They were rotting in that prison. Children lying on the cold floor appeared hungry and weak.

"They might have been locked-in for months, years. Who knows!" Orion felt sick in his stomach.

He heard someone coming. Orion went behind a pillar. One hooded man covered with black cloak appeared. Many more came. All covered with black cloaks. No one noticed Orion.

"Who are they? Why are their face almost fully covered except their eyes? Should I follow them?" Orion became more disturbed and afraid.

"That's the one. Bring him to the King. He must pay the price. Umhhh...a big price." A man covered in black cloak waited in front of a cell and chuckled.

The guard opened one of the prison cells and took out a man with rough look in his twenties. He had an innocent face, strong body, and sharp look. Anger, agony, and despair were printed on the face.

"It is your time, Ishan. Let's go."

The man came out in chains, was guided through the hallway in another direction.

Orion bent and quickly moved away toward another room. The door behind him closed automatically with a thud that made him nervous. He felt helpless when he heard the distinct click of the latch locking by itself. Frightened, Orion wanted to run. He felt hungry and thirsty. He came out of that room and started to run. He saw a staircase. He hurriedly went up the stairs. He did not know where to go. But he wanted to run. Wanted to go far away from this place. To a place he knows for a long time. His own home.

He went through the iron gates. Came out through another door at a distant corner. Now he was in a patio. This place seemed a bit normal to him. People were walking around, busy in their work. Ladies were carrying baskets. A bazaar was opening at a distance. More and more people were on their way to buy or sell their stuff.

Yet they had a sad smile. They were talking among themselves. Others were approaching the lake to catch the water wheel. They appeared scrawny, haggard and it was clear they all were slaves. Living under persecution. Their diffusive look and brittle voice told Orion a story of tyranny, and subjugation.

The people looked at him with suspicion. Rarely did they turn to greet him. Barely anyone smiled. No one said much except hi or hello occasionally.

Orion started walking. At a distance he noticed a large crowd. People gathered. They were discussing something.

"They are going to kill my grandpa, going to kill him. Please help, do something." A young girl in her teens was running desperately in tears and pleading to everyone for the life of her grandfather. Her mother was sobbing at a distance. Another woman was holding and consoling her.

Orion took cover. He noticed a few guards standing in front of the house. In minutes, they pulled out an old man and threw him on the street.

"Dominican! You are a traitor. You betrayed the King. Must pay the price." Their leader screamed.

The old man stared at them for help. With his wounded arms and broken legs, he was limping and screaming. They made him sit up on his knees. The sad eyes, the rolling out tears depicted a picture of innocence and desperation of that old man. Morning light reflected from his face filled up the air with a golden heavenly touch. The man appeared frail and weak.

After a long pause, the man said, "But what did I do?"

The chief guard took out a paper from his pocket, showed it to everyone and then read it aloud.

A few pictures were painted on the paper with some writings:

A Dagger: Unite and use it.

A stone: Turn the tide: throw it.

An arrow: Aim it well, it will get there.

The chief read out loud from the decree.

"Found guilty as charged."

The guards took him away. "If anyone is found involved in doing anything against the King like Dominican, will meet the same fate." The guards declared before leaving.

Orion stood there for a few minutes. He spotted a creepy looking man making his way through. Orion managed to have a quick look at his suspicious face before he disappeared in the crowd.

Orion started walking away. He took a turn and approached a road. It was a tree tunnel. Soon the road ended on a bridge. A river was flowing by. He walked up to the bridge. Stood there.

Orion murmured "Who is running this land? Why is it so dark and depressing? Where is light?"

"Yes, it is dark sir! Light only comes to them who seek it sir. I don't think anyone is seeking light here sir. The only thing people seek here is to find a way to be saved from the torture of the Devil King."

"Who are you?" Orion couldn't see anyone.

"The voice continued, "Destroy the Shadow Kingdom, kill the Sleeping Prince and win the entry to the Land of Nines. I'm sorry to say, but that's what they are supposed to live for! If anyone thinks otherwise, they meet the same fate as Dominican. You just watched him taken away. Soon he will die. The same fate sir. No one can. Not allowed to." A voice talked to him from behind.

Orion turned back in fear and noticed a bird with a human head and two large wings walking behind him. He was shocked to find out a strange looking creature was talking in human voice and was having a conversation.

"Who are you? I see you can talk like humans." asked Orion.

"I only come to those who seek light sir. I'm no one sir. I'm just no one." said the human bird with a breathing voice.

"Please don't call me sir! My name is Orion. But who are you? What do you want from me?" Orion was feeling angry.

He paused and looked at the strange creature again. With two brown, white strapped wings, tall nose, drooping deep eyes the creature appeared harmless.

Then he said, "Do you have any idea who I am? I am King Orion. Yes, that's my name. I don't even know how I came here or who brought me and why. Now tell me who you are and what you want from me? Are you a ghost or something?" said Orion in a brittle voice.

Orion took a pause. He was feeling upset and losing his temper.

"Stay positive sir. Yes, that's the way. I'm Yoko, Yoko they call me. I used to be a normal human being. I'm the sister of the King Sculptor, and the rightful owner of the throne of this land. My father gave me the throne before he died. But my brother conspired against me, took the throne, and threw me out. He is still untouched. But not for long. Long story short. He is the Scorpion King Sculptor, yes, that's him sir. No, he cannot escape no more....not his greed and lust. That will bring him down sir. The King does not want me here. People love me and that adds to his anger. He took me as an enemy, put me into prison. Then expelled me out of his kingdom." Yoko finished in a breathing voice.

She was looking at Orion. Then said again, "I live out there, sometime in the ocean, sometime in space. I only come here when I hear a call from someone who seeks light. When you said: 'Where is light?' you turned to me. I heard your call. I'm here." With that the body of Yoko had an aura, a strong pure light that made her special. It was even hard for Orion to look at her. Slowly the light subsided.

There was a pause.

"But how did you hear me even if you are not here?"

Yoko continued again. "Yes, I can sir. I can read people's mind and answer them in their dreams. I can do many things, but mainly I am a singer for the people. I can fight, fly, read other's mind, put out fire or even start one. Since the King does not like me, nobody wants me to be here. They think I might get killed...Which I also worry about sir...You know whom I'm talking about? The King sir, the Devil Scorpion King Sculptor."

"Don't call me sir!" shouted Orion.

"Alright sir."

Orion gave up, "I'm sorry to know, but how did you find me? I do not even know how I got here or who brought me here! I just arrived only hours ago. My name is Orion. I'm sorry, what is your name again the extra-ordinary lady?" said Orion with a question on his tone.

"I am Yoko sir. They call me Yoko, the magician. But I am not a magician Sir. I am just an ordinary lady, although I don't look ordinary. Do I? The way I look now, is due to the curse from the wizard saint king. But he also gave me a rare gift. I can see the past, the present and the future. That's not all. If I want, I may know all his plans, but I can't help him. I can't, I'm sorry sir. I just stand here helplessly as he tortures millions. I can still help you if you want me to. Yes, Yoko, remember my name, I'm Yoko sir, a friend of those who seek light. Remember: light only comes to those who seek it. The other side of light is darkness. Darkness begins when light loses its freedom." the human-bird said in an ephemeral tone.

"Good to know, thank you Yoko, thank you. I am hungry, thirsty; can you tell me where I can find some food or water?"

"Keep walking in this direction sir, you'll see a sign. Not until you see that place, the dark palace of black obsidian. It has food, clothes, jewelries, people, children, their grandchildren... almost everything sir."

"Everything?" Asked Orion. He became interested.

"Almost everything. Remember, you can find almost anything in there, but not love, hope, or light. You remember that sir. Love creates hope. Hope gives light."

"I don't know anything." Yelled Orion.

"Of course, you know sir. Yes, you do. You know. Happiness follows love. Beauty follows happiness. Peace follows beauty, sanctity follows peace. Blessings follow sanctity, and the history and hope follow blessings."

"How do you explain such things?"

"It is easy to know sir. We just don't look for it. We don't. We don't want to."

"Look at this place that has almost everything. But appears so depressing….it got nothing. Nothing at all." Orion expressed.

"Keep going." Said Yoko. "You are getting there."

"You mean to say, they, I mean the King wants it this way… dark, gloomy, depressing and deserted? What's wrong with him?"

"I think you are getting it sir. I think you will get to know his way. A way, elusive, yet painfully attractive."

"What do you mean? What is his way?"

"His way is painfully attractive sir. Very simple."

"Tell me."

"He looks for the sign. The sign of anger. Anger feeds hate. Hate feeds cruelty."

"Keep going."

"Simple sir, simple. Division feeds distrust. Depression follows. Just like service follows salute, bigotry follows discrimination. Justice follows equality and signals hope, anger follows resentment. When people throw away the blessings of trust and hope, they begin to embrace violence as the new way of hope and equality. Unless trust, love and respect meet with fear, diversity is a fantasy sir. Just a fantasy."

"You sound different. You are telling me something I have never heard before." Orion was having a flashback. How he lost his god mother, the only person he loved most as a child. Was that his real mother? To date, he does not know. He heard from other sources, that could be his mother, his real mother, the biological mother. She was the most trusted person in his family. Then someday, she fell ill and died. Orion gazed at his finger. He was looking at the ring she gave him at her death bed. "Son, you are my love. Always will be. Take my name and whisper. It will grant your wish." She was still holding his hands, as she took her last breath. Soon after everyone forgot her, but to date Orion remembers her face and everything she taught or told him. Even today he feels pain and his heart becomes heavy when he thinks of her beautiful face.

"Knowledge comes with clarity sir. Clarity in thinking, seeing things differently without bias. Without clarity knowledge got no power sir, no power."

"So, what are you up to?"

"I'm waiting for the bright moment. The right moment. When everyone will seek light. Seek clarity. Seek freedom. Freedom for their own self. Freedom for others. That's the moment I'm waiting for."

They continued their walking. But there was no sign.

"Where is your sign? Asked Orion.

"You'll see a sign sir. Patience sir. Patience is the key."

"It will direct me toward the right place?"

"You will know when you reach there. That's a dangerous place to be, sir. This entire kingdom is dangerous. And his territory, sir. You got to be careful out here, but I can promise in that palace, in that ballroom there will be food, beverages and much more. Much much more sir, much, much more! It will be an enticing moment for you. But hope, love, or freedom? I don't think so. Be......careful out there...about what you eat, drink or what you do.........or even what you say......or think..."

"Why?" asked Orion.

"Oh, yes. Very soon you will find out. Darkness will be trying to sneak upon you. Evil will ask you to follow. Beauty of peace and sanctity will be a rare gift to reach out to. Be careful of what you say. Proper use of right words at right moment brings in the sound that is like music sir. It can lift you. It can take you to the land of hope. It is like a mosaic of divinity sir. Just by proper use of words you could start a war or could bring peace and prosperity. It is mightier than the sword or the pen. Oh, yes sir! Words can make a huge difference. Look at the exquisite beauty of freedom people enjoy today. It is all because of proper use of words. You know. You could go by the rule of thumb: greed precedes anger ..anger precedes loss of hope....which precedes loss of conscience. They could very well turn you into one of them. Be careful sir, be careful! I shouldn't tell you any more sir! Soon you will find out on your own. Now I got to go. I might

have told you too much sir. If the king....my brother... finds out
he will be upset sir."

"Where is he? The king, your brother? Is there a way to meet
him?" Orion asked.

"Be careful of what you wish for, sir. I'm not supposed to
tell you anything sir... not supposed to.... not supposed to sir,
not supposed to.... ...." Yoko took a turn and moved in another
direction.

"Bye then, take care of yourself!" said Orion as he watched
Yoko taking a turn and walking away.

Then he screamed, "Don't ever call me sir, do you hear me?
But how do I find you again?"

"You will find me only when you truly need me, when you
seek light, seek love and hope, seek freedom....only then...."...
by then Yoko had vanished behind the black walls.

CHAPTER IX

Orion captured

Confused and hungry Orion walked for a few more minutes in the same direction. He passed through deserted buildings, porches, and then came over a canal. He crossed the bridge, entered another part of the kingdom.

The huge iron gate in front of him was closed.

"Who are you?" A strange looking sentry with four legs, and long droopy nose scanned him through his goggles. "Allowed." Popped up in his scanner.

Before Orion answered, the gate opened.

"No weapon? Hmm. You look tired...hungry, bruised... you are not a spy!" He laughed. "From the Shadow Kingdom and the Land of Nines? I don't think so. You are alright. Go ahead. Scorpion King Sculptor's ministry greets you!". The sentry said.

"Don't make too much of a noise here. The King is already upset. Look at the dark cloud. Today is a bad day. Bad day for you, me, everyone." The sentry murmured.

""May I get something to eat? Could you direct me?"

"See you have already started making noise. Don't even try. If there is extra food, of course you will. But yes, only if there is any extra." The sentry chuckled.

Orion passed the gate and came to the front of a huge black palace.

"The sky doesn't look happy." Orion thought. Dark clouds were hovering across the horizon as he watched the thunderstorms. He got up, walked back up the wide stairs and went past the front gate to the lobby on the second floor when it started pouring.

He approached a door. The door opened by itself. Orion entered, passed the empty large table, came to a huge brown chair, and sat down. Tired and exhausted Orion lay there for some time, didn't know how long, and then decided to move on. He came out of the ballroom. Immediately he got wet. Yet, he walked by a few trees and plants. The wet birds were looking for shelter behind the balcony. He went past a deer farm, two duck ponds, and a lake. In the middle of the lake was standing a huge dark stone.

"What is the place? I feel crazy. Where am I?" he muttered.

"In the palace of Black Obsidian." A whispering voice murmured in his ears.

"What happened? How on earth did I even get here?" Orion was talking to himself. He kept walking in the drizzle.

This part of this kingdom was better maintained. The gardens had fruits and flowers. Orion walked to one of the palatial buildings that drew his attention. The nameplate 'The Palaces of Smokey Quartz' was reflecting sunlight. With many strange looking creatures curved on the palace walls and gibberish writing next to them.

He took the shining black stairs and walked up to an open courtyard. In front of him lay several passages. He went through a passage to find himself in front of a large door. He hesitated and waited. Then he pushed the door and entered. It was a ballroom.

Orion had no idea where he was. He drew in a chair from a corner, sat down, closed his eyes, and tried to think. He felt a headache. He felt weak and hungry.

On the large table he noticed unfinished plates with food and drinks. "Maybe a dinner had just been served." He thought.

"Many types of food, fruits and vegetables were on plates. Big jugs of many kinds of drinks, juice and wine were sitting on the side.

"Some people must have just finished eating here," Orion was thinking. The look at food made him hungrier. He sat there for a few minutes, looked around, stood up, and hesitated. Then he rushed to the table, sat down, took out a plate and filled it up with food. Swiftly, he finished and refilled the plate. Thirsty as he was, now reached out for the drinks.

Varieties of drinks were on the table. He started checking the labels….. *Anger of insanity, Rebirth of shadows, Lovers of sanctity, Hatred from the volcanoes, Disgust of lovers* …….and many others. He hesitated for a moment and then picked up the *Lovers of sanctity*. He poured some on his glass. Red bubbles with a clove like smell began forming. He started seeing all colors of balloons of signs of love and hope everywhere. Then they dissolved. Puzzled Orion picked up the glass and started to drink the beverage. He felt relaxed. Very much relaxed.

"But who lives here?" Orion stood up. He was feeling little dizzy. He felt something different.

"Hello? Is anybody there?" He yelled. "HELLO?" Orion hollered. But there was no answer.

Suddenly a nicely dressed woman appeared from the kitchen.

"Do you need anything Sir?" She asked.

In Orion's eyes the woman appeared many. She was a symbol of love and hope. As she approached him, he started having strange visions about the woman, first he saw his wife Zenithia…. she was biting her lower lip, full of love….her red cheeks, her body with very little cover…her sensation made him crazy.

The woman paced toward him slowly and in a lucid voice she asked, "are you alright sir?" She stared at him closely and asked again, "Sir? Everything alright?"

Orion came back to his senses. He looked at the lady. She was not his wife. She was coming close to him and smiling…he felt passionately attracted to her…her deep hazel eyes….her full red lips…her golden cheek….everything became alive. Then he felt sad. Understood it was just a dream.

"Sir, is everything ok?" The lady asked again.

Orion came back to his senses. He jerked open his eyes. Shook his head. He glanced at her and said, "Hmm..yes, yes. I'm fine. Feeling little different, different …… I'm fine. But where am I? Could you tell me a bit about this place? What is the name of this place?" He could barely keep his eyes open.

The lady had a beautiful smile. She gazed deeply into his eyes. Came close to him and whispered, "You are in the Kingdom of King Sculptor. Inside the palace of Starburst Obsidian sir." She sat down next to him

Then softly said in a sad voice, "I'm here, take me with you. I'll come. I want to leave this place. We all do." Then she smiled again and said at a higher pitch:

"It is the drink sir. No worries. Just relax a bit. It will take a few days to completely come out of it. Soon your dizziness will go away. Be careful what you drink sir, be careful what you think too." She waited for a few moments to see the reaction from Orion.

"My name is Faith. Remember my name. Faith. You can find me here. In this palace of Starburst Obsidian. Come and get me if you find a way out of here. I want to come with you." Her eyes turned heavy. Before king Orion understood anything, she kissed him on the cheek. And then went back toward the kitchen. With each step, she turned back and gave him a smile.

From her appearance and the smell of her apron, Orion understood she was busy in the kitchen. He was having visions again. The woman turned into his wife Zenithia now. She sat down next to him. She was staring at his eyes with a loving look.

He opened his eyes still full of love and hope.

The woman standing at a distance glanced back with a lovely smile.

"Be careful of what you eat, drink or say in this land sir." "I'm here for you. Will come if you ever need me."

"But how do I find you?" Orion screamed.

"You'll find me if you ever truly need me. Faith is my name." She stared at his eyes, then gazed at the drinks on the table with a crave for a few seconds, smiled at him, and then she was gone.

Orion rubbed his eyes. Wanted to take the last look at the beautiful woman. She was gone. Devastated Orion looked at his glass. It was still half full. He wanted to drink more. He stretched his right hand and picked up the bottle. But at the last moment, he changed his mind. As he was trying to put down the glass, it stayed locked to his hand. Using his other hand, he wanted to take it out. But it stayed glued to his right hand. Orion wanted to throw it away. But could not. The glass did not move, or the liquid did not get dispensed. Orion felt crazy.

He gazed at the other drinks on the table. One of the bottles marked '*Disgust of lovers*' was shining. With his left hand still free, he picked up the bottle, poured the liquid in a glass. Bubbles started forming and a black smoke came out with a hissing sound in front of his nose. He could smell the sweet bitter candy floss smell and took a sip. Immediately he felt better. His eyes turned red, and fumes started coming out of his face and head. Within few seconds, his symptoms subsided.

But now the glasses were glued to his hands. Orion didn't know what to do. He started picking up and drinking all other drinks with his fingers, ... *Anger of insanity, Rebirth of shadows, Hatred from the volcanoes* one by one. *Anger of insanity* made him angry, his red eyes almost popped out in anger and frustration. He started pulling his hair out. *Rebirth of shadows* made his eyes watery; he discovered himself surrounded by his clones. *Hatred from the volcanoes* made him jump and jump as if he was inside a fireball. Now five glasses were stuck to his hand, arm, and shoulder and he couldn't get rid of any of them or their liquid.

Orion felt crazy, looked up and down, everywhere. He rushed toward the opposite wall and made a blow with his right hand. The glasses fractured; the liquids came out of the glasses. Everything started floating in the air and evaporated. He made another blow with his left hand. Slowly all the glasses fractured, the liquid and the pieces of the glasses evaporated in the air.

Orion fell on the floor with his bloody hands. Blood was dripping out of the wounds. But before it hit the ground it was evaporating too. Slowly he regained strength as he observed his bleeding stopping. He stood up and paced toward the table and sat down.

Orion was still carrying the sword he found. He put it down on the table and stretched out on the chair. Orion looked up at the ceiling. Finally, he felt confident that he was not going to be killed. He turned and gazed out to the blue. Dark clouds were gathering at the skyline. Another storm might be on the way, he thought. His eyes were closing, he was slowly falling into a sleep......

Then behind him, he heard a chatter that woke him up. As he turned and peeked through the huge door, a water wheel came down the river and anchored at the port. Orion picked up the sword from the table. For the first time he noticed, his name inscribed on the steel. "Vulcan Dynasty. King Orion." He got spell bound and almost dropped the sword. What is it all about? He stared at the steel again he was holding. Is it true? His own sword that he carefully locked in his own cabinet in his palatial estate in Eridanious is right here in front of him? He rubbed his eyes repeatedly. Yes, it is his own sword that his father gave him as a gift. He could even identify the bright black mark appeared on the steel when he had to fight with his master as a teen to earn his trust. Orion stared at the half open door. The people were getting closer, their conversations were now more prominent. He quickly put it back into its holder strapped around his waist. He moved, took shelter behind the curtain.

As he watched, people poured out of other water wheels. All were in a hurry, walked in different directions. Many approached the gate and moved toward the same ballroom.

The faces were rarely visible. From head to toe, entire body covered with black cloaks, they entered the room, walked past

Orion, went through another door and disappeared. None of them was aware of Orion who was hiding behind the curtain.

Orion waited a while for the last person to pass and then came out. He looked at the harbor. The water wheels still anchored there, all empty. He tip-toed out of the room through the door; then ran and jumped into a water wheel. The moment he got in, the waterwheel started spinning, shook vigorously and made a tremendous sound. Orion could not stand still. He had to hold on to the handle of the steering wheel tightly. The sound went up and up, intensified and the waterwheel went flying high in the air as it was spinning. Orion felt dizzy. He was hoping to use the water-ferry to get out of there. In a few seconds, Orion found himself thrown out and lying on the ground.

He glanced back at the palace he came out of. Many faces were visible, watching him from their windows. They must have heard the sound.

Once Orion was out of the water-ferry, the ferry moved to the original location next to others and sailed away. Orion laughed in a pale look at the last water wheel as it departed, and then turned back toward the ball room. All the doors now closed; he was uncertain if he would be able to get in.

"Palaces of Smoky Quartz!" written on the wall.

Orion went in and stood in the hallway. A staircase rolled up next to the sign to lead to the second floor. Alarmed and afraid Orion took the stairs. He went up and stood still for a moment before he decided to enter one of the rooms. He tried to concentrate to collect his strength and finally pushed the huge black door. With considerable effort the heavy wooden door opened. A cracking sound filled the air. Orion walked into complete darkness. For a few minutes, he could see nothing. His eyes adjusted and the room appeared empty. As he was walking around the room, he stepped onto something. Orion jumped and yelled in fear. He looked down but found nothing.

Suddenly appeared in front of him a grotesque man. The

man had a dark evil appearance. Orion bolted to another direction in fear, and then he heard a human voice.

"Come closer," the human voice was asking. "I won't harm you."

Orion turned and stepped back. He started running looking for an exit. His eager eyes were adjusting to the darkness. Lamps began popping up across the room. A series of pictures became prominent on the wall. One depicting the kingdom with the seven palaces in the background. Another one with seven unique stones standing in the lake pointing toward the seven palaces. The third picture illustrated the celebration of the arrival of a new royal baby. The beautiful queen was carrying the newborn Prince in her lap. Another picture of the crowning ceremony of a Prince. Next to it was hanging a picture that had the celebration of the Prince's wedding.

Orion followed the man who was now seated on a black throne studded with gold and jewels.

"Is he the same man?" He questioned.

He walked close, very close to the man. Then he noticed something. There were many. Many of them. The evil-looking man had multiplied into many identical dummies. All sitting on thrones side by side in a circle. And it was hard for Orion to recognize which was the original man that he was talking to.

Then one of them moved, stood up and stepped forward. The man had a well-built body, but he was limping, had one of his legs injured, and one of his eyes was made of blackish green stone which was glowing red. His breathing was coming in wheeze. The other dummies remained immobile and speechless. Orion came closer at a slow pace in trepidation and was astonished to see that they were not trying to attack him.

The man moved his fingers and all the windows popped open. It had stopped raining. The sun was setting over the ocean. A flush of light from the setting sun gushed into the room. Then he signaled him to sit down. But Orion didn't want to sit. He was afraid.

The man initiated, "well, well, well, look who is here. Sit down Mr. Orion Vulcan. I believe you are still little drunk. Aren't you? After trying all the drinks that are available in our kingdom. Now, please sit down." He said again in a commanding tone.

Slowly, startled Orion found himself a chair and sat down.

The man had a hoarse voice: "I believe being an outsider, you don't like to be here. Do you? No, you don't. I understand! Yes, this place is not where you wanted to be. It is not familiar to you. Possibly you are completely at a loss! Welcome to the Palaces of Smoky Quartz!"

Orion now slowly realized that huge ballroom was full of many people that came out of the ferry. Behind black cloaks their ugly faces were lurking with greed, anger, and hate.

"Zuno! Tell me what you got. Tell me everything." The man ordered.

A man covered in dark cloak moved forward and made his face visible. He had broad shoulders, a rat tail and red eyes filled with hate. He exchanged looks with Orion. Came forward, bowed, removed his hood, and started.

"Your majesty, every enemy needs to be hunted down. Our beasts are making their lives miserable. Darkness shall be their last restitution. Grave will be their resting peace." Ha, ha, ha..... he started laughing and screaming.

"Need a strategy. Now tell me about the strategy." The King questioned.

"A simple thing. Bring hell to The Shadow Kingdom and the Land of Nines. Ruin and run. Destroy in disguise. Attack when they are expecting you the least. Learn from their weakness. Crush their confidence and hope."

"Then what are you waiting for?" The King was annoyed.

"Spy. The right spy. The man who can move in silence like a snake. In secrecy. But adamant and fearless. Can hide his emotion but determined with passion. Can play with danger but can conceal his identity. At the same time ready to meet his fate, his destiny. I am waiting for that man." Zuno finished.

"Yes, I understand." The King replied. "You need someone who can infiltrate into the inner circle of the Queen. Someone she can trust. Someone she might even allow. Allow to get close to the Prince Anish's chamber in the Diamond palace. Or get to the Wizard Saint King's mummy and his power. We need someone who can be trusted as an insider. Be there when we need him. Who can unlock the mysterious magical power of the Wizard Saint King. But who could this be? Do we have such a man? The man that we can trust and so could the Queen? Answer me. Answer me Zuno!" Thundered the King.

"For a few moments Zuno remained silent. Then he turned, advanced toward Orion and said,

"Maybe this man? This Mr. Orion Vulcan?"

"You think so?" The King said in a surprised voice.

"Now with this man standing here, we might be lucky!" He finished in a thoughtful voice. Zuno folded his hands and stretched them toward Orion. "Maybe this is the man. Maybe he could solve the puzzle that we have been struggling with. Maybe he is the man Your Majesty. The man that we have been waiting for." He said smiling.

"Then why don't you put his family tree up there on the wall and explain everything to Mr. Vulcan? Hah?" The King asked. "Once he understands who he is, and why he is here, things might be easier for him. Isn't it Mr. Vulcan?"

"Sure, as you say your majesty." Zuno said.

"Look at me ..look at my eyes …closely." Zuno approached in front of Orion and said while staring at him with a creepy smile on his face.

A green, yellow ribbon formed around Orion, flew back to the distant wall, and started writing something.

A huge family tree started being printed on the distant wall. There Orion found his name glowing in the fire. It took him some time to understand what was going on.

But as he went up the chart, he could see the names of all his fathers, and grandfathers, great grandfathers…great great grandfathers.... ....the chart went on and on and on and finally at the very top was written Sleeping Prince.....

"Look again, Mr. Look at the chart." Zuno said.

"Why me? Why are you showing me all these?" Orion screamed in a timid voice.

"I am sure you don't know our King, or who we are and how you got here. It's a dangerous place Mr. Orion Vulcan! This Kingdom of seven Palaces of Smoky Quartz!. Unless allowed, no one, can enter or leave this place! And only a very few can even go back alive. If that answers the questions in your mind. If you wish to live, want to see your family, cooperate! I guess you want to go back and see your family again, don't you?"

Zuno had a sinister laugh and took a pause. "Our king is the master of this Kingdom! He wants to reclaim the right of the Endless Stone and regain his own land. Someday he will be the force behind the planet. That day is coming. The shadow kingdom of the sleeping Prince will be there no more. Guess who will be ruling. It is our King! Now all we need to do is destroy Prince Anish?"

All those who were present in the room cheered, "Destroy the Prince!"

"Destroy the whole family."

People cheered, "Destroy the whole family."

"Destroy his kingdom and his followers."

People cheered, "Destroy the Kingdom. Destroy the followers."

"Destroy the Sleeping Prince. Destroy the family. Destroy the kingdom and the palaces.........................." The cheering continued.

Minister Zuno was breathing heavily. Fiery speeches were coming out of his mouth and fumes were forming all around him. He appeared evil and dangerous.

Orion glanced around. Endless series of people wrapped in black cloaks were standing. He could not see the end of the room. All evil looking eyes were on him now. He could see many faces filled with anger, greed, and hatred. He remembered the creature and what it told him, *'in that ballroom there will be food, beverages and much more. Much much more sir, much, much more! But hope, love or beauty? I don't think so….be careful there…about what you eat, drink or what you do……….or even what you say……or think… Remember, you can find almost anything in there, but not love, hope, or light. You remember that sir.'*

"Order, order, order." Said the King. "Silence!"

"Mr. Vulcan. Look at the chart carefully. You carry the bloodline of Prince Anish; you can get in and out of the Shadow Kingdom and trick the force-fields. Do you follow me? We are asking for your help!" Zuno said in an alluring voice.

"Me, Prince…. Shadow kingdom, force-field, blood relative… you must be making a mistake. I'm from Eridanious. I don't understand. Why me? I am just a common man." Orion screamed the words out of his lungs out of desperation. He did it after collecting lots of stamina. Once done, he leapt backward. He was sweating.

A lady covered in black, and red appeared from nowhere and stood in front of him. Her entire body was fuming with different colored signs of shooting arrows. With the mask of a lioness and a black cloak printed with hissing cobras covering her entire body. Only her long black hair, deep eyes were visible through the shining dark red glass walls of her mask. She winked at him. Or did she? She bowed her head to him and the king as a protocol. Orion shook his head. Is he still drunk? He asked himself. He bowed back. He started floating in the air in his dreams and was having visions about the woman he met before.

"I think we got our man. He would be able to penetrate the defense system of the Shadow Kingdom. He got the right track record and a matching DNA with the Prince as a blood relative." As she was talking to the King, she took out a scanner from her pocket, scanned him. Then she pointed the light from her scanner at the bottom of the chart and started reading…."50% with the father, 25% with the grandfather, 19% with the great

great grandfather. She kept going. ....0. 3% with the Prince's great Grandfather. ....0. 1% with the prince's father.......and.... 0.01% with the Prince.

"Excellent news Amihan! That's enough." What else are we waiting for?" The King remarked. Then he turned toward Orion and said, That's my daughter Amihan. She is trained in every martial art. And so is my son Benjiro.

"But, ...I think you are making a mistake." Orion said helplessly. He came back to his senses.

No one paid any attention to answer Orion Vulcan's concerns.

"We will train you, and in a few days, you will be on your way and ready to face anybody in this world. We will give you the protection you need." Amihan finished.

The King came up to him with an awful expression and a sarcastic grin attested to his face as he exchanged looks with Orion. Then he gave a smile and took out a black stone from his pocket.

As he held the stone on his hand, he called out, "Circinus where are you?"

A bright black grisly serpent figure started forming on his hand. Slowly it got larger and larger and wrapped around his hand and neck.

"Go and bring me back the latest information from the shadow kingdom Circinus! I need to know everything." He smiled. His blackish teeth sparked with hate, anger, and fury.

The serpent sniffed King's face, glanced around him, slowly uncoiled, and flew out of the window. The horn on its head and the two red eyes started shining as it continued its journey. In a few minutes it disappeared behind the clouds.

The King watched the serpent for a few moments, smiled and put back his black stone into the pocket. "Soon we will know what we do not know. We will see what we have not seen yet, and we will hear what we are not supposed to."

Then he looked back at Orion. He blinked furiously at everyone and said, "Time. Sure, give him time. He will learn. I know he will. Let him understand the value of this place." He stared again and laughed.

Amihan stared at Orion. Orion started having visions again. The more he thought about the beautiful face of the lady he met before; he became lost in his dreams. But then again as he stared back at the King, he came back to his senses. The vicious look of the King, his red flashing suspicious eyes, dark long hair, and creepy laugh were making Orion jittery.

Zuno's hoarse gasping voice came out.

"Our King needs to know everything that goes on behind those closed doors of the forbidden palaces. He needs to know how we can overcome their force-fields." Zuno said. The men standing in the room grinned slyly.

The King had a jittery laugh. The sarcastic laugh echoed through the doors, windows, gullies, valleys—across the dark kingdom.

Everyone started laughing with him.

The King couldn't stop laughing. He sipped from the bottle of rum in his hand, smirked. "Go and get that map out Brody! Get it out of the cabinet and hang it on the wall! Would you? And let Zuno explain it all."

One guy with a walker stepped out, went over to the cabinet, and brought out a map. He put it on the table. The King stretched his hands. A thin dust of silvery particles came out of his hands and hovered across the room, made the map float in the air. The map got larger, wider. floated straight to the opposite wall. Colorful stars began to shine at different locations.

"We are here," Zuno explained, pointing at one of the stars on the map with his long silver rod that now formed on his hand. He could extend or shrink the silvery rod at his will. "Our people could reach these places and storm them quickly. But we need a guide. Someone who knows everything about these palaces. Their strengths and weaknesses. Their vulnerabilities, their exits, and entry-points. We need someone who can let us in and out of those palaces without any detection." Zuno paused.

"I am tired! Tired of my people getting killed," the King ended with a thumping voice. Everyone was staring at the map. The King was explaining, the different points of the map were becoming bright one by one. The golden color of the beautiful Shadow Kingdom and the Land of Nines was lighting up at a distance from the dark grey colored palace of smoky quartz on the map.

Orion couldn't speak for a while. He lost his voice completely at the gravity of the situation. He wasn't sure what to tell or how to answer. Was it real?

He stepped back in fear and said, "Please let me go. I don't understand. What are you saying? Please tell me what you want from me. I am just a common man. Yes, they call me King Orion. But in real life I am no king. Just a common man….a common man…just a commoner. Kindly let me go, please." He was shivering in frustration and fear. His eyes were getting watery.

"Calm down, son, calm down, calm down. Don't be afraid. I am not a bad person, never was, never will be. You trust me, don't you? It is the hatred and darkness in me. That takes me over. But I'm not a bad man!" Scorpion King Sculptor screamed in fury. Then he gazed straight at Orion's eyes. Orion felt a deep sensation in his head. He screamed in pain.

The King made a clap. Orion spanned around and flew close to the king. With eyes closed, the King made a fist, and then opened his palm with the word "*The Sword!*" A sword figure started to form on his palm, it came flying at Orion and merged with the sword hanging from the waist of Orion. The King moved his hands once more and the unlocked sword from his waist came flying next to Orion Vulcan's neck. His lock of hair was waving back and forth in the air close to the sword. He understood that Scorpion King Sculptor was getting upset. Slowly the sword came back to his holder in the waist.

"Take a seat." Immediately Orion found himself seated on a chair not very far from the King.

"My daughter Amihan will be with you. And so will my son Benjiro. Right Benjiro? You will train him."

A young-looking man named Benjiro came forward and stood by his sister Amihan. He bowed his head to the King and Orion to follow the etiquette, stood still.

"They will give you the power to be invisible, fly, or reach anywhere you want in a second's time." The King continued. "They will protect you from any danger."

Orion turned toward his side. He took another look at Amihan and Benjiro. Benjiro's entire body was covered in dark cloak. Only his dark red eyes were visible that were filled with hatred.

Scorpion King Sculptor turned to Orion and said, "Come closer my friend. Closer. Let me show you. Who we are and where we come from."

The black-red cloak from his body came off, floated in the air.

Scorpion King Sculptor examined everyone in the room. Then he turned to his children. He took his mask off and threw it in the air. The sword hanging from his waist suddenly came off and started floating alongside the mask. As the King moved his fingers, the sword raced back and forth through the air and sliced the mask and his cloak into many pieces. The pieces of the mask and the cloak began to dissolve into fumes and vanished.

Then an amazing thing happened. The dark room started glittering like gold. All the masks and cloaks from peoples' body fell loose came out into the air and started floating. The King's sword raced to find each one of them, sliced it into pieces and moved to the next one. In a few minutes all the masks and the cloaks dissolved into fumes and vanished. Men and women in that dark room hiding behind their cloaks and masks came out of their darkness. Men moved forward to talk to their ladies in the room and started conversations. A newlywed couple was among them. The Devil King and his dark kingdom destroyed their wedding and every dream. The priest present at their wedding captured by the Devil King's soldiers was now free. Another old couple slowly walked out of the shadows. They were very tired and exhausted. They could hardly stand for a long time. They had no choice but to follow the orders. Their outfits and age were telling a different story. It was obvious, they were not ready for any of this. Among all these new and old people in their eyes, there was no sign of greed written.

Scorpion King Sculptor came out of the curse. In front of Orion was now standing a young handsome man who was not limping anymore. He had no facial disfiguration and had perfect eyes. A tall muscular handsome man was standing there whose entire body was covered with a dazzling royal dress. He appeared cheerful and gracious. This man had no resemblance with the dark, demon looking person he watched a minute ago. Scorpion King Sculptor greeted everyone with a smile. Then he noticed the old couple and approached them.

"I'm truly sorry for what you had to go through. But now I release you from my bondage. You are free to go or move anywhere." With his signal, a royal minister (Orion was surprised to see it is the same Zuno with a rat tail who was a vicious person a few minutes ago) took out a pad and paper from the table, and advanced toward the King. The King signed the paper and gave it to them. "This will release you from being captured anywhere in my Kingdom." The black stamp of the Kingdom of Smoky Quartz in red was visible at the center of the paper, but it was dazzling with gold ribbons.

The couple were incredibly happy. They bowed and thanked the King many times. Slowly they turned around and walked out of the room with a smile on their face.

The King then noticed the newlywed couple. He came near them and asked, "tell me your name. And explain what happened."

"I'm Adrija and he is Deneb. Halfway through our wedding, King's soldiers came in horse and arrested us. Our wedding was never complete. Since then, we have been asked to be present at every gathering your Majesty in case you need us."

The King listened to their story carefully. Then said in a humble tone, "would you please accept my apologies? Your journey into new beginning needs privacy in peace. You can't be any part of this war. Go back. Find a place at the very distant corner of my Kingdom. No one will ever disturb you." He handed them another copy of his signed release order.

The couple hesitated for a moment. They felt ecstatic. They started kissing each other. Everyone cheered. Then they bowed to the King, thanked him, and walked out of the room with big smiles.

"And you. You can leave. I release you." The King was speaking to the priest. "The war is not for you." The King blinked at his eyes and gave him the signed release order form. "Go back to your monastery and preach to your followers and the children. Tell them about all the great things that this planet has to offer."

The priest was puzzled, did not know what to say. He appeared pale and weak. "I'll pray for you and our Kingdom." He hesitated.

"Go ahead, take it." The King ordered.

The priest accepted the signed copy, bowed to the King, and turned back. Soon he was gone.

Scorpion King Sculptor walked back to the window. He stood there looking at the sky which had turned bright golden red. Then he took steps to walk on the glittering golden floor. The kingdom outside was no more depressing or dull. Gentle breeze had started. A beautiful music was filling the air. The magnolia, violet, Azalea, camellia and many other flowers were blossoming in the gardens. In the reflected lights from the lakes of the setting golden sun, the entire landscape in the Kingdom of seven Palaces of Smoky Quartz appeared stunningly beautiful.

In that beautiful dazzling landscape, Orion noticed a large crowd. The same prisoners that were being tortured or killed in the dungeon were free now. They were streaming out of the prison cells or the poison chambers.

The guards that wanted to kill people a few minutes ago, were now handing them over clothes, food, and water. People were waiting in lines with a blissful smile. They appeared hungry, sick, and weak yet patient. It was a beautiful scene. The music of divinity was filling the air everywhere.

Scorpion King Sculptor was now standing in the middle of the hall; his young appearance made everyone breathless. Next to him were standing his handsome son Benjiro in a Princely dress and his divinely beautiful daughter Amihan as a Princess. The people in the ballroom all appeared good innocent people, their black cloaks and ugly looks were gone. They emerged well-fed, with well-built bodies and smiling faces. No touch of evil could be spotted on them.

In that Kingdom of seven palaces of Smoky Quartz, the central courts, city walls, porticos, sidewalks, gardens, canals, bridges; all were now gleaming like gold. The mosaics on the floors of every palace were ornamented with diamonds and jewels. The people started coming out of their small huts, poured out on streets. They all looked happy and graceful, busy with their own work. The hungry, tormented men, women, and children that Orion watched a while ago were coming out of the underground dungeon in smiling faces. Kids were in a mood of jubilation. The entire kingdom and its people, the palaces, coliseums, greeneries, orchards, roads, meadows, and mountains together seemed like a perfect place to live.

Orion looked through the window. He spotted thousands of troops standing idly in unison at a distance on a field, ready to take orders. He was amazed to see that the king had such well-organized armies. They were dressed in dark black, red, and grey.

"You see Mr. Vulcan, this is a great country, a great kingdom of wonderful people. The military and the people that you see now are a great success story. They are invincible. Each one of these soldiers is self-protected from the enemy by its own invisible armor." Scorpion King Sculptor was walking back and forth as he was gazing at the sky. A dark smoky wave was cutting through the evening clouds. It was the serpent Circinus. The King stretched his left hand.

Circinus landed on his palm. It a wavy motion it went up his arm, coiled his neck and stayed there.

"What did you see? Tell me everything that you have seen Circinus."

The snake made a hissing sound.

A flash of sound and light came out of his mouth. It started to take a shape. Soon everyone saw a movement. The picture of Tyler and Ella standing by the window in a huge palace room.

"The chosen ones are here. Very soon the Prince will wake up." Circinus muttered slowly in its broken hissing sound. The crowd was listening in a silence at the background.

The King stared at the two kids. For a few moments he didn't say anything.

But something was wrong. The beautiful music that filled the air, suddenly stopped.

"They look harmless. I am not even sure if they are the chosen ones." Amihan said softly with a blissful smile. "Maybe Circinus is wrong."

"Noooo!" A scream came out of the mouth of the serpent. "Circinus is never wrong. Never will be."

"They are too young to be the chosen ones." Benjiro said aloud.

"But they are." Screamed Circinus again.

"It is not how old they are. It is who they are and where they come from." Scorpion King Sculptor spoke in a concerned tone. He felt remorse and depressed. His eyes began losing its charm.

The King stood still for a while looking over the beautiful landscape. Took out the same black stone from his pocket. He moved near the high table, put it on the top in front of a mirror.

"Enchanter's Stone! Wake up."

"A light started to form as a blueish golden black woman's body emerged. The woman gazed at the King. Eye to eye. Then she smiled.

"On each call, I answer only three questions. And you can call me only nine times. This is the first question. Remember." Her beautiful smile came back. Her dominance over the King was apparent.

"Bring me the news of the Chosen Ones from the Shadow Kingdom." He ordered.

She emanated with full force and streamed across the sky. In a few seconds the woman streaked back through the sky, came back to the King, and landed next to the stone.

"The chosen ones have arrived, soon they will meet the queen." She smiled with her beautiful white teeth shining. It was a wistful smile.

"I told you! You need to trust me." Circinus was sad and angry. Its tail tightened as it came hissing at the King. "You need to trust me, need to trust me." The sad snake slowly uncoiled and left King's body. It drew near the window and flew out into the vastness of the sky. Soon it disappeared.

"Enchanter's Stone, tell me how to get to the Sleeping Prince." Scorpion King Sculptor asked again.

The beautiful bluish black woman gazed a minute at the King. Her face was bearing a footprint of melancholy. This time she dissolved into a blue glow, emanated with full force, streamed across the sky. After a few seconds the blue glow was back. It landed next to the stone on the table. And she reemerged.

"He is protected. By the power of the Diamond palace. The power of the Diamond palace is protected by the magic of the endless stone.

"Who can break through the magic to get to the Prince?" The King questioned.

"Only a pure soul can pass through its barriers. Anyone else will be scorched to death. Find the Gold Magic, the chosen ones. They own the Gold Magic. Only they can allow you to get to the Prince's chamber. No one else can." The woman answered slowly. Her voice was breaking up. "I must leave."

The eyes of Scorpion King Sculptor almost blew up in rage. "How can I get to it? How do I bring them here?"

"They are protected by the force of the Gold Magic, a hard thing to break into." Her daughter Amihan answered calmly in a grave tone.

The King glanced at the melting away woman for a few moments. His eyes became red.

"Enchanter's Stone, Bring the mask, Put the cloaks, get us ready, Devil the hope."

The woman's body began melting away and disappearing into the stone. The halfway melted woman smiled again. By now she already had lost one of her legs, both her hands. Her head was still visible over her torso. She stared at the King for a while. "Think again." She heaved, took a pause, and said in a shattered voice.

"Devil not the power.
With time it fades.
Mask will stay
Fail or fall.
Only pure can bring them
Back from the call.
Bloodline can win
Might be the way
Yet, Purity is the key
Nothing else will sway."

A blue light started at the black stone, jumped into the bodies of every person in the room. Then it streaked out through the evening sky and moved at a lightning speed to touch everything in the kingdom. Finally, it came back to the king and got absorbed into his body.

The King stretched his hands. Immediately black cloaks and masks came flying from the sky through the window.

They wrapped around the bodies and faces of everyone in the ballroom including Orion with only their eyes visible.

When the blue light hit Orion, he had a strange feeling. As he opened his eyes, he found himself standing in a beautiful kingdom. There he met a gorgeous queen who had just finished talking to two young kids. Are they the kids he met during his voyage in Adora? Orion was surprised.

Scorpion King Sculptor swung his arm with a scream. A cry out of despair. An angry reverberation started to fill every corner of his kingdom. Wind began blowing. Fire broke out at many parts. A storm set off. Uprooted trees started falling. Rivers were surging again. Huge tsunami rolled in flooding shorelines. Scream and horror broke out. Helpless people started running everywhere out of fear.

The beautiful picture of the kingdom visible a few minutes ago disappeared. Instantly, the dazzling appearance of the kingdom started to fade. As evening drew in, a dark velvet descended over the land. The dazzling seven palaces sitting inside the Kingdom of Smoky Quartz started losing their glory. Angry demonstrations started. People were screaming out of despair, pain, and anxiety.

The quiet and well-behaved guards were now active again with their brutal force. They were rounding up the prisoners, hunting them down like animals either to kill or to send them back to prisons.

The story didn't end there. Fireballs started rolling out of the top of the Devil Tower toward the sky aimed at the Shadow Kingdom of seven palaces. As the soldiers rushed out of their barracks, they turned into beastly creatures. Many more dreadful creatures came out of the forests. All started roaring across the dark roads of the kingdom.

. Scorpion King Sculptor's mask and black cloak that vaporized reappeared in his body. The long double-edged sword came right back to the holster where it was hanging from his waist. He started limping again. Only his heinous, deep, and red eyes were visible. He picked up the black stone from the table and put it back into his pocket with a creepy smile.

King's handsome Princely son changed back to the ferocious greedy looking young man Benjiro. But his beautiful daughter didn't undergo any metamorphosis. Though her royal dress was now gone with her body covered with a dark cloak, her beautiful innocent face remained unchanged under the mask. She retained all her charm and beauty. No one was aware of this.

Orion was still in his dream. He was not conscious the one-eyed evil looking old limping Scorpion King Sculptor was standing only a few feet away staring at everyone.

One large black bird with raptorial beak flew in through the evening sky from somewhere and sat on his right hand. Scorpion King Sculptor patted the bird while talking.

"Need a plan. Need a plan. Shadow Kingdom and the Land of Nines. Yes, all will be mine. I will recapture the Gold Magic, the Purple Magic and rule the world. But how? Show me the plan Zuno?"

"Greed and lust will rise. People will dig into their follies. Darkness wins. Stay close to the Enchanter's Stone." Zuno laughed.

"The darker the power, more powerful is the destiny. It is the future. They can't resist it." Benjiro was talking.

"Let greed be their wisdom, lust propel the power, their hope. Let hunger for lust drive them to their last....their destiny ... Scorpion King Sculptor started laughing.

Perplexed Orion stood there motionless.

Scorpion King Sculptor, the devil king who had a clean, innocent face a few minutes ago, was gone. His open jaws, black teeth and sarcastic grin expressed the evil smile and intention on his face.

"You see Orion. This is my bird Rabaga. I gave him a new name, Neohi." Notorious Scorpion King Sculptor was talking to Orion. He was pointing at the dark black, red bird perched on his hand that flew in from the ceiling. It was a two-faced creature, had no tail. From one of its face, fire was streaming out. From the other, a long tongue visible behind its teeth was hissing out to smell and catch.

"Rabaga-Neohi. Rabaga is the bird. Neohi is the snake. My two-faced bird creature. Are you listening to me? Orion?"

The high-pitched voice of Scorpion King Sculptor broke his dream and brought Orion back to his senses. King's dark-blue face, cynical smile and corny looking hair made Orion worried and uneasy.

"Look at this bird. How he can change back and forth from a bird into any other creature. He was our beloved servant, the right-hand man of my father.

Then he turned at the bird that was perched on his hand. "You betrayed. Lied to my father when he needed him most." The king was patting the bird as he was looking at him. "Now he is at my mercy if he wants to get back his original stature. A small price to pay." The king smiled.

The bird's face turned red. Fire and fumes sprinted out of its mouth. It hit the King's face. But did not do anything.

The King laughed and continued. "My father was a good man. He gave him another form to repay his debt. His strength can match anyone in this world in strength and stamina. He can form something out of nothing," Scorpion King Sculptor paused and murmured…"yet, he can't break into the temple tower, go near the endless stone or get into the Diamond Palace……………..we need a path forward." he started to ponder…..King's voice reverberated across the room.

Then he whispered, "But why? This Wizard guardian King is dead. Yet his spirit, his magic is alive. The spirit. Waking up every night. Guarding the Diamond Palace, Ruby palace, Amber palace…every palace. The entire kingdom. Are you listening to me? Orion?"

"Oh, yes, yes, yes." Orion spoke in a trembling voice.

"You like the dark. Don't you? The dark lives. The dark rules. The dark wins. Wins always."

Orion repeated, "yes, dark rules. It wins always. Wins always." By now he had forgotten everything that Yoko had told him.

"Be on my side. Won't you Orion? You have the advantage of the same bloodline. You know that. Don't you?"

"No...I don't..." Orion murmured, and then looking at the King's eyes sluggishly stated again, "Oh, yes, yes, I know...I do."

"I know you do." The King raised his finger and Orion started spinning and flying in the air. "Be faithful. Stay on my side."

Neohi jumped out of the ceiling and turned into a huge monstrous two-winged lion. He was almost on his way to jump over Orion.

"Wait. I'm only testing him. Don't hurt him yet." Sculptor yelled. "But if he chooses otherwise, he will have to pay. Pay dearly." King's voice was stiff and rude.

Orion was trembling in fear.

"Forgive me your majesty. I don't think that would be necessary. Afterall he is our last hope. Maybe he does not know how to talk to a king yet. But in time he will. His knowledge will surpass your expectation. He is a private citizen without any prior expertise your majesty. Maybe..... we should send him for a complete training under Neohi." King's daughter Amihan remarked humbly with a smile on her face.

"Hmmm...not a bad idea. Well, let him go Neohi. Let him go." Scorpion King Sculptor was breathing heavily.

Neohi left Orion and jumped back to the ceiling. Soon he turned into a small insect and was not visible...slipped into the crack.

Scorpion King Sculptor blinked at Orion, and he was bolted on the chair next to the King.

"But what if he fails?" Benjiro shouted out of frustrations.

"I don't think he is an idiot." Amihan shouted at her brother.

"I've checked his background. He comes from a royal family in this life too."

"He looks like an idiot." Cried someone.

"Yes, he does look like an idiot. Doesn't he?" Another person said loudly.

"Kill him. Kill Him." Someone started to shout.

"Bad, Bad, bad. That would be a bad mistake. It took us almost a thousand year to find someone who is from the same bloodline as the Sleeping Prince Anish. If we lose this chance, it could take another thousand years to get someone like him. Until then we will have to stay here and rot. Do you want to go through that again?" Amihan remarked.

"Well, well. You all are losing patience my friend. Respect our guest. He will learn. Give him time!" Scorpion King Sculptor laughed. His haggard facial expression was more visible this time as he laughed to induce terror inside everyone in the room. His cracked and hoarse voice sounded like someone else's.

"Yes, I mean, sure, yes," Orion could feel his head spinning. He stared at the man without any more word.

He watched Neohi now sitting on a window, then slipped into a crack. In few minutes it came out through another crack from the roof and hung from the ceiling. The creature stayed there for a few minutes, then expanded and expanded. It got heavy and fell on the floor. The creature tried to stand up. A moment later, a giant six-winged wolf was standing on the floor next to Orion.

The wolf stood there for a while staring at everyone and then slowly walked forward and stood with the rest of the people in the room. A dark spotted cloak was covering the body of the wolf. Orion watched speechlessly and waited to see what might happen next.

The wolf had its body covered with a black cloak and its eyes were glowing in the room with dark looks. Orion noticed the wolf had wrinkles all over its face.

Orion shivered out of fear and distress. He didn't know what to do or say.

"We want you to go to the Shadow Kingdom. You need to be tactical, and elusive, arrogant, aggressive, cruel but hideous. You're the one. You must learn how to sneak into the library. Look for the Book of Ten. From there on I do not know. No one knows." Paused Amihan looking at Scorpion King Sculptor.

"Be one of us," Sculptor proclaimed. Bring me the Endless Stone. I will let you go....... bring me the Endless Stone.........."

Gently, the people around him began chanting. "Join our force. Be one of us!" their chant echoed across the palace.

Suddenly the door behind Scorpion King Sculptor opened. One of his followers came forward and gave him a map. The Dark King walked restlessly. He was angry. He was upset. He screamed out of anger and threw out the map toward the opposite wall.

A dark cloud started forming. It slowly enveloped the entire room. It was a map of the enemy kingdom.

Then a scene appeared. The picture of the shadow kingdom and the land of nines emerged over the ocean as an illusion made of light and fire. The cloud stayed scattered.

Everyone could see the entire kingdom.

Amihan started explaining.

"Here is the Diamond palace. And here is the Prince's chamber. Look at the positions of the guards. And here is the Ruby, Sapphire, Amber, Pearl, Emerald, and Topaz. Look at the stone sitting on the lake in front of each palace. The stones bring in the energy and light for the palace and the kingdom. They also protect the palaces and the Kingdom. To get in and out of the palace you need to be a blood relative. Someone that can pass through the palace eyes."

Scorpion King Sculptor stood there watching.

Amihan continued, "the chosen ones are here at the Sapphire palace. Before it is too late. They can go in and out of every palace. If we can capture any one of them and bring in here, we will have the power to get to get anywhere in the Kingdom. And maybe to the Queen and maybe we will be able to get to the prince!"

"Get going. Bring me a plan how we can storm the Shadow Kingdom. You have one week. The clock starts now. Be Ready."

Scorpion King Sculptor pointed his sword toward the wall. The door opened in front of him. The King went through the door and disappeared. The opening closed and there was no trace of Scorpion King Sculptor.

His followers started to disperse as they walked toward the black wall behind them. Soon all disappeared behind the black walls one by one. Orion didn't know what to do with himself or where to go who was the only one left in that room.

Orion stood there speechless. All the lamps started going out one by one.

The room turned completely dark and empty.

In a few seconds, Orion noticed he was the only one standing in that room. The next thing he knew, he was standing in the middle of a forest in another land. Another man was standing next to him covered in a dark cloak.

"Let's hurry, Mr. Vulcan, we got work to do!" The man stated in a calm voice.

Orion now understood, he couldn't escape unless he followed their orders. With a big heave, he just accepted his fate. He looked again at the back of his cloak; a small dark Scorpion King Sculptor figure was visible clearly. The picture was alive, Orion was stunned. It was him, that snake, that wolf. That man, Neohi!

CHAPTER X

The Journey begins

A woman in a startling lace dress, walked in with a basket of flowers. She laid down the basket on the same table Tyler was hiding under. After filling up the vase with water from the fountain of the painting, she walked up to the picture. A low humming sound was coming out of her mouth.

She transferred the flowers into the vase and then wiped the furniture. With a fresh white cloth, she cleaned the table. Next, she turned toward Narasingha, the human faced lion. As she moved, she noticed something was out of place. She pondered for a moment and then her face turned white. It was the bronze statue of the lady on horseback was missing. Terrified, the woman screamed. Rapidly she turned and examined around the room. With a cautious eye, she approached the door. The door opened on its own. The moment she got out, it closed automatically. From her dress, it was obvious she was not just any house cleaner.

Tyler came out and ran to the window. He noticed the lady leaving the building and running toward the gate. Soon the lady was seen talking to the guards while pointing toward the building.

Immediately some guards approached the front gate of the palace to make a fortified barrier. One of the guards came off the horse and walked up to the door. He pushed but the door did not open. The heavy mahogany door didn't budge.

"What is happening?" He screamed. "Maybe we need to break in!"

His voice could be heard as he screamed in high pitch.

"Be respectful!" The prince is asleep." A heavy voice echoed everywhere.

Immediately the guard mellowed down. He turned back and left the area.

At the center of the seven distant lakes the stones seated were glowing. They were lighting up each palace in front of them and every corner of the kingdom and the heaven.

One of the main guards turned toward the Ruby palace on horseback. A beautiful middle-aged woman in royal dress was seating on her throne in her courtroom. She was the Queen. Queen Eleonora. Two monstrous looking guards Jori and Himari were standing next to her. Her nine ministers, Prithvi, Birsa, Imani, Bidziil, Aphiguna, Hoag, Afjal, Ayoreo, and Najeebah were seated around in the chamber.

A commoner standing in front of her was asking for justice.

"Explain to your Majesty what you have to say." Minister Bidziil said.

"Two days ago, they came. Knocked on my door." The commoner was explaining. "My wife opened the door. They came in and started asking questions. The questions that we could not answer." Before leaving they told us, 'The King sent us. The Devil King. Never tell anyone that we visited you. Or you will die. Get us the answers. We will be back again.' Then they came again last night. We could not answer any of their questions. Enraged, they kicked me, threw me out of my house. Then they killed my wife, put my house on fire and took away my daughter." The man was sobbing.

"How many?" Asked one of her ministers named Prithvi.

"Six of them. Looked like soldiers."

"Did they come on horses? Or on foot?" Asked minister Imani.

"They all came on horseback your majesty. Before leaving, they even told me, "Remember our name, the *Flying Devils.* Go and tell everyone."

Queen Eleonora looked at the farmer. Then asked, what did they want?"

"They asked me to give them information where to find the Queen. The prince. How to go to the temple Tower of Magellan or how to get into the palace of Sapphire. Asking about the source of our phytoplankton. These kinds of questions your majesty."

"We have heard of them before. But we could not apprehend them yet. You can go now. The Kingdom will do everything to help and protect you." Minister Prithvi said.

The man bowed and left.

Queen Eleonora turned to Prithvi, "Deploy guards at every corner of the kingdom."

"Who are they? These people?" Asked one of her ministers named Birsa.

"Devil's hand is long. Can reach anywhere." Minister Hoag said with a concerned look.

"Won't be surprised if these are his men." Minister Bidziil said.

Queen Eleonora stared at him and then continued her discussion about the state of the kingdom with her ministers.

Her eyes shifted at the guard when he entered the courtroom and raised her hand asking everyone to be quiet.

The guard slowly approached the queen and bowed.

"Say what you have to say." Prithvi said.

"Your majesty, Ritu just noticed the bronze statue of the lady on horseback is missing from the ball room of the *Sapphire* palace."

Queen Eleonora stared at everyone.

"Devil never sleeps. Never does it get tired." She uttered gradually in a grave tone. "Send Ritu. I want to talk to her."

She turned toward her chief minister and asked, "Prithvi, send someone to check out the situation. Give me a complete report. Is it a breach or something that we all have been waiting for!"

"I sense the same. Maybe the day is coming that we all are waiting for!" Birsa said.

Prithvi rushed outside.

The head of the palace guards Perseus approached him. He was a tall, well-built man. With broad shoulders and long hair and mustache, he appeared invincible. Perseus was also the general of the queen's infantry.

Prithvi explained the situation. Perseus left on horseback, reached the Sapphire Palace, and heard everything. Then he approached the door and pushed.

He was unable to open the door. "Hmm...strange, he grinned. "Wait here. Let me go back and report to the queen. Until then, keep an eye on the palace and guard the surrounding area. Also talk to everyone and anyone. Did anyone see any strange thing? Out of ordinary? In last few days or last few hours? We need to know. Know everything, anything."

Perseus turned back. As he returned and entered the court room, he noticed, Ritu was standing next to Queen Eleonora.

"Are you sure? The Bronze statue of Ashwini on the horse is gone?"

"Yes, your Majesty. I swear your Majesty." Ritu answered.

Suddenly one of the guards brought in a commoner.

Everyone looked up.

Queen Eleonora stared at them with a curious gaze.

"What do you have to say?" Asked one of the ministers named Ayoreo sitting there.

"He has noticed something flying out of the Sapphire palace." The guard replied.

"What is it? Minister Imani asked.

"Don't just lie to get some reward or a gold coin from her

Majesty." Minister Afjal chuckled. He had a strange look on his face as his glasses slid on his nose.

"You might repent later if you do that." Lady minister Aphiguna squeaked. Her sinister laugh with sweet delivery added to the skepticism.

"Come on. Say what you have to say. Her Majesty is waiting." Remarked Perseus with a grin.

"I have seen something strange your majesty. Early this morning I have seen a man and a woman flying out of the Sapphire palace."

"Hmm…. interesting it is. Are you sure about this?" Hoag, the old minister asked. His head turned as he almost lost control of his glasses.

"Yes, I am." The commoner repeated.

"Are you the only one? Or there are more who watched them leaving?" Asked one of the ministers

"I'm not sure your majesty. Every morning I look at the sky to do my Surya-pronam (my salute to Sun God). That's when I noticed this. I thought it is an illusion. I rubbed my eyes and checked again. And yes, the man and a woman were flying out on their Pegasus as they disappeared in the horizon."

Queen Eleonora stood up and hinted the commoner to come forward. There was a brief silence. It was a man with a wrinkled face, long nose, pierced ears, and reddish hair with a ponytail. His eyes were rough with irritation but stating that he was not lying.

"What is your name?" The Queen asked.

"I'm Neil Murphy your Majesty."

"You remember what happens if you lie to our queen, don't you Neil?" Queen's personal assistant Prithvi asked.

"Yes, I do. People may die. Or turn into a plant, statue, or an animal if they lie."

"I do not think he is lying. He is telling the truth." Queen Eleonora sat down on her throne.

On her signal, Prithvi asked one of the fellow men to award the commoner.

"Hmm...interesting to know. alright Neil. You can go now." Prithvi told.

Neil bowed and left. The guards left the room with the commoner. The door closed behind them.

Birsa said, "interesting, remarkably interesting. They were flying on Pegasus. They knew each other, could be friends or could be spouses."

"Possible" said Hoag. "Very much so."

Queen stood up, walked back and forth. Then sat down on her throne. The personal assistant and third in command Prithvi and the eight other ministers, four men and four women, all sat on their designated chairs.

"Now what do you make out of this Hoag?" Queen asked the old minister again.

"I think it is time." Hoag bowed and answered with a humble voice. The Queen gazed at his deep eyes, his wise face, his kind appearance. As if she became convinced. Yet she wanted the opinions from others.

"Maybe. But is it? How do we know for sure?" She muttered.

"What do you think Afjal?"

Eleonora's eyes were now fixed on Afjal as she looked for an answer.

Afjal laughed. Then got back his composure. "Yes, ...yes, Your Majesty, it is possible. Hoag could be right. Anything is possible. Several things. It might be a trick of the Devil Scorpion King Sculptor? What if he sent out one of his spies to steal the statues? It is difficult, yet not impossible. I'm not arguing, the time could be near, but I doubt if this is more than anything but a trap." Afjal answered while nodding his head with a strange look. He was stoking his beard with a wrinkle on his face.

"Exactly. That is the point." The Queen said.

"You, Aphiguna?" Queen Eleonora asked for an answer from the beautiful black lady sitting at a distance.

"I agree with Hoag. But to be sure, we need to wait for the rest of the prophecy to come true." Apiguna replied in a lucid voice.

"And you Ayoreo?"

"My thought is in the same line as Hoag. If there is any chance for saving the Prince, it is time. The chosen ones should be here any day now. It is that time of the year."

"What is your thought on this Prithvi?" Eleonora stared at Prithvi.

"The month of May, the time for red blood moon. Good and evil; anything is possible." Prithvi said in a convoluted voice.

"What do you mean?" Make yourself clear!" Queen was losing patience.

"Your Majesty, I still remember the day the Saint King was talking to you. As you were praying for his mercy, this is what he said.

Prithvi stood up and his voice started to reverberate through every corner of the room and the palace.

"As the kingdom fails and falls
Deep into a sleep, Devil calls
Kingdom moves, go down deep
Prince sleeps, as they all grieve
Water, ice, air move with force
Storm comes, temple the source
Water rises, pandemic strikes
Famine comes, hunger bites
Enigma of six save the siblings
Each with a sign, carry the markings
Red the color, distress comes
Carry them through the land, carry them through the sun
Chosen are they two, bring back His soul
Prince is the body, three times the goal
Palace will defend, so shall He
Devil or Prince either can win

Only the two can make their call
At the end of it all, one shall fall!"
At the end of it all…..one shall fall….one shall fall.'

I think it is very interesting what will happen next. If they are here, they need our support, every protection. But before anything, we need to make sure it is them."

"So, you Birsa?"

Her calm and eloquent voice was attested with a command.

"He is right….a*s the kingdom fails and falls*

Deep into a sleep, there will be a call…..a call…a call….

We need to figure it all out before it is too late…"

Minister Birsa said as if he was reciting a phrase.

Queen Eleonora stared at Najeebah for an answer. Najeebah's eyes were reflecting.

Slowly she uttered…..

"Kingdom will move, rise from the fall,

The chosen ones will come,

There will be a call.

The door will not budge,

Statues will fly,

Butterfly and leaves

Bees will not be shy."

Najeebah finished.

"I need a definitive answer?" Queen Eleonora asked in an appealing tone.

"Did anyone look at the garden?" Hoag smiled humbly.

"Remove the drapes." The Queen Eleonora ordered.

Birsa and Najeebah stood up and removed the drapes.

The beautiful spectacular garden surrounding the palace was dazzling with green trees, flowers, and fountains.

"The time is near."

Said Najeebah and Birsa in unison.

Everyone stared with amazement. The trees had new leaves.

Flowers started blooming. But no sign of bees and butterflies flying anywhere.

The personal assistant to the Queen Eleonora Prithvi stood up. He was a handsome man with roman nose and sharp eyes. He appeared determined and focused.

After a brief silence, he replied, "Maybe the bees and butterflies will only come when the Prince wakes up. It is a good sign. Time might be near. But we are not there yet."

"Time is near for the Prince to rise from his sleep if the Chosen Ones are here. We need to be ready." The Queen commented.

"But where are the chosen ones?" Birsa asked.

"Without them, Prince Anish will never come out of his deep sleep. Even if he does, he will fall back into sleep again." Ayoreo remarked.

"They are already here. In that room." Hoag's calm remark made everyone startled. "Your Majesty. Now is the time to protect them. They are our only hope to wake up our Prince Anish."

Queen Eleonora glanced at him. Her eyes turned watery. She came back to her throne.

"Let the guards know not to kill anyone in the kingdom, man woman, or even an animal. Send out the message by secret golden leaves. Now is the time to be humble and pray. Ask everyone to go to the Temple-Tower. It will be our chanting for revelation, prayer, and meditation."

"Sure, will do." Afjal signaled Afiguna to make a note.

Aphiguna nodded her head and said, "will do your majesty."

Queen Eleonora left with Prithvi. Hoag, Ayoreo and Birsa followed. Afjal, Afiguna and Najeebah started walking together in another direction. "Let us go and visit the Shappire palace. I can't wait to see what is happening there." Najeebah nodded in a curious tone.

"Well, it could be good, could be bad or could even be ugly.

You know?" Afjal asked. "I'm not sure if anyone should even go there now."

"Why not? Are you crazy?" remarked Aphiguna.

"Well, the door is locked from inside. But why and how? Is it by a spy? A notorious spy of Scorpion King Sculptor? Or by even himself? Who can guarantee that it is safe there?"

"I can't believe what you just said. In broad day light Scorpion King Sculptor will be here? Don't you know the force field and what it can do to any stranger who does not belong here? Are you even thinking?" Najeebah got angry.

"Well, don't think I am stupid. From what I know, that could be a possibility. Why don't we first investigate what or who is out there? Next, we can of course visit the palace."

"Sounds good to me." Told Aphiguna.

"Well, then why don't you send out your top general Perseus? If necessary, ask him to break in. But I think, that won't be necessary. He is a very distant cousin of our Prince. Just ask him." Said Najeebah.

"A thorough search should reveal. Don't you think that would be a prudent thing to do? As the home minister, you are the only one except queen to give such an order." Afjal smiled.

"Of course, I'll. I will investigate it and do the necessary." Aphiguna smirked and turned toward Ruby palace.

Najeebah and Afjal continued walking toward the lake.

"What are you thinking?" Turned around Najeebah and asked Afjal.

"Nothing." His eyes were fixed on her.

Najeebah brought her mouth close to his ears and said softly, "It must be something." She had her eyes glowing with raze. They turned red and then slowly turned back to normal.

"I just can't let it happen again."

"What? Tell me."

"You will know in time." Afjal chuckled and walked away.

Angry Najeebah stood there in silence. Her eyes were fixed at the huge landmass surrounded by seven palaces.

CHAPTER XI

The invincible dress from the Queen

The guards that cordoned the Sapphire palace did not lift the barricade. They were still waiting for the order from the Queen.

Everyone noticed thousands of golden leaves flying out of the Ruby palace. They were heading in every direction.

In the meantime, Ella came out of her hide out and stood beside Tyler next to the window.

"What's going on?" Tyler's tone was anxious!

"Maybe we are trapped." Ella glanced at Tyler and remarked.

The creature hidden under the floor had a brief smile.

"I don't think anyone can get in or out now." She was not looking outside anymore. Her eyes were fixed on one of the portraits on the wall.

A faint memory reeled through her mind. A memory full of many voices, many faces, many incidents. She became unaware of her situation.

"Look, thousands of gold leaves are flying in every direction. See, not sure, it is the wind or something else. Watch!" Tyler pointed his finger.

Ella had a nudge. She turned back to the window. Many golden leaves were floating in the air. Slowly the leaves were coming down to everyone, men, women, children. People gazed intently at the sky, and then snapped the leaf. They stared at it for moments as if they were trying to read something. Then the leaf melted away in the air. The kids who picked up any leaf, brought it to their parents. The ones picked up by no one, slowly melted away.

"What is it, Tyler?"

"Not sure. A message? All coming out of the Ruby palace, but why?"

"Could be. Or a secret code. Might be a force-field trick. I'm confused." Ella paused. She was looking down at her waist.

She discovered something stuck to her dress.

"Watch, a spider!" She yelled.

The huge spider was moving rapidly. Ella was finding it difficult to get rid of it. No matter how much she tried, the spider came right back and clung to her dress.

Ella gave up in desperation. In a few minutes, a gorgeous small dress made of spider silk was visible held by the spider's two legs. It was a beautiful floral armored dazzling dress with red ribboned protective apron, black tunic, and grey baldric. The spider slipped out of her dress, fell on the floor, grew larger and larger. In a minute it was as tall as Ella. It stood up on two legs, bowed down with folded hands.

Tyler and Ella realized the spider appeared harmless. They could hear it opening its jaws.

Then a voice came out of nowhere, "Let your heart speak."

Tyler and Ella heard a woman's voice reverberating across the room.

"Here is your invisible cloak, Ella. Do you remember the last words that you said? Scorpion King Sculptor stormed the palace as you took your last breath:

'Time will talk to uphold the truth.

Bring me the invisible cloak from your root.

Evil will fade, end will come, Prince will rise

Rise Lyra, rise to be with the win and the wise.'

I am your humble servant from the Shadow Kingdom,

remember my name?" I'm Lyra. The guardian saint King turned me into a spider." It folded the gorgeous dress and handed it out to her.

Ella was in awe. She carefully extended her hands to accept the dress. The dress almost flew toward her and wrapped around the body. In her new dress Ella appeared invincible.

She patted the back of the spider. The moment she touched the spider, a beautiful girl emerged! "Today your pure touch made me free! I'm not bonded to the slavery of the Wizard Saint King anymore. You are my boss." The girl smiled with joy.

Then continued, "The time is nearing for the Prince to wake up. I'm so glad that I found you. Have been waiting in this room as a spider for almost thousand years. Finally, the time has come, and the waiting is over! Welcome to the Shadow Kingdom and the Land of Nines. Welcome our beloved Chosen Ones."

Ella didn't know what to say. A sweet, soft voice filled with awe came out of her mouth, "thank you!" She was looking stunningly beautiful.

"At Queen's order, I have been holding this armored dress for you for last thousand years. It will keep you invisible from anyone you wish to be or from the crowd. It will never leave you, appearing on your body at wish. It will act as a shield to protect you from harm's way. With your shield on, no one would be able to touch you. You can fly high above to go to stars or touch the sky or dive deep under the ocean. No one would be able to destroy it. Neither will it ever get wet. It will save you from fire and storm, hail or thorn, any weapon or fall."

In the meantime, a lizard showed up on the distant top wall above Tyler's head. It had been watching all these. So far it was not moving and stayed still. Tyler didn't notice anything. The lizard jumped on the drape and quickly came down to the ground. It stood next to the Spider and paused. As if it was trying to say something.

"Who are you?" Asked Tyler.

The lizard gave a brief smile and spoke in a human voice,

"I'm Sharpnil." It grew taller and taller. With folded hands it bowed at Tyler and Ella. When it unfolded its hands, on the top of its palm, was lying a beautiful armored black dress.

The lizard said:

'Endless stone, remember the sun?
Seven palaces sank, as we all ran,
Separate stones formed to guard
Diamond, Emerald, Amber, Pearl
Ruby, Topaz, Sapphire all
Temple-Tower Magellan had a fall
Vulnerable Prince, protected us all
As Prince fell, so did his horse,
came out his voice, came in due course
"Stay with me Tyler, kingdom will rise
Dead be evil Sculptor, hunting would be wise
Kill the Scorpion King, he would not be the last …
..save your kingdom Tyler…you two be the first….
Save it from disgrace, horror, and shame
Endless stone, but not the end."

"Now the time is near, Tyler. Dead be the evil Scorpion King Sculptor." Sharpnil took a pause.

"Look at me Tyler, look at me." Sharpnil continued. "Try to remember me, I'm your friend and your personal guard, Sharpnil."

It offered the dress to Tyler. Tyler accepted the armored dress with humility. While looking at it, as he swung his hands, the dress rapidly unfolded and wrapped around him. It was a perfect fit. He took the lizard's hands and shook it with thanks.

A royal guard emerged from the lizard. Sharpnil bowed to Tyler and smiled:

"This is your armored cloak, Tyler. It can do miracles, appear, or disappear at wish. It will let you fly or go under the ocean. It will make a shield around you and protect you from any harm.

It can read other's minds, take its own decision, and make you invisible from anybody who could be a threat to you. If you wish you can overpower it. Just ask. It will follow your orders. With its own mind it can read its surroundings. It can read the mind of a man, woman, any creature.... may it be human, half-human, animal, or half-animal...or even can look out for you against any weapon ...coming at you! It will protect you from any danger. It will be up to you to stay visible or remain invisible. It can read your wish too!"

Sharpnil and Lyra stood there smiling.

After a long pause, Ella said, "Great. It's awesome!"

"Yes! It is! Thank you both." Repeated Tyler. Both were smiling with a humble note.

A galloping sound came in. As time passed, it was being prominent. Tyler looked outside the window.

Then he turned and said,

"Guards are coming. They will be here soon. We need a hiding spot. Hurry."

"I know one!" Lyra shouted. We all can hide inside the belly of the human-lion Narasingha. The only question would it allow us?"

"I don't think so." Said Tyler. "Why should it?"

"It is a tough call Lyra." Reiterated Sharpnil. "We appeared into this room after one thousand years! You still think the Narasingha will remember us? Are you crazy?"

"Does not hurt to try. What other option have we got? Huh?" Ella jumped in.

Outside the window, the horsemen were now in front of the palace gate.

"The riders are here." Tyler cried.

"Now whatever you want to try, hurry." Ella spoke.

Lyra shifted close to Narasingha. With folded hands, she prayed at Narasingha eye to eye and begged: "We are here. Your old friends. Open your belly if you remember us. The *Chosen Ones* are here. Save us, help us, protect us!"

They could hear the footsteps of the guards. The mahogany door was now being pushed with heavy force.

And they knew, this time it will not hold.

The red eyes of Narasingha started to blink. It moved its head, scanned them head to toe one by one. Suddenly its belly popped open and sucked everyone in. It was dark inside. Tyler and Ella felt safe in that tiny space.

Just at that moment, the door opened, and the guards stormed in. They combed through the area.

One of the guards looked familiar to them. With an evil looking figure tattooed on his neck and a concerned look he was disappointed not to find anything. Two of his associates had poisonous snake tattoo on their face and arm.

"Search everywhere, every corner." The captain of the royal guards shouted.

The guards searched all over the place. A few of them even tried to feel the human-lion by pressing its belly. After a while, they left frustrated. While leaving, the evil-dark looking man turned back and took another look at the human-lion. He nodded his head with frustrations, looked back with a question on his face as they left the room. The door closed. The sound of their footsteps disappeared at a distance. Everyone came out of Narasingha's belly.

'Not sure how to thank you!" With an expressive smile Ella gave Narasingha a hug.

"I'm thankful too! Only because of you, we are still alive!" Tyler smiled at Narasingha.

Narasingha moved its head and blinked twice.

Lyra and Sharpnil faced Tyler and Ella.

"From now on, we will be always near you, and remain invisible as your shadows. If you need help, please call out our names. Hail, or storm we are here to protect you at any place or at any time." finished Lyra.

Sharpnil shook his head in agreement.

"Remember our names: Lyra and Sharpnil. We are here to

protect you as your bodyguards. Now with your permission, we must leave." She repeated.

Tyler and Ella glanced at them in awe. Then said in unison, "yes."

With a meaningful smile attached to their faces, their bodies slowly melted away and disappeared.

Tyler and Ella got a spur. Their eyes fell on their shadows. The shadows became thicker and larger. A memory from the distant past triggered their minds. They could hardly see any face or recognize anyone. It was a ferocious battle. Scorpion King Sculptor was storming the Shadow Kingdom and the land of Nines. Every palace was under attack. Even the diamond palace. Thousands of dark Scorpion King Sculptor followers were trying to break open the palace gate. Then it all went dark.

"Did you feel it?' asked Ella.

"Oh god! Yes, I just did!"

Tyler stood motionless. Didn't say any more word.

Then sprinted toward the mirror.

But to their dismay, there was no reflection.

"We are invisible!' Screamed out Tyler.

"Yes, we are!" Shouted Ella! "But fortunately, we can see each other. It is just awesome!"

Tyler wished to be visible. And there he was! And next to him was standing Ella smiling.

They enjoyed their new power for a few moments. Tyler jumped to touch the ceiling. Ella floated in the air. Then they chased each other in every direction moving through the space of that huge room at lightning speed. It continued for a while.

Finally, they became tired.

A sound was bothering Ella.

"Do you hear that?" She asked.

Tyler could barely hear it. He put his ear next to the wall. Then smiled.

"It is the sound of the waves. Remember it is a place

submerged under water. Water is hitting it from every direction. That is creating this sound which is coming out of thin air."

Slowly the sound subsided.

"We need to get out of here!" Tyler paused. "There must be a way!"

He pushed hard but the door didn't budge.

"I don't think you can open it this way!" Ella pushed Tyler to the side, came forward and glanced at the gibberish writings on the tiles next to the door. Every tile was lit. As she touched one tile, a sign came up. A sign of an arrow. She touched the next one. A sign of a Lion came up. Then she touched the next tile. A sign of a deep dark red chakra came up.

"This might be the one." She punched the tile with full force. The tile color shifted from dark red, to yellow, then maroon, to white.

"WELCOME!". A beautiful soothing woman's voice vibrated through the room touching every corner and the ceiling. A writing of words came on it, "BE QUIET! You are inside the Sapphire palace. Our Prince is asleep in the kingdom. Be respectful!"

A faint deep voice was rolling out......the words....

Suddenly, the two doors and six windows across the room swung open. A flood of early morning sunlight filled up the room. They were facing a pretty sight.

People were out doing their chores; sun was shining in the sky. At a distance over the blue lake seagulls were flying. Anxiously they walked out of the room into a hallway. They had no idea what was waiting for them. The door behind them gradually closed and then completely disappeared. Another set of words appeared on the wall: 'The guests are on the move.'

"Did you notice that?" whispered Ella. The door is not there! It totally disappeared.

"Yes, I did!" Said Tyler. "It feels like someone is in control. Everyone is under watch."

"Could be a good thing. Too early to tell." Tyler remarked.

They turned back to the room they came out of. It was one part of the beautiful Sapphire palace.

The elegant staircase made of marble with stunning ceiling and amazing paintings was in front of them. They took to the stairs and came down to the front courtyard.

The sun was lighting up the sky. The clouds were forming and then dissolving in the blue vastness of the emptiness. The sudden early morning sunlight blinded them and made them blink multiple times. It was such a shock for Tyler and Ella.

Tyler and Ella were invisible, they scanned their environments. They were standing at the back of a flowery garden that encircled the palace. In the middle was a gigantic cascade of fountains. The palace gate was not easily accessible from any side. Fortification walls supplemented with defensive Temple-Towers was protecting the road between each gate and the palace.

Tyler and Ella noticed a regiment of soldiers were marching down the road. The road led to a bridge over the river and then to a huge Temple- visible at a distance. 'The Land of Braves' engraved on the top of the Temple was glowing.

"I think they are getting ready for a battle."

"They don't look too friendly." Said Ella.

They moved behind a bush next to the fountain.

The regiment passed with their marching song. They approached the long bridge over the river. Once they reached the bridge, they broke their stride and did not march in unison.

"Why did they break their stride?" Asked Tyler.

"They must, due to the bridge. Don't you know? Their marching can cause the natural frequency of the bridge to amplify its vibration and it might collapse." Ella explained.

The soldiers crossed the bridge and reached the front gate.

"I wonder where they are heading to." Said Ella.

"Watch, the Temple-Tower gate is opening. Let's see what happens next." Tyler spoke.

The Temple-Tower bell started to sound. The soldiers moved

and encircled the Temple-Tower. The main entrance to the Temple-Tower opened. People started coming out of their cottages. All headed toward the tower.

"It might not be a bad idea to sneak in and check out. We need to know what goes on inside that Temple-Tower.

"In minutes, the Temple-Tower gate will close. I agree," nodded Tyler.

They flew into the ground in front of the Temple-Tower, stayed invisible. Once inside, they moved to the center stage. The priest was lighting a huge oil lamp. They sat close to the center stage and became visible. Someone almost took their seat seeing it empty. Then he watched them seating. He and his wife raised their eyebrows and moved on. So did the people behind them.

Everyone took to their seats. The main priest was now seated on the high platform with his eyes closed.

Tyler and Ella noticed the dome of the tower had thousands of small rooms stacked on top of one another. A slow array of moving people was taking stairs and filling up those rooms one by one. Once inside they were sitting down in the posture of padmasana in a mood of meditation with eyes closed. A small lamp was lit in front of the person in every room.

Tyler sighed in relief, "Finally we have little time to explore what is going on here. Look each room has a lighted lamp in the middle in front of the man or the woman."

The room turned dark, and the prayer began. The main priest rested in padmasana, was now flying high in the air as he slowly started chanting very slowly but clearly. His few repetitive words started reverberating across everywhere:

"Ohm, Shanti, Shanti, Shanti! Ohm Peace, Peace, Peace....... Ohm, Shanti, Shanti, Shanti!...... Ohm Peace, Peace, Peace. ....Ohm, Shanti, Shanti, Shanti! Ohm....Ohm...Ohm.... Ohm...Ohm....Ohm....Ohm..."

The meditation session started. It was all quiet. Except a continuous mystical sound of the word Ohm filled the air.

Tyler and Ella watched the meditation session for a while.

"We need to keep moving." Ella signaled with her finger.

By then they turned invisible.

Through a back door, they came out. A guard chatting with one of his friends was blocking the back exit. He couldn't understand the reason of his sudden loss of balance or what forced him to move aside. It was Tyler. He had to push the guard to get out.

"Are you alright man?" His friend asked.

"Yes, I'm, I'm." He laughed with his sharp teeth as he looked around him.

Tyler and Ella set out to explore the vast span of the land unknown.

Chapter XII

Meeting new friends

"A beautiful place for meditation. Have never seen anything like that before." Tyler said.

"I know! I'm not sure where we are or where this place is!" Ella took a deep breath as she passed the remark. She was feeling restless.

In that early morning, the roads and sidewalks were mostly empty. Young kids were running around and playing. They appeared happy and healthy.

"This place is amazing! I am not sure who lives in those other palaces!" Ella was thinking. She was staring at the other six palaces visible across the landscape surrounding the main Diamond palace.

Tyler and Ella started out.

In few minutes, they were walking by a lake. At a distance, appeared a strange looking old man. He looked tired, had long hair and mustache. He was leaning on the top of a billboard hanging from a pillar next to the gigantic lake. The moving shadows of enormous pillars were reflecting from the blue water of the lake into the billboard.

The old man had a feeble and far away voice. He was having difficulty standing at one place. His glasses were slipping from his nose. With a hat covering most of his face, he appeared to be in a hurry. Unable to read the sign, the disappointed man sat down on the roadside with a grim face.

"Look at this! What is this place? No one can even read a sign!" He was screaming.

"No wonder the guy couldn't read it." said Tyler. His eyes were fixed on the billboard.

"Must be written in an ancient language." Ella uttered bitterly looking at the sign.

"Must be. But you just made a guess? Tyler asked.

"I know many things brother." Remarked Ella with a chuckle. "Remember, I was taking foreign language classes."

The writings on the huge billboard were distinct. But the white marble was continuously changing its color and shape. Tyler also realized it must be an ancient language. Neither of them knew which language it was or how to read it.

Tyler approached the billboard and touched the writings. A flash of spark went through his body. He felt dizzy and his head started spinning. Memories started flashing back into his mind.

"Are you alright?" asked Ella.

"Oh, yes, yes, I'm." He had a blank look. As if something was taking him over. It took him several minutes to recover himself.

The old man must have heard them. He hollered, "Hello, is there anybody?"

He made a failed attempt to stand up and began gasping for air. Tyler and Ella came out and became visible. Tyler took out his water bottle and handed him over. The man had a sip, recovered a little bit.

"Thank you. I am very tired. Not sure where I'm. Who are you?" He uttered with much of a difficulty.

"Do you live here?" Asked Tyler.

"No!" the man answered in a weak voice.

"How did you get here?" Questioned Ella.

"Don't know! I am not sure exactly what happened!" The old man scratched his head. "It all started in my voyage. I was playing poker with my friends. Our ship was in the middle of a storm and then caught fire. It was seriously damaged. Then the captain announced the ship might sink. He asked us to escape in lifeboats. I do not remember what happened afterwards. I woke up and found myself lying here on the road." The man managed to say in a broken voice.

Ella and Tyler exchanged looks.

"What is your name?" Ella asked. She felt his pain.

"Coma, my name is Coma Servantes." He answered and cracked a smile with tethered brown teeth. His eyes lit up. "I don't know how I landed here. Help me to get back home." He started to sob.

"I think, you have been transported here the same way. They brought you here by mistake. Just relax and soon you will head home," consoled Ella. "We all are looking forward to get home soon."

The old man stared with a sick and gloomy look. His brown broken cheekbones, wrinkled forehead, and watery eyes touched her heart. Ella leaned forward to see if he is running any temperature. She felt his forehead. A bluish electric spark went through and almost burnt her hands.

"Oops, what's wrong?" She screamed. She looked at the old man. With eyes closed, the man lay motionless tears dripping out.

"Is he dead? What is going on?" Asked Tyler.

"No idea. It is bizarre. Must be an evil spirit is trying to take him over." Ella reacted. They stood by the man's side as Tyler sprinkled more water on his face. Slowly the man regained consciousness.

"We don't know what's going on here. We need to find out!" Said Tyler. "Why don't you wait here? We are going to look for some food and water. We will be back. Until then, please come and stay here under the shade of this tree."

Tyler and Ella helped the old man to get under a tree and lie down. The man thanked them with his yellow teeth and rotten egg smell.

A brief cracked smile appeared on his face.

"I want to go back home, please let me go home! Please let me go home." The words were coming out of his mouth slowly as he closed his eyes.

Ella tried to console him.

"We will. Please stay here. Ok?" Ella smiled in a lucid voice.

The man opened his eyes, slowly nodded his head, stared back at them in a blank desperate look and asked, "who are you? who are you? Tell me." But due to heavy wind and his feeble voice neither Tyler nor Ella could hear him.

"Now, we need to figure out how to venture into this unknown land. We have a responsibility to send this man back to his family if possible." Ella was talking to Tyler as they walked out of that area.

"Yes, you are right!" Said Tyler.

"Need to find a place to eat something. I'm getting hungry."

A cottage was coming up on the hillside behind the trees. They dreamed of fresh breads, smell of butter, hot coffee.

No one was nearby. They went to the back gate. Tyler silently went in and peeked.

"It is empty."

Couple of young children were playing at a distance by the river. No one noticed them.

"Let's check if we can find something to eat." Ella whispered as she silently followed Tyler into the cottage.

It was a small house, with only two bedrooms and a kitchen. The oven was still hot. Smoke was coming out.

"They must have finished eating just before leaving." Tyler said. "We need to be quick. They can return anytime." Tyler leaned forward to open the kitchen cabinet.

"Look! Fresh bread. Wow butter too!" Tyler was excited.

Ella opened the pantry. A set of stairs went down.

"Must be the basement." She murmured.

"Let me check what they got down there." She yelled at Tyler.

"Fine with me. But hurry." Tyler said.

Ella carefully walked down the stairs. She walked past bags

filled with axe and other weapons. Bows and quivers filled with arrows were hanging from the walls. Bags filled with spears and swords stacked at another corner. Next to the pile of weapons, multiple bags of grains: wheat, rye, barley. Eggs in another basket.

At a distant dark corner, she noticed a small door. Ella pulled the handle and unlatched the door. It opened to a tunnel.

"An escape route." She murmured.

Ella gradually walked in and paced toward the wall and opened another hidden cabinet behind walls. There she found a staircase going down through the dark passage. The sound of water waves was coming.

"Wow. We should revisit this house in near future." She uttered with a smirk on her face.

"We have to leave." Hollered Tyler from upstairs.

Ella turned and came up.

At the kitchen, it was another story.

Tyler had finished making a few toasts and omelets. Now started making a drink.

"I have found a hidden passage down there. But we don't have time. We can always come back later." She paused.

"What is it? Coffee?" Then Ella asked.

"Kind of. But smells good. Found it sitting at the counter. It will keep us going. I am sure it will make a good drink. I vaguely remember drinking it when we are in Canopus."

"Are you crazy? We can't take it. They will figure out. It is too risky."

"Of course, it is risky. But I can't wait to have some fun. I'm thirsty Ella." Said Tyler.

"Trust me, this drink is good." He took another sip.

They finished their breakfast quickly.

Tyler remembered to pick up a few leather waterskins filled with water while leaving.

"Let's take some for Coma." Tyler packed a small basket with bread, and toast.

"Ella, why don't you go and give him this breakfast?" Tyler said.

"Sure!" Ella grabbed the basket, the waterskins and flew away.

"Don't be late." Tyler screamed.

Tyler came out of the house into the alley, flew to the nearby falls. Beautiful waterfalls were coming down from steep high red mountains. Red leaves were falling from the trees, birds were flying, sunlight reflecting everywhere. In that breathtaking view of a backdrop of the mountains, waterfalls and the blue lake, Tyler stood there with an amazement.

Then he rushed to the top of the snowy mountain.

The other side of the mountain was steep that went down into the lake. At a distance he noticed another Tower. The pinnacle of the tower was emerging out of water. A black smoke hovered over the top of that tower.

Tyler was not thinking of Amba. He felt her presence, captivated.

"I'm here, near you. Always will be......" he heard a faint voice murmuring in his ears.

With a jolt, Tyler woke up. There was no one. He was standing alone. The deep blue lake, the cavernous forest was standing beside him.

Her beautiful face and how they lost her during their escape from the ship became vivid. Tyler was feeling sad...he sat down beside a tree.

At the ruin, when Ella approached Coma, he was gasping for air.

"Help me, help me!" There was a scream and then he stopped breathing.

Ella ran and sat down next to him. She felt his pulse and tried to feel his heartbeat.

His heart was pounding with an irregular heartbeat. She didn't know what to do.

Ella looked around and was relieved to see that no one was watching them. Her heart melted down for the old man. She looked at him once more, at his closed yellow eyes, wretched face, dirty torn out clothes. She wanted to save him. She stood up and ran back and forth on the road for a few minutes.

Then she noticed the ruin of an old tower. Gently she picked up Coma and flew to the ruin.

The ruined tower had very few entries, part of it destroyed during wars. Ella found her way in and took the path heading toward a fountain. From the severely damaged fountain, occasionally water was dripping out. A beautiful golden black statue of a woman on horseback in armored dress was standing next to it. Part of her face was missing.

At a distance was visible a long series of black statues of soldiers all riding on galloping horses with a prominent person.

"The King must had been sprinting through the area with his knights on horseback" Ella thought.

As Ella moved, the statues became alive, and they all turned and rolled their eyes. Ella did not notice any of this.

She stopped at a corner and glanced at the room that was still intact. She paced toward the room. Sunlight was beaming through a broken window.

She walked carefully over the shattered glasses and then gently put Coma down on the floor. The man was senseless.

A fractured glass vase was sitting on a table. A few chairs around the table were mostly untouched. Ella picked up the vase, part of it fell off.

She stared at the broken glass then paced toward the fountain to fetch fresh water. As she approached the fountain, the flow of water in the fountain intensified. It took her by surprise. She filled her broken vase and turned around. Before taking her steps, Ella spun around and noticed the flow of water in the fountain went down. With a wrinkle on her forehead, she came back to Coma and sprinkled water on his face. Coma twisted, turned, and then opened his eyes. After a while, he revived. Ella gave him the waterskin and the bread.

With a heavy breathing, Coma started talking in a broken feeble voice.

"Stay here, do not go anywhere. Let me eat the food."

He sat up. Started eating his bread.

Ella handed him some juice. Then he had enough strength.

Coma started talking.

"I am hungry. I need more of water, juice, and supply of food. And you don't go anywhere. Stay here. Protect me. You protect me." The old man said in a weak tone.

"Of course, I'm here. But you need to take rest. I have brought you enough food and drink that will last for a few days. Once we figure out a plan, we will come and get you." Ella said slowly in a lucid voice. She was getting nervous; 'the poor man might not make it', she thought. She looked at him again. "How did he get here?" She was thinking.

Coma stared at Ella. He stretched his arm.

"I want to thank you." He grabbed her hands. His eyes lit up.

"I know what you are thinking. You are thinking, how I got here."

Ella startled.

Coma smiled expressing his old yellow teeth.

"The same way. The only way. You know. Don't you? But tell me who are you? Are you the chosen ones? The chosen ones....? I am looking for them. The chosen ones. They can help me. Protect me. Save me from this torture." His voice broke down and became rough. As if someone else was now speaking. His eyes lit up again.

"Let me go. Would you?" Ella shouted with a startle.

Ella's hands turned red. She had a scorched feeling. Her palm turned painful. She turned to move her hands away. Then she had a strange vision. She watched Ryan, their guide, smiling at her. "Where have you been Ella? Where is Tyler?" Then, it was the King Orion from the ship was now laughing and talking to her. "Do you remember me? I'm King Orion....."

The next moment it was the same fragile old man lying on the floor with yellow eyes open staring at her.

"Who are you? Please tell me. I am looking for ...no....I'm not looking for anyone. It is just me...just me....a man without a name....just me...just me....." The man was breathing heavily, his eyes were bulging out. He was shaking.

"We all are from the same place, the outside world just like you. But stop. Let me go." She fought herself out of his grip. The old man's sarcastic grey smile faded, and he turned motionless.

"Is he alright?" Ella thought.

She felt his pulse. Checked his eyes. They were still. She became nervous and splashed more water on his face.

A few minutes passed.

Then she saw the man slowly opening his eyes.

"Are you alright? Stay here, get rest. We will be back soon.

Ella was relieved and silently left the place.

"How is he doing?" Asked Tyler.

"He is going to make it. After eating breakfast, he should be ok. I have moved him into a hidden room inside a ruined tower. A ruin not regularly visited by people. He would be able to survive there for a couple of days." She paused.

Then said again, "but something is strange. Each time Coma touches my hand, I get a strange feeling. My hands turn red, and it is painful. Not sure what is going on."

"It is your imagination Ella."

"No, not my imagination. You know it!" Ella's tone had annoyance. "I doubt if someone did cast a spell on him. I'm not sure."

"In time we will find out." Said Tyler.

They headed out. In front of them lay a huge unknown land. A land submerged under the ocean yet dry and habitable that was completely unknown to them.

A musical sound started emanating from the tower. It was

to declare the end of the meditation session. Gradually the soldiers marched out of the area and dispersed. Citizens began coming out.

Tyler and Ella followed a road. A road shaded with leaves. The interlinked roads ribboned out diagonally under canopy of trees. They were connecting the kingdom to other palaces from all directions. The landscape was beautifully decorated. Distinct forms of sculptures and statues made of gold, bronze, and other precious metals were overlooking the landscape. The roads covered with trees connecting the landscape went in different directions. Distinct waterfalls, fountains, and pillars engraved with mythical features were visible.

They began walking toward another gate.

They went past the main gate and walked into a bazaar. There were craftsmen, miniature painters, goldsmiths, blacksmiths, food courts…. almost everything.

Tyler and Ella turned back at the palace in distance.

"See, look there. At the middle is sitting a huge diamond inside a lake. No wonder, they call it the Diamond Palace." Ella said with an expression.

The dazzling architecture of different palaces in the background stunned them. They realized the whole landmass was sitting right in the middle of an ocean. The oceanwater with gigantic waves were pounding behind the huge walls all around the perimeter of the Kingdom. As if an unknown force-field was holding the water back. The land mass was sitting in the middle of the ocean just like any other land, with open sky, trees, forests, rivers, lakes, grassland, agricultural lands with livestock.

The dazzling palaces with their own unique colors were reflecting the light in every direction.

The sun was shining brightly in the sky. People were returning home from the Temple-Tower. As they moved forward, the road was getting crowded. A few people came on their way. The people looked around in surprise but couldn't see anyone. They shrugged it off.

Tyler and Ella moved on. A few equestrians passed them. Kids were playing. Seniors were chatting with their friends. Seniors were engrossed in playing own games. An old man was reading a book on a balcony. Another girl was trying with her flute in her house. Mothers were carrying children in their arms. One man was playing hide and seek with his granddaughter.

What caught their attention, the people were not from any single race or color. All kinds of people emerged from the Temple-Tower. Some white, some with darker skins, some had a yellow tone to their skin. From their appearance it was easy to understand they all had a mixed origin. They appeared healthy, normal people. They also found some dwarfs and some very tall people.

As they moved, Tyler and Ella emanated to another area covered with trees and bushes. Not many people were around. Ella wanted to take some rest and she leaned against a pillar. She was thinking how far they could go. She was trying to remember how to go back to that old man they left behind. What if they are too late or can't find the way back to him? She was getting worried.

Tyler walked away and entered at a slow pace into the nearby garden. The strikingly beautiful, ornamented palaces were dazzling across the horizon. Small ponds and lakes were visible one after another. In the distant islands, he spotted a swan flying in search of food. Then came another. Soon he noticed, many types of birds were flying.

In the nearby forest animals were roaming around. Ella was happy to see deer, buffalos, and many other creatures. The structural design of the buildings was spectacularly attractive. The golden statues of kings, queens, captains, priests, or soldiers told the story of an ancient civilization.

"They look alive!" thought Tyler. "I can't remember ever

seeing any statue that appears so alive!" he was looking at the statue of a witch.

He felt a pressure in his chest. His heart started pounding. He heard a whisper, "Come to me! Come to me!" Tyler felt a jerk. Did he hear something? His ears were still ringing.

Colossal columns were standing in the middle of magnificent gardens. Many figures were carved on the mountain walls. Many columns were wrapped with expensive jewels. Carved out lions, zebras, elephants, and many other mythical figures were displayed.

"The intricacies of the carvings on the palace walls are captivating. The startling color of each palace is unique. Each one reflecting the color of its own at night." Ella was saying standing next to him.

"A rich kingdom." Smiled Ella, as she stared at the stagecoach passing by. The coachman was resting under a tree. His horses were gazing at the adjacent field.

An argument broke out among a group of old people at a road corner under the shade of a tree. Tyler and Ella smiled.

"The same old thing!" Tyler nodded his head.

"Time to be visible." Ella murmured at Tyler as they took another turn. No one was nearby.

They discovered themselves walking inside an alley. Cottages made of stone and brick stood side by side.

People stared at them or even smiled at them, as they came out of their invisibility.

"It's interesting. They know we are strangers, do not belong here. Yet they didn't say a word." Tyler paused.

"Hope that is a good sign." murmured Ella.

"This civilization is old...not sure what happened to them or how it got destroyed and ended up in the middle of the ocean. Yet, I think it was an advanced civilization. We are looking at people or things from the ancient time, they look little different, but not much. Notice their postures, body structures, make up, artwork, their clothes, their customs." smiled Ella.

"I can't believe it! It's utterly amazing!" said Tyler.

They went through a cross section and then entered a forest. At the very front of the forest stood a huge statue of a white horse fighting with a giant python."

It was the picture of the python. An arrow pierced through its chest. Blood was dripping out as the horse was coming out of its grip."

"The sign does not look friendly." Commented Ella.

"You are right. Let's wait here." Tyler and Ella sat down under a tree next to the sign.

Suddenly they heard a babble. A few youngsters were coming their way. One of them appeared to be their leader.

Tyler and Ella greeted them with a friendly smile. A tall boy was carrying two golden fruits in his hands.

"What kind of fruits are these?" Ella asked with a smile.

But no one answered. From their expressions, Tyler and Ella understood the kids didn't understand what she said.

The boy offered them the fruits. Ella took one for her and gave the other one to Tyler. Their fingers touched. She had a strange sensation. Her heart was racing, her palm became hot. She was having muscle movements around her eyes that she had no control over. Her cheeks turned red.

He felt very thankful. But as they were going to bite, the boy raised his hands and laughed.

Tyler and Ella understood something was wrong. They exchanged looks. Tyler tried to reply by making gestures. It seemed the boy understood. But it was obvious that the boy was interested in Ella. He kept looking at Ella's face.

The boy wrote a sign on a stone and gave it to Ella. Ella stared at it. But it was not Sanskrit. The writing changed into English. It said: *'Nice to meet you! I am Nigam.'*

The boy then made gestures to write their names on the other side of the stone. Ella wrote her name, put a star next to it, followed by Tyler's. She gave the stone back to the boy. Her name changed into some strange looking language in front of their eyes.

"Ella" He gazed at Ella and squinted! Ella nodded her head.

Then he pointed at Tyler and said "Tyler".

Tyler said "Yap. That's me!"

Ella glanced at the boy. With his oval face, big eyes, straight black hair, the tall boy was smiling.

Suddenly they heard the noise of galloping horsemen. At a distance, a dust cloud was rising. The sound only became more and more intense.

"Run, hide. Could be friend or foe. Be careful." The boy Nigam stared at Ella, leaned forward, and uttered quickly. The boys and girls ran toward the forest. In minutes they were gone. Ella felt something inside her chest. She became thoughtful. She remembered seeing him somewhere but couldn't remember where it was.

Ella and Tyler became invisible. But they did not move. The cavalry came. The horsemen armored in short fur black trimmed jacket, ring mail and helmets. They searched the area. At one point, one of the equestrians almost met Ella. She barely saved the touch by swinging to another side.

"Must be hiding somewhere. I got the news." The leader shouted.

"Who are these people? What are they doing here?" One of the soldiers asked.

"Hmm….The Chosen ones. Came to save the Prince. Gold leaves were dispersed this morning carrying special messages." Another one spoke as his horse neighed.

"Save the Prince? A Prince who is asleep for last thousand years? Who is going to save him?" A soldier laughed out hysterically. "They all are going to die. Our King is going to kill them. Kill them all." He laughed again.

"Shut up!" The leader shouted. "Find them. Search every corner of the Shadow kingdom. Wait at every entry point of the seven palaces. I did not hire you to fail. The king wants them. Alive."

"Take them into custody before they move anywhere." The leader was still shouting. Ella and Tyler recognized him. The same man with tattoos of skull on arms. They had seen him inside the Sapphire palace.

He was fuming out of frustrations. With chattered teeth, he instructed everyone to leave.

"Let's go. To the Topaz."

The horsemen left with suspicion.

"They are gone." Ella paused as she fixed her eyes on their turn by the river.

Ella and Tyler became visible. They sat down under a tree and as hungry they were, began eating their fruits.

It felt different. Their heads felt heavy, they fell on the ground. When they woke up, they found Nigam and his friends were smiling. Ella took help from him and stood up. Their fingers touched; eyes met. Ella's heart was pounding hard. She could not take away her eyes from the boy. Neither could she stare at him for a long time.

Now they could understand every word their new friends were discussing. This kingdom looked familiar. Ella had a flashback and saw Nigam a friend from her distant past.

"It's amazing. I can understand what they're saying." Tyler was jubilant.

Nigam came forward seeing them talking in their language.

"This was a test. We wanted to find out if you are our friend or enemy. Anyone from the enemy side eating that fruit will die instantly. We are so pleased to meet you. But where are you from?" Nigam asked.

"We are from another world that is very different than yours. We don't know how we got here and what this place is all about. We are still trying to figure it all out." Ella explained.

"We know. We met people like you before. It is the search-work of the force-field of the wizard Saint King sitting as a mummy inside the Temple Tower of Magellan. He is dead. But his mummified body is still active. It scans the ocean and bring in people to save the Prince. We are running out of time. If Prince dies, so do we. There is not much time left." Then he stopped.

Tyler and Ella stared at him with curiosity. They did not know what to say. Their eyes turned bright with interest.

"I do not think you understand anything I am saying. You are standing in the Shadow Kingdom and The Land of Nines. A Kingdom of seven palaces. Once it was under a wizard Saint King. Long story short, the whole Kingdom is under his spell. The Prince who can save this land and its people, is cursed. He is asleep. Prince could come out of the spell only if he gets help from his friends the Chosen Ones who can bring him the pure water from his past from the land of divinity. Otherwise, he will perish. And so will all of us." Nigam's eyes turned gloomy. "The force-field is continuously scanning the whole ocean to find anyone who can fulfill the prophecy." Nigam finished in a sad tone.

Then there was a silence.

"This is Ara." Nigam pointed at a girl. "And this is Bootes, Lintus, Marycui, Abidemi, Meghna and Alheri. He pointed at his other six friends, three boys and three girls.

They entered the forest with their new friends. On their way, they met some two-faced creatures, half-human, half crocodile. The creatures were taking naps under shades next to a water hole.

"Don't be afraid. They are harmless. They protect this forest from our enemies." The boy Bootes said. "We call them Monoceros."

Nigam smiled. "The creatures look harmless now. But if our kingdom is under attack, they could turn out to be the most ferocious animals anyone can think of."

Then he stopped facing the lake and turned at Ella.

"It is very nice meeting you. We need to turn back. It is

getting late." His beautiful smile and deep look made Ella's heart pounding.

"But wait. How to get to the land of Divinity? Where is it?" Asked Ella. They gazed at one another but couldn't hold it for long.

The handsome boy standing in front of her made a deep impression. "Is he feeling the same way as I am?" Ella thought.

"The route to the land of Divinity is not revealed to just everyone. For that someone must first go to the Tower of Magellan. There lies the mummy of the Wizard Saint King. If the mummy is pleased it will reveal the codes. With that codes he must go to the library and ask for the book of sanctity. The route to the Land of Nines is described in that book. That's all we know." The boy Bootes said slowly with an assertive voice.

Tyler smiled. "But which road leads to the Tower of Magellan ?" He questioned.

"That you need to find out of your own. It will be revealed to you in time if you need to know. Remember all roads lead to the Land of Nines." Nigam said.

Tyler noticed his sister was at a loss. "Are you alright?"

"Hmm...yes I'm I am." Ella said softly. Then said, "let's go."

Everyone was facing the lake watching the blue whales. Huge dolphins were jumping out of water and diving down.

"Such a magical place. We are glad to be here." Smiled Tyler.

Excited and puzzled Tyler and Ella were talking to each other. When they turned, they realized Nigam had left with his team.

Ella's eyes searched for him everywhere. She felt her heart was heavy.

Chapter XIII

The Flying Devils

At a distant part of the Shadow kingdom and Land of Nines something strange was happening. The golden leaves started flying out to every part of the Kingdom.

People came out of their huts, houses, cottages, caves, forests. Came out of everywhere. The golden leaves flew to each one of them. Male, female, boys, girls, children everyone. Some of the leaves went over the forest and made a canopy covering the trees and floated above and moved. Many other leaves came down on the lake as a cloud and floated very close to the surface of water as it covered every part of the lake and was talking to the animals in the water.

"I know where to go and how to find them Tucan." That afternoon, two girls named Padmasree and Tucania were talking facing each other sitting on pasture on the countryside next to the lake. They were in a jubilant mood celebrating the news of the arrival of the Chosen Ones.

"Did you hear the news? The Chosen Ones are here. They will save our Prince. Our Kingdom. Save us all!" Padma continued.

"Yes, I have heard Padma." The other girl Tucania said. "That is wonderful. That's what we have been waiting for. Isn't it? My only concern is the Devil King and his spies." Her anger was prominent in her tone.

As they looked up, they watched thousands of golden leaves floating in the air. Two golden leaves continued floating their journey and came to them.

Padmasree stood up and grabbed one. Tucania stayed where she was. The leave floated over her head for a while and then came down to her. She snapped it.

The golden red color leaves were beaming with glow. Words became prominent on the leaves instantly as they touched. The wizard saint king's face became visible inside a white mist. A slow soft lucid voice came out. "Chosen ones might be here. Be respectful to everything in the Kingdom. May it be human, animal, a tree, or a statue or even water waves. They could be in any form: person, male or female, children, animal, trees or even statues. Do not disturb or destroy anything. Even if they do not look familiar or treat you differently."

"See, that's what I was telling you Tucan. They are here. We need to protect them." Padmasree said.

"But how. We do not know them, Padma. They do not know us. Where do we find them? How do they look? We do not know anything." Tucania said.

Suddenly they saw some horsemen coming their way at a distance. Six people riding on horseback. All carrying swords. The riders were in a hurry. They were going through every barn, farmhouse, poultry, silo everything.

"Searching for something or someone." Tucania said. Her gaze was fixed on the riders. The drums of the hooves were gaining strength.

"Maybe we are in trouble." She took out her small sword that she carries everywhere she goes.

"We need to go." Padmasree stood up, whispered and crawled toward a bush. "They do not look too friendly."

"It is too late. I think they have seen us. We just cannot run. They will get us no matter what. We need to face them." Tucania said.

"No, I'm leaving." Padmasree stood up and started running.

Tucania followed. She was still screaming at her, "It is of no use. How could you outrun them? They are on horseback."

The horsemen were now cutting through the grassland. They have noticed the girls running. Padmasree and Tucania ran through the agricultural land, green meadows, bushes, and came to a river. They stumbled onto the rocky surface and fell into the river.

They crossed the river and soon headed toward the lake.

"Why the lake?" Tucania asked. As she was following Padmasree and gasping for air.

"I know someone living there. Know him for a long time. His name is *Teslange. He* will protect us. He is always there."

They continued running. But soon became tired. They could hear the drum of hooves behind them.

The lake was not very far now. Only fifty yards. They looked back. The horsemen caught up. One rider slipped over the road to block their way.

"Who are you? What do you want?" Tucania asked. "Let us go." She already drew her sword.

"What's the hurry?" One of the horsemen asked. His creepy smile was evident as he drew his long sword.

Tucania raised her sword.

"Scared, huh?" Laughed a man riding a grey horse.

"She had good training. But how could she even defeat them. Six? Is she crazy?" Padmasree was thinking as she stared at her.

As they were talking, Padmasree walked past them and moved toward the lake.

"What are you thinking kid? Evade us? Dive into the lake? Save yourself? Tell us where the Chosen ones are. You know who they are and where they could be. Don't you?" The leader laughed. His grizzly laugh could be heard from a distance.

By now all of them were standing very close to the lake. Padmasree was desperately looking at the lake for help. She was praying hard. Her eyes were moving back and forth from the bandits to Tucania to the lake.

"What are you looking at kid? Where do you live? I know where you are from. The Emerald palace? Aren't you? That's it. I know it. That palace is always fortified. Must be something going on there. Hmm?" The leader was laughing.

Then his attention shifted toward Tucania.

"And you? Answer me!" He did not make any attempt to hide his anger.

"I am from the Pearl." Tucania said slowly. Her eyes were fixed at the leader. Her hand was holding the sword in a tight grip. "I can take him down any minute. Or wait?" Tucania was holding her breath. She looked at the leader again. A man in his forties. Broad shoulders with long arms. The man had rough oval face with many scars. Tucania looked at his red bulged eyes. She was losing patience.

"Pearl? That's interesting. Then I'm sure you would be able to tell us where is the Queen? Or which passage she takes to move from one palace to the next. You know it. I know you do." He laughed again.

"We have not seen her for a long time. She must be busy, huh?" One of the riders laughed.

"Take them in." The leader ordered.

Laughter and smile showed up in each face. They were pleased and were waiting for such an order. Everyone moved and reined their horses. Slowly the horsemen started circling the two girls. One of them was massive. He was wearing a long black coat. His black teeth and ugly smile could make anyone anxious. His horse was huge. The grey horse was sensing the situation as the man started to talk to them.

"Don't be scared. We won't harm you. Once you tell us the truth, we will let you go. No worries. You know it. Don't you? Or you could very well serve our King! Hmm? That's a possibility not everyone gets. What do you say about that?" He laughed again sarcastically.

He extended his right hand toward Padmasree.

"Come on. I will give you the ride." In the blink of an eye, Tucania was on top of him. Her sword sliced through his arm. Half of his right arm was hanging. Blood was everywhere.

The gigantic man fell from his horse. His shout and laughter turned into a scream. By then Tucania was on the top of his horse. She pulled up her friend and sprinted through the field. The horsemen were not ready for any of this.

"Take him out of here. Go to the mountain and transport him to the King." The leader shouted.

One of the riders picked up the wounded man and left. The rest of the riders followed Tucania and Padmasree. Soon they caught up with them.

"Go back to the lake. Turn back. Go back to the lake." Padmasree was screaming. "I trust him. He is there. Teslange will save us. Just go and dive into the lake."

The riders were on their tail.

"Kill them. Kill them both." The leader was shouting.

Tucania directed her horse toward the lake. The huge horse was galloping at high speed. The lake was near.

But the riders were faster. They came upon them. The leader's knife flew by Padmasree's neck. Another rider moved with a spear. He wanted to strike the horse. He was coming. Getting close.

The blue lake was shining only thirty feet away, then twenty, then ten....five.

"Dive in!" Screamed Padmasree.

The horse jumped into the lake. With a scream they both flew out in the air yet came back on the horse. The horse was still galloping on the surface of the water as if it was a normal road. Soon they were at the center of the lake. Next to them was sitting the enormous Emerald stone beaming with light. Tukania pulled the rein. Stopped the horse.

The horsemen stopped at the edge of the lake barely saving

themselves from a free fall into the lake. The drum of the hooves were loud. The horses groaned.

It took the riders by surprise what had just happened. They never expected a young girl would be able to defend herself and that too with a small sword. But when the girls dived into the lake with their horse, the leader was assured their end was near.

Now the watched the girls did not drown. Rather they were standing in the middle of the lake.

"We can't just let them go. One of us must jump into the lake and get to the girls.

"That's a bad idea. We can never catch them." The leader screamed.

"Don't you see they can even ride on the waters?" Another one shouted.

"If they can ride over the lake, why not us?" One rider screamed.

"It is a trap. Trap of the wizard saint king. Have you ever seen a horse galloping over water?"

"What do we do now?" Asked one of them staring at the leader.

"We will wait here. Wait until they come out of water. We have the whole day ahead of us." The leader said.

The riders came down from their horses. One rider sat next to the water with his feet dangling over the lake.

The others were chatting. They were looking at different direction.

Suddenly there was a scream. Everyone saw a huge monster snake turtle coming out of water. In the blink of an eye, it propelled through the water at high speed, opened its jaws and swallowed the man sitting on the edge.

The rest of the horsemen screamed. The leader attacked the snake turtle with his sword. The snake turtle swung its strong heavy tail at the bandit leader before diving down into water. Next thing, bandit leader was flying in the air and fell on the ground fifty feet away.

The half-conscious leader somehow grabbed the rein of his horse and immediately left the area with his followers.

Padmasree and Tucania saw the snake turtle coming to them. They were riding the snake turtle. It carried them along with their horse to the edge.

Padmasree hugged the snake turtle. "Thank you." Because of you we are alive today."

"Good job Teslange! Love you!" Tucania said.

CHAPTER XIV

Visiting the Prince

Tyler and Ella moved on. They passed through porches, courtyards, sidewalks, gardens, and came down to a river surrounded by a riparian forest.

A market was visible on the other side of the river. A narrow hanging bridge was the only connection. Tyler swiftly crossed the hanging bridge and signaled Ella. As Ella started walking over the bridge, and came to the middle, the bridge started vibrating. She toppled, slipped through a hole, but grabbed a part of the hanging rope from the bridge with her right hand at the last minute and pulled herself up. She was sweating and could feel heat on her neck.

It was a market square full of activities. An elephant fight was about to start. People were taking their seats to watch. Everyone had been waiting all dressed in a festive mood.

The local community leader came out and announced the fight had been moved to the following day. He requested everyone to come back to the same place at the same time.

Tyler and Ella did not want to catch unnecessary attention. They dressed in familiar clothing and mingled well with the crowd. People did not pay notice to them. Tyler and Ella made their way through and came out of the market.

A crowd was gathering in front of another palace at a

distance. "Look over there!" Tyler gestured to Ella. Ella noticed the congregation and said, "I would like to know what's going on over there."

"Why not? "Let's check it out."

After a short walk, the two were at the palace gate. Dozens of people were walking in and out of the gate. Tyler was confused by this. The two approached the gate. At the palace spire, a golden arrow of fire was constantly shooting out toward the heaven.

They glanced at each other and winked. They turned invisible. The guard could not spot them, and they easily slipped through the gate. Once inside, they flew to the second-floor balcony. It was a quiet area. Tyler and Ella stepped forward. And as soon as they did, their surroundings changed unexpectedly and spectacularly.

They were now standing in front of a great hall. The walls were golden and white mix.

"We are inside," whispered Ella.

A grand staircase was visible in the middle. It had walls lined with paintings, murals, and ancient texts.

"Someone important must be living here! A welcoming humming voice I hear! Something different." said Ella.

"I am not quite sure, but I sense it too." said Tyler. And moved to a corner.

"Ella pondered for a minute, "no, not sure if trespassing would be a good idea."

"Yeah, I guess you are right…"

As soon as Tyler finished his sentence, a low-pitched tone began to play and in front of their eyes, words began to appear.

'The Chosen ones. Palace welcomes you, Tyler and Ella Demarest!

Now face the unknown……face the destiny….face the truth….or face the death……'

They stopped and quickly moved around. No one was there.

"Wha . . . whe . . . where are we?" stammered Ella from behind.

"I don't know, but something is going on. Wait! It could be a trick! "Or a ghost! It is triggering us to go in that direction." Tyler answered.

"Then, what should we do?"

Something quickly slipped through the corridor from one side to the other. It happened so fast Tyler could not comprehend what it was.

He pointed at the room in front of them.... Stopped.

He stared at Ella and said, "Look Ella. It might not be a bad idea to check out this room. I mean, why not? Huh?"

Tyler paced.

As Tyler strolled closer to the room, he could hear the echo of his footsteps. At a slow pace, he took out his sword, moved to the room. Ella was right behind him with her bow and arrow.

A voice came out of the room with a smoke, *"Leave Now! Leave Now! Unless you are the chosen ones."* The words took shape in the smoke, turned golden red, flew right at them, and floated in the air for a while. Then it melted away in the air.

Silence fell.

Slowly emerged two beautiful girls on two sides of the door.

Dressed in royal dress they were holding two bluish white rocks engraved with blue handprints.

On top of each stone was penned:

Princely Path

"Entrance to the Prince's room
Or
Exit to the heaven."

For a few seconds, Tyler stood there hesitated. He noticed a beautiful smile on the girl's face, felt strong. He took a deep breath, and then put his left hand on one of the handprints.

Immediately he felt a push from behind. Someone was trying to force him to move away from the stone. Tyler could not move.

With one of his hands stuck on the stone, he was flying in the air while he was still holding his sword with the other. His face turned red and started giving out fumes. It changed from its original color to blue to dark green, then to yellow, red, golden, and then to golden white.

"Do not leave the stone." He heard a murmur in his ears.

Ella paced forward with her eyes fixed at the other girl's face. The girl had a beautiful, strange expression that made her uncertain. She watched Tyler was shivering in pain with his firsthand on the stone. S

Yet, she felt an enormous desire to move forward.

"What are you waiting for? Come on! Closer." The beautiful smiling girl was staring at her.

Ella paced forward; decided. Nothing could stop her. She must know. Know this place, the kingdom, the Prince…. everything.

She closed her eyes and put her left hand on the stone. A spark went through her body. A black smoke came out as a strong wind to smash hard on her face. She began to fly in the air.

Her hair became straight, she felt a jerk as if someone were trying to force her to move away from the stone. The stone became hot, had a fire burning. Soon her scar mark and her fingers turned golden red. She watched them but could not move or say a word.

"Do not leave the stone." She heard the same murmur in her ears.

In seconds, the fumes from the stones absorbed into their bodies. The stones changed back to their original shape and color as they flew out of the stones to hit the ground.

Tyler and Ella turned back to look. They noticed the two beautiful girls transformed into two winged witches, one black and one purple. In place of the two stones, they were now holding two giant golden black king cobras. One cobra spit out a sentence:

"Prince will die, so will the queen.

The second cobra followed:

Sculptor will reign, dark will shine."

The deep dark red eyes of the witches were fuming with rage, anger, and hate. Soon the witches melted away only to vanish with their cobras in the vastness of the empty room. It was all silent again.

"ONLY THE BRAVE AND THE HONEST CAN ENTER THIS ROOM TO FULFILL THEIR DREAMS." A text appeared in the air.

'Am I brave? Am I honest?' Tyler doubted. A whispering sound talked to his ears, "Are you brave? Are you? Are you honest? Are you? Are you? Are you?"

Tyler stared back, a shadow behind him disappeared, he couldn't see anyone. He was unsure and stared restless.

Silence fell again.

Tyler stood and pondered for a moment. He was reflecting. His eyes were rolling, and his hands were sweating.

Two more rocks moved out and separated from the wall. They flew at high speed toward them and stood still right in front of their noses.

It was so close, Tyler almost got knocked out.

"It was a close call." Ella said.

The rocks spoke in a gibberish voice:

"Brave you are, ready for fun.
Timid you are, you better run."

Tyler and Ella paused. They didn't know what to do.

"Catch the rock! Grab it." Shouted Ella.

Tyler rapidly jumped on one of the rocks. Ella grabbed another. The flying hot rocks were moving at high speed as they were spitting out fumes and sentences in a whispering human voice.

> "Good in heart, better you all
> Bad in heart, make it a call"………
> "Prince is ready, ready for light
> Dark that king, out of sight."……………..

"Look at this! My hands are already numb." Ella shouted at Tyler who was also flying close to the ceiling just behind him. Ella was breathing heavily, and so was Tyler.

"I'm not sure, if I can hold on to the rock much longer….but we have to." Tyler screamed.

"This is the only way to pass through the force-field I believe." Ella shouted back.

The whispering voice came back. Tyler and Ella exchanged their looks. They could hear, but could not see anybody. It was saying:

> 'Chances come, come to those.
> seek it, love it, Trust it close."

"But how would I know?" Tyler sputtered. As if he was talking to someone.

"Are you alright?" Ella asked from the side.

Then she heard someone speaking to her:

> "Right or wrong, know in heart.
> Conscience tells, have a good start."

Tyler was sweating and breathing heavily. He did not answer.

> Force can shadow, lust and greed
> win or lose, Dark is deep
> fight the dark….fight it all

listen in you, golden call…..golden call…..golden call……… "

Ella was in sweat, her hands red, practically sleeping out every moment. She was having a tough time to hold onto the rock.

'I tried my best to save my sister when she was almost drowning in the ocean." Tyler sissled. His face turned red.

Ella felt the heat of the conversation. But she did not notice anyone. It was all dark.

'Clearly think kids! You are not coward; you are not dishonest. Honest you are, brave you are!' The voice echoed in every direction. A golden light triggered across the room and made them confident.

The flashes of their recent past reeled through their minds. The ship reck, the storming ocean, the tsunami sized waves, the hidden rock bed, the tearing and falling apart of their small lifeboat, the emergence of the wooden log as a chair and its mimicry as an elegant, majestic throne……all reeled through.

The rocks stood motionless for a few seconds and started moving again. It went through different parts of the palace, slipped through the corridors and doors, passages, hallways, and then came to a cafeteria. Tyler and Ella could see people seated in groups and eating down there. No one looked up or noticed them, and the rocks moved. They passed to another section of the palace.

It was quieter here. The doors were heavily guarded. In between every two rooms with their doors was standing a bridge made of molten lava or plasma. As they came close, the doors opened. Once they passed through, the doors closed again by themselves. They had to go through nine different doors, rooms and hallways that opened one after another.

While moving Ella noticed the guards stood motionless for the time being as if hypnotized. By the time the guards came back to their senses, Tyler and Ella had moved through into the next room and hallway.

Finally, the rocks took them to a dark place. The rocks

spanned heavily before they were thrown onto the floor of a dark corner of an empty space. In front of them was standing the last gigantic door. Two golden hands were holding the door from behind in place as if it was about to fall.

Tyler was still holding onto his sword. Ella was armed with her bow and arrow. She came forward and pushed the door by touching one of the hands. It didn't open. She pushed again. Immediately she was sucked into the doorknob and then thrown off into the ground a moment later completely unconscious. A creaking strong noise announced the door hinge fell. The heavy door started to open.

Tyler stared at Ella. He hesitated for a few minutes and then advanced to enter the room. It was completely dark.

Slowly he stepped foot into the room. A few tiles fell off from the top of the ceiling. A few bats came flying at him. But just before they stopped short of hitting him on his face, all melted away in the air. The tiles that came flying stayed in the air for a while and then vanished before melting away too.

Tyler waited with anxiety. He was curious to know what would happen next.

A fireball emerged in front of him and began to melt away into darkness spontaneously as a wave in every direction.

Then a wind started to blow. It came and whispered at Tyler in his ears.

Suddenly, a three eyed snake came flying by and tried to bite Tyler on the face. A sudden force pushed him away just in time. Tyler almost lost his balance. By then his eyes had adjusted to the darkness. In that dark room, he noticed he was standing on the edge of a steep boiling volcanic island in the middle with a drop off canyon that went deep down to the seafloor. In the middle of the island was standing out a tower made of glaring golden rock. And on the very top of the tower was sitting a man in saffron cloak on a golden chair.

"Who are you? Are you the force behind the force-field?" Tyler screamed.

"Ha, ha, ha. Force field! No force-field. Nothing. Only force! My force can win over any force-field. Anyone!"

Tyler stared at him, could not answer. Only silence fell.

The boiling volcanoes stopped pouring out toxic gases as they receded. Now he was riding a boat over a stormy ocean through a rocky floor. He was the only passenger. Gusty wind and snow were hitting the boat. Huge waves rolled as the boat moved at high speed. Tyler looked everywhere. There was no trace of his sister.

"Who are you? Where am I heading? Answer me!" Screamed Tyler.

His boat slammed onto the rocky island in full speed as Tyler flew out on the stormy ocean. He dragged himself onto the rocky seashore. He was now lying alone on the dark island facing a gold seat. The seat turned toward him as a gigantic figure emerged. With long bushy hair, tall golden beard, saffron dress, and red burning eyes the figure made itself comfortable on the seat. With a declamatory voice it stared at Tyler. His defamatory look, the poisonous laughter and the creepy sensation made Tyler afraid. But Tyler didn't show any expression. He didn't want to look weak.

Tyler paced back slowly.

"It is good to see you after almost one thousand years. I've been waiting for you all along. I knew you will come Tyler Demerest."

"Who are you? Are you the Wizard Saint King? That's I'm looking for?"

"Not so fast boy. I'll tell you, tell you in time. But come near. I need to see you first. I want to make sure it is you."

The man extended his right hand holding a golden stick. And then he lifted it. In the blink of an eye Tyler was floating in the air and started leaning toward the canyon. He then got sucked into the force-field and emerged seated on a chair next to the figure.

"Sit down." The figure asked.

Just like a doll, Tyler fell next to the man on the chair.

"Now close your eyes. Meditate. Truth will be revealed."

A lighted sphere appeared around him, and he started to float like a dust in the middle of that bubble.

Tyler stared to the side. He noticed his sister was awake and is also inside another bubble meditating just like him.

As he closed his eyes, he met a king and a queen. Then he observed the birth of a Prince, the kingdom in celebration, a saintly man moving through the crowd....then all went dark.

The bubbles melted away. At this time, Tyler understood he had an illusion, and he was the only one sitting next to the gigantic man.

"What happened? And where is my sister?"

"She will be here any minute, relax."

The man smiled and gazed at Tyler.

"You are an exceptionally good soldier. But fighting for the wrong cause and with the wrong side. Now give me your sword and your armor. As you see, we are now sitting in a land of peace. We don't want to disturb the force-field, do we?"

The man stared eye to eye with Tyler. Tyler slowly got hypnotized. He took out his sword and left it on the top of the rock by his side."

"Excellent, my boy. You are doing very well."

"Now remove your armored dress and leave it on the rock too." The man moved the golden stick he was holding.

The gigantic man was watching and smiling at him.

Tyler started taking off his armored cloth.

As he was slowly removing his dazzling armored dress, he heard a scream.

"Don't! Never give up your weapon. Don't you remember what our guru said?"

It was Ella. By then one of her arrows pierced through the chest of the gigantic man. They watched in the place of the man lay there the dead body of a transfigured one-eyed wobbegong carpet shark.

The tower with gold seat disappeared. Instead, they found themselves sitting in a dark room.

"Who woke me up? Tell me your name. It is not time yet. Don't you see? Not sure? What are you doing here?" A human voice threw all kinds of questions at them.

They did not know who was talking. At the deep dark corner of the room appeared a figure slowly approaching.

It was an Elephant seal. Slowly it moved in front of them. It was talking in a human voice.

Tyler took out his sword while looking at the Elephant seal and was going to kill it. Suddenly Ella pulled him away.

Instantly the room lit up and they discovered themselves inside a beautiful room with a mosaic ornamental floor surrounded by many guards.

All the guards moved sharply. Their spears pointed toward them.

"Wow, wow, wow! Not them! They are the chosen ones! Don't you see their outfit?" Now the elephant seal had transformed into a handsome royal man. "Look at them! They belong here! Can't you see? Let them in!"

The guards saluted and retreated. The royally dressed man walked into a room, Tyler and Ella followed him.

"Don't be scared kids. My name is Cygnus, I'm the elephant seal that you noticed a few minutes ago. Her Majesty has ordered me to come and help you. I'm here to make sure you guys aren't lost! Her Majesty released me from my bondage for these few moments. But very soon, I must go back to my form. Please come in. Soon you will be entering the room of our sleeping Prince! He is asleep for almost one thousand years. Only a few more years to go. Soon it all will come to an end!"

Then he came forward and touched the scar mark on Ella's forehead.

"Yes, here you are! You are the chosen ones! Remember that scar mark that you got while fighting with Scorpion King

Sculptor to save the Prince? Yes, I'm pretty sure, you are the chosen ones! You are, yes, you are!"

Tyler and Ella were exchanging looks. They didn't know where they were going, who he was and what they should say or do. They were lost!

Then Cygnus turned toward Tyler.

"And you? Remember your star on your wrist? The mark that stays with you forever! Even in these thousand years you should have it if you are one of the chosen ones! Let's check it out! I'm sure you are! Otherwise, you would had been killed the moment you came through the gate when Aquila scanned you with his eyes! But let us check it out!"

Cygnus's eyes lit up with a glaze. He took Tyler's right hand, turned it and kept his palm over Tyler's right wrist. As he projected the blue light on his skin, Tyler felt a strong sensation. The blue light turned to golden yellow, went through his body. His wrist was getting hot.

Moments later, Cygnus raised Tyler's arm and a bright blue star mark was now visible on the wrist of Tyler. A blue light was coming out of it. The bright ray of light receded by itself and so did the mark.

"There it is! See? I told you! You are the chosen ones! I have seen many many visitors in these thousand years, but none like you! You are different! Yes, you are!" Smiled Cygnus.

Tyler stared at Ella and questioned, "but why are we here? Who brought us here? What are we supposed to do?"

"You're trying to tell me you don't even remember? You gotta be kidding! Lives fade, but memories stay! Our lives are full of memories! You, the two chosen ones! You'll know. I'm not supposed to tell you much! I'm here just to show you around and take you to the room of the Prince without getting killed. Without my permission, no one can pass through the gate that you just did.

Ella was going to say something.

Cygnus interrupted in the middle, "I know, I know! You must

be thinking what's all this? No worries. You will know once your memories come back. But we must leave soon. Once you meet *WELCOR, the Enigma of six....*" He was going to say something more but didn't finish his sentence. He pushed the palace door carved with expensive stones and gold plates in front of them.

They took another turn and entered a half-dark room. One oil lamp was burning on the side.

It was hard to see anything more in that dimly lit room.

"I can't see. It is too dark." Slowly uttered Ella.

"Soon you will." Cygnus replied.

Then the oil lamp started to grow brighter and brighter. The whole room began to glitter like gold.

A group of ladies came in with lamps. They looked at them, smiled.

Tyler and Ella noticed a handsome Prince in imperial dress was asleep on the bed with his eyes closed. He had a charming face of a fearless young man. His majestic appearance was giving an indication, that he could wake up any minute. A beautiful woman was sitting on a striking gold-plated chair next to the majestic bed.

Tyler and Ella bowed their heads and stood there speechless for few minutes. Memories were flashing through their minds.

Slowly the ladies tuned back and went away with their lamps.

"We need to go."

Startled Tyler and Ella woke up in that dimly lit room. Cygnus was talking to them.

As they turned, Cygnus was talking, "remember, you two are his closest friends. You are his saviors! Only you two can bring him back to life and wake him up! Remember your promises?" With a reflective meaningful smile Cygnus paused.

In an awestruck look, Tyler and Ella were listening to Cygnus.

They heard Cygnus was reciting:

'Enigma of six save the siblings

Each with a sign, carry the markings

Red the color, distress comes

Carry them through the land, carry them through the sun
Chosen are they two, bring back His soul
Prince is the body, three times the goal
Three times the goal, three times the goal…three times the goal.'

Cygnus looked at them deeply for an answer.

Tyler and Ella didn't know what to say. They kept quiet.

"Alright, alright. I know, it has been many many many years and you don't remember much! Do you? That's alright. But I shouldn't say no more!"

He was losing strength. His voice became wobbly.

"Running out of time, need to get to the garden, before I pass out! Rush!" Cygnus was turning pale. Tears were coming out of his eyes. He started to run.

Tyler and Ella followed Cygnus, came out of the room, passed through the passage, and turned. Then went through a few more doors and two more hallways, took to the stairs and came out of the palace. In front of them was a beautiful garden with a fountain standing by the blue lake. The sun was shining in the sky. They looked for Cygnus. But he was nowhere to be seen!

For the first time Ella and Tyler were amazed. The seven beautiful palaces were standing with grace. From their majestic styles it was obvious these were imperial residences. The humming river at a distance and the soothing sound of the flow of water in the blue lake, the grassland, the flowerbeds, the canopy of large trees and silvery clean roads mapped all around, captivated their imagination. The ocean right above and around them was visible through the blue dome. The whales, sharks and many other amazing sea creatures were swimming by in the blue lake.

They decided to move on.

CHAPTER XV

Attack by Devil King

Tyler and Ella were now coming down through a hilly forest toward a valley. High mountain peaks gleamed at the distance as streams babbled about.

Ella was a bit tired.

"I'm thirsty!" She spoke as she sat down under a tree.

"Wait! We are close to a village," said Tyler. "I can see movements. Seeing a river, people are swimming."

Tyler carefully approached the flowing body of water. He went up and down across the forest and the river. The water was clear. The mid-day sun was reflecting.

"Woah, look up there," said Ella who came down to the river behind Tyler.

A dark cloud started appearing in the sky.

"Another storm must be coming." Ella said.

It appeared odd to Tyler. "On such a sunny day with a blue sky you normally don't expect dark clouds! It's kind of funny, isn't it?" Tyler remarked.

Tyler and Ella were busy looking for a container from someone to fetch water.

One woman was walking in a hurry carrying two containers and a couple of waterskins.

"We're very thirsty. May we borrow an extra container in case you have one? We would like to get water." Asked Tyler.

"Sure. The woman smiled and replied. "You can borrow mine." She handed them over one of her buckets and two waterskins.

By then, the dark clouds grew larger. Then a strange thing happened. A part of the black dark clouds ripped apart and fell on the lake with a strong lightning and thunder on the other side of the mountain. The earth beneath their feet shook heavily like a major earthquake.

Tyler and Ella watched the mysterious event.

A vast number of cavalry soldiers and beastly creatures with weapons were coming down to the lakes hidden behind the clouds.

High above in the sky, the clouds were moving fast. Wind started blowing, soon picking up speed. The tower bell sounded to alarm people. People ran for cover.

"Follow me. Not the river. We collect water from the waterfall hidden behind that rock." The woman pointed at the beautiful waterfall at a distance. She turned and ran to fetch water.

"You two should get home! And you can keep the bucket and the waterskin." She screamed at Tyler and Ella running behind her.

Tyler and Ella stared up to the sky. By then, the dark cloud got thicker, darkness drew in. The rustling of leaves was murmuring into their ears.

The woman was fetching water from the waterfall. She was knee deep. Tyler and Ella waited at a distance.

Suddenly six equestrians appeared on the top of the mountain. One of them shouted off to his friend, "there she is. Get her!" They pushed their horses, came down the rocky mountain toward the woman.

An evil smile was lurking on their rough faces. Tyler and Ella caught the glimpse of the first two riders reaching the waterfall.

"They are coming after you. Get out of there, run." Tyler and Ella screamed.

The woman raised her head and noticed the equestrians, but it was too late. The huntsmen went into the waterfall and held the rein tightly to stop the horses. One man stretched his hand to grab the woman.

"Help! Help!" The woman was crying out. She ducked under the feet of the huge horse, filled her bucket, and splashed at them. The equestrians laughed. It did not stop them from chasing her. They were waiting for the right opportunity to pick her up.

The woman slipped and fell into the waterfall. Tyler and Ella could not see her anymore.

"We need to save her." Shouted Ella.

She flew and drew her arrow. It moved all the way through the air and knocked out one of the equestrians with a cry. Blood splattered from his right shoulder. The other rider looked at Ella, laughed and continued chasing the woman with his sword. Tyler flew, jumped on him, and his sword ripped through his jacket. He fell from the horse screaming.

But that did not stop the others all wearing heavy armors. With a heavy jacket, long hair, and broad shoulders one of them appeared invincible. He was laughing while chasing the woman with his axe. Tyler and Ella were busy fighting the other huntsmen.

Then suddenly the woman was up. She threw her water filled heavy bucket in full swing at the man. It flew in the sky and struck the man. He lost his momentum and came onto the other horse. The riders and the horses lost their momentum and came onto each other.

Tyler and Ella quickly took her hands and helped the woman to get out of the waterfall. The woman ran toward her friends screaming.

The riders stood up, looked back at the woman, Tyler, and Ella.

They swiftly dragged their wounded huntsmen out of water onto the horse, took the mountain path, and disappeared behind the mountain.

"We should follow them." said Tyler. "Come on." He was ready to go after the huntsmen.

"That would be too risky; we do not even know this part of the land that well." replied Ella. "Rather, we first need to figure out everything that goes on here."

Ella and Tyler walked into the waterfall, started drinking water. They filled their waterskins.

With wind blowing, there were severe thunderstorms across the horizon.

What they did not notice, a dark cloud was gushing through the sky like an arrow, and it was heading toward them. And behind it there was another one. And then another. By the time, Ella noticed, it was late. She screamed, "Run!"

Tyler and Ella rushed through the forest. Went up the hill. The dark clouds were pounding behind them as shooting arrows. Soon they found themselves in front of two Palaces. On one side it was the palace of Amber. On the other side was standing the palace of Topaz.

"Which one should we go to?" Tyler screamed.

"Get into the Amber. That looks closer." Shouted Ella.

They turned around. Another dark cloud was emerging from the horizon. It landed behind them on the mountaintop like a shooting star. Angry soldiers were rolling out of the mountain from the waxy mud with weapons. Their only objective was to kill people.

Then emerged marching beastly creatures, the Cropions, and Snapions. The cropions were the beasts with scorpion type long grasping pincers, thorny tail, human type face and the body of a crocodile. The Snapions were the beasts with snake type long thorny body with a tail, human type face with two legs.

Everyone was running in fear and screaming, "run, the gates are closing."

Tyler and Ella were sprinting toward the gate. But it was still far.

"Run!" Screamed Tyler, "only a few more yards."

People were rushing to safety in fear of their lives. The angry creatures were destroying everything and killing everyone on their way. A gusty dark storm of wind and snow was roaring down across the entire kingdom.

"It does not look good," Ella was saying, "the soldiers are out fighting and sacrificing their lives."

"They are doing everything they can." Tyler was talking, "with their parsing swords, bows and arrows, axe, spears, and many other weapons, they are defending their palace, their land. But I am not sure if they will be able to save their land, their kingdom."

The palace guards behind the fortification walls were shooting flaming arrows at the angry monsters. The haunted soldiers did not lose hope, appeared determined and were ready for a fight.

More beastly creatures and cavalry were coming out of the lake, the mountain, the forest.

"Fill in the moats, let the beasts fly." It was Perseus. He was flying over every palace sky on his black Pegasus with his fellowmen and issuing orders.

Water came gushing and filled in all the moats across all the palaces. Huge crocodiles and alligators flooded the moats and started swimming in the moving water.

"Soldiers be ready. We are under attack. Drawbridges will be moving and turning across. Citizens, get to your safety immediately. Her Majesty is ordering for an immediate evacuation, All Palace and Tower gates will be closing soon." An announcement came to everyone in golden leaves.

People started coming out of their villages. They poured in from every direction to cross the drawbridge to reach to the safety of any palace. The guards took positions at every fortified tower.

"Let's go." Tyler said urgently. "We need to decide, help them. It is the time."

"Everyone is running away from the beasts." Ella screamed!

"Let's get inside the palace." urged Tyler.

"But what about Coma, that old man? Hmm? All alone there? We promised him safety, food and water remember?"

"Ella, I know, I know what you mean. But unless we save ourselves, how we would be able to save him? Let us get inside the palace before it is too late!"

"No, I am going to get him. We promised him. I cannot leave him there all by himself!" Before she finished her sentence, she flew out to get Coma.

When Ella reached the ruin, it was all dark and covered with snow. Frightened animals had taken shelter. Ella spotted snakes, lions, hyenas, and jaguars. The abandoned ruin had trees and plants all around that completely isolated it. She somehow managed to climb her way in to get into the room where Coma was asleep.

Unaware of the attack, Coma was sleeping peacefully. A moaning sound was coming out of his mouth. He was shivering in cold.

Ella looked around. Then she went to the window and glanced outside. The enemy soldiers were pouring in from many directions. Their numbers were going up by every minute.

"But they are not coming this way. Gosh! What a relief!" She murmured.

She gazed at Coma again. Then she went to the next room. The room was upside down, broken pieces of furniture, paintings, utensils, clothes all scattered across the room. Ella found one of the cabinets intact. She pushed and opened a drawer. It was empty. She opened the next one. Inside were lying few papers with a map written in an old language. She quickly glanced at the map; numbers, words and red arrows were flashing. She decided to take it and tucked it inside her pocket. Then she put it back.

In the next drawer, it had another map lying inside. It looked the same. Then the next one…she opened all other drawers one by one. All had a map lying inside. Same color, same words and numbers flashing with a different background. She closed it and opened the next one. At the very last drawer she found lying a few ancient paintings.

As she was shuffling through the paintings, she found the king, queen. The people in the palaces. The royal wedding. The next one the Prince with his parents. The Prince and the queen. The Prince alone. The next one with the photos of two young kids. It was them! The painting she was holding had two recognizable faces. One was her brother Tyler. And other one of herself. It was them! She almost lost her breath. Ella looked around. No one was watching. She was relieved.

Ella rushed to the next room. That room had a better luck. As if someone had saved it from destruction. There at a corner she found a series of cabinets. One of the cabinets was full of many clothes. She took out one blanket, came out of the room and paced toward where the old man was asleep. She covered and wrapped Coma with the blanket, escaped out of the ruin and flew toward the Topaz palace. She had noticed before guards rescuing wounded soldiers and taking them to the Topaz palace.

Coma woke up. He opened his eyes to see dark gloomy sky. Arrows and spears were swinging by them.

"Where am I going? Where are you taking me?" Then he saw Ella's face and did not say anything anymore.

Ella slipped through the palace gate of the Topaz palace.

"Is there a treatment room here?" She asked one of the guards.

"Go down the hallway and it will lead you to the room of healing." Ella went to one of the distant rooms. It was a difficult scene. Wounded soldiers lying on beds were screaming in pain.

Ella put Coma down there on an empty bed at a corner.

"You will be better off here. It is safer."

She looked up and saw one of the nurses.

"Take loving care of this old man. He is sick. Needs food, water, and medicines."

"Of course. We will." The nurse came forward, nodded, and said calmly in an assertive tone."

"Stay here. Rest. They will take care of you. Once things get better, we will try to send you back where you came from. Until then, rest." Ella put her hand on his head.

"I must go now. Ok?"

Coma nodded his head. A few tears dropped out of his old yellow eyes. This time he did not try to hold her hand.

Ella ran toward the gate.

"How do I get to the Palace of Amber?" she asked one of the guards.

"The other side, ask the security. Take this. show him this as your ID." The guard gave her a gold coin. It had the picture of the queen engraved.

Ella gazed at the eyes of the guard with an inquisitive look. He smiled and said, "I know who you are. Queen's order."

Ella ran to the other side of the palace.

A few ferry boats anchored at the lake were transporting people from one palace to the other.

She handed over the coin to the sentry and got into a ferry.

Soon she was at the Amber palace gate.

Tyler was with Nigam, and his friends They were rescuing and carrying people through the gate. They were flying and getting through the defensive layer covering the shadow kingdom sky to funnel them into the Amber palace.

Ella flew toward them and joined.

"Where are you? Could you bring him? Tyler asked.

"Yes, he is here. Safe in the treatment room of the Topaz palace." She screamed. "How are we doing here?"

"People are pouring in." Tyler said carrying three children on his back.

"Guards, retreat. Citizens, take a path to reach any palace.

Her Majesty has ordered for an immediate evacuation. All Palace and Tower gates will be closing." An announcement came to everyone in golden leaves.

Within moments all palace gates became deserted. Guards standing in front of every palace announced, "the gates are closing. Come inside if you want to survive."

But before Nigam, Tyler and Ella could reach the gate, the gates slammed shut leaving them and many other families outside. Among them were seniors, women and children who had nowhere to go.

People were screaming out of fear. Old people hid behind bushes and tall pillars. The kids stayed wrapped under the cover of their mothers. Few brave men picked up their weapons and stood side by side with Tyler and Ella to defend themselves.

Snow was coming down heavy. The sky was dark with thunderstorms roaring across the horizon. The dark cloud was hovering above the mountain as increasingly beastly flying creatures poured down from the air. They had bows, arrows, axes, clubs, spears, and many other weapons in their hands.

Unexpectedly an opening formed by the side of the gate and a guard with evil looking tattoos on the neck came out. He picked Tyler and Ella up in the air with his arms and ran back into the palace. He dropped them on the palace floor and said, "Queen's order. Now, hide, run!"

Tyler and Ella paced back to the main hall.

A woman in purple and white striped dress flanked by two black guards was consoling them. The monstrous guards standing next to her were keeping an eye out for any disturbance.

"Must be the queen." Ella whispered to Tyler.

The Queen was talking to the people to console them. Even in that distressed situation she had a smile attached to her face. Her golden-brown eyes were lighting up as she was talking to everyone in a majestic but humble tone. With black hair, fair skin, an oval face she looked beautiful.

Tyler and Ella stood by the window. They were at a loss.

"Not sure how to stop the rampant attack or what to do." Ella was saying.

Fireballs, and arrows were coming down at every palace and hitting them hard.

"I am not sure how long the palaces will hold." Tyler whispered at Ella.

Ella turned and noticed one lady walking toward them. With her deep look and resolute personality, she said, "her Majesty would like to have a word with you. Please follow me."

They followed her to a magnificent room and stood on a side. Queen Eleonora arrived with her bodyguards within moments. She stepped toward them with a beautiful smile.

"Very nice to meet you Tyler and Ella Demarest! I know it is an inconvenient time to talk or discuss anything. It is so good to see you both after so many years." A joy was pouring out of her words.

"I hope you have heard little bit about who you are, and why you are here." She had a question attached to her face.

Tyler and Ella were silent. They wanted to hear everything from the queen.

"You two are the Chosen Ones. You are here to fulfill a prophecy. Lift the spell, wake up the Prince from his long sleep." She paused. Then continued, "It is you who can save the Prince, me, the people, the kingdom, everyone. Only you." She was now looking straight at their eyes. Then she glanced out of the window and said in an absorbed voice, "yes, only you can do it. That is what we know."

"We have heard part of the story, not all." Ella said.

"Good. It has been many many years since you two left this kingdom. I was living every moment in this cursed kingdom with my people and my son. And the only thing that kept me alive was someday, and yes, someday you will come, and I will see you. And you two will be here to save my child." She paused and then continued.

"Now the time has arrived, and by god's grace you two are

here. Without your help, there was no hope for my son. You two are the chosen ones. Please help my son to live, help me, help my people, help this kingdom, your kingdom." She paused. Tears were rolling down her cheeks.

"I will tell you everything in time. But now we need you to do something to save us from this disaster."

"Tell us what we can do." Tyler said.

"This kingdom is in the middle of an attack. If we can help, so be it." Ella continued, "we are ready."

Tyler said, "Yes, we are ready."

Queen smiled again, "then go, save your Prince, save the kingdom."

Tyler and Ella bowed and said, "As you please your majesty."

Tyler and Ella closed their eyes and called for their armor and the weapons which appeared in their bodies and on their hands instantly. They went out running.

CHAPTER XVI

Faith be the guide, wisdom be the source

In the meantime, few other families managed to pass through the gates. A secret opening was formed at each gate. A man standing at the gate was scanning and letting people in. The same thing was happening at Amber palace. Then the opening closed, and the scanners had to go.

"But why?" Asked Tyler when he noticed it.

"The Queen's order. Sorry!" Screamed out one of the guards.

Many other families had reached the gate. They ran from a long distance to get into any palace. Their villages, cottages were on fire. The enemy soldiers were plundering village after village and ravaging through the entire landscape.

"Open the gate. Take them inside!" Screamed Ella. She was asking the guards to open the gate. The enemy soldiers were moving closer to every palace.

The bald fat guard came close to her and said, "Thank yourself that you are safe! Worry about them later, ok?" He had a terrible accent, and he was screaming not talking.

Ella took a deep look at the fat huge man. With almost no hair, giant spike of arrows tattooed across his neck, and elbow he was laughing. His ugly yellow teeth and grizzly laugh made Ella tearful! But she was determined.

"No, we can't do that. Tyler, we need to bring everyone inside." She screamed.

Sharpnil, Lyra, Bernard and Ashwini emerged by them in horseback. Two other horses appeared by their side. Tyler and Ella jumped on.

It was a horrible scene. Dead bodies were piling up everywhere. Any wrong move could kill them.

"Guard the gate. Do not let anyone in except Tyler and Ella or Nigam and his friends. Remember." It was Perseus. He was waiting for the Queen's order.

"Look, it is Queen Eleonora. She could be at one place or could be everywhere at the same time." Said Lyra.

Everyone saw a beautiful woman appeared in front of every palace. In dazzling armored dress saddled on a white horse she started to speak.

"Citizens! We are under attack. Our country is under attack. The Devil King wants to capture Prince Anish, capture the Chosen Ones, and capture me. He wants to take over this land. He wants to take away our freedom. Freedom. Freedom that is hard to come by. He wants to take you all as slaves, as prisoners.

Time has come. Now is the time. Fight. Fight to your last breath. Save your country, your kingdom, your Prince, your family. Help your country. Your Prince. Your friends and families. It is you who can save the Kingdom, save the country and its Freedom."

Then she paused.

"Perseus and Pratap, my two army chief commanders will lead the attack from two fronts. Follow them. Follow their orders. Fight. Fight to save your country, secure your freedom."

Abruptly a few equestrians came flying out of thin air in front of each palace. They started throwing every kind of weapons at the Queen. The weapons came bouncing back from the palace force-fields. Few made it through. It was hard to know if anything happened, but gradually her image faded away and disappeared.

Perseus advanced with his huge army. Hidden soldiers were coming out of secret holes beneath the huge forest and grassland. The palace soldiers started hammering on the enemy defense. With loud grunts and roar Perseus and his soldiers were ripping apart the enemies. They attacked the enemies with their weapons, swords, lances, spears, axes, daggers, flanged mace, with everything. The archers stationed at the palace gates started to nock, draw, and loose thousands of flaming arrows at the enemy. Because of the rain the ground turned into mud that slowed down the enemy soldiers. The flying arrows created a havoc on them who were advancing toward the palace gates.

The palace guards gave them extra cover from their defense. Arrows were also coming out of the defensive turrets of every palace and slaughtering the beasts. The beasts that were trying to cross the moats became food for the crocodiles. Even then, a few of the enemy soldiers made it to the other side and were trying to break open the gate. Flaming tar and heavy rocks came down from the top of the palace terrace and burnt them alive.

Ella, and Tyler became visible. Sharpnil and Bernard were guarding Tyler. Lyra and Ashwini were by the side of Ella.

Arrows, and spears, were coming down like rain. A flying sword barely missed Tyler's head. Another axe came in at high speed that was stopped by Sharpnil. Tyler noticed a family with children that had nowhere to run. He grabbed the child and the woman. He asked the man to grip his leg and flew back. Sharpnil and Bernard gave them cover from each side. They all could make it to the safety of the palace.

Ella flew in another direction with Lyra and Ashwini. One spear came flying. Lyra moved quickly to swing her mace to stop it. Then a knife raced by her neck that Ashwini caught in time.

Ella went down to the man standing with his wife, and their son. She took the woman holding her child in one hand and said, "stay with me, don't let go." She picked up the man with her other hand and flew back toward the palace. Lyra and

Ashwini stayed with them and gave protection. They rescued many families and brought them to safety.

Finally, it came down to the last few families.

"We have to save them." Determined Ella looked at Lyra and Ashwini.

They flew toward them. Huge fireballs were flying in every direction. One pounded the Amber palace at high speed and part of the palace came down. Before Ella could reach, one sword came flying and beheaded the man and killed his son. Then another row of arrows came down and killed the rest of the people in front of her.

Enraged Ella flew at a lightning speed through the battlefield and started shooting arrows at every direction. With her armored dress she was moving like a fireball. Lyra and Ashwini gave her cover while flying and killing as many as they could. Tyler flew like a storm through the sky. His sword came down in high speed and slashed every beast on its way.

Ella was looking for the general leading the enemies. It was Zuno. He was moving through the field on a lion faced hyena as he shook his entire body. Red fumes were coming out of its mouth. The beast was tearing apart anyone who came on the way.

Ella came down to strike Zuno. Zuno was fast. He turned around and saved himself with ease.

"The Chosen One! Not bad!" In a single strike, his spear knocked out the bow from Ella's hand.

"Now let's see who saves you, Chosen one!"

In one snap, Zuno's sword barely missed the neck of Ella.

Ella rammed through the air and crashed onto Zuno. Now her hands were on top of Zuno's armor. Zuno was having trouble to come out of the tight grip of Ella.

"Your time is near." Ella shouted.

She clicked her finger and took out the staff from Zuno. Her staff pierced through the chest of the Tigeana that Zuno was riding. The monster beast with the face of a Tiger and the body of a hyena fell to the ground.

Zuno fell on the ground. He stayed there motionless. Blood was dripping on the mud from his neck. He was having difficulty to breathe. But the next moment he was up with his axe.

Zuno opened his sharp black teeth and cracked a smile.

"We are not done yet, Chosen one!" He screamed. He came at high speed and hit her dress.

Zuno picked the flanged mace. He flew toward Ella. Next, he was on top of Ella. With empowering rage, Zuno used all his power to put Ella face down. With her face pushed against the mud, Ella's throat went dry as she was gasping for air. Zuno was ready to make his final strike. He was waiting for the right moment to bring the end.

Ella slowly took out the small knife from her waist and pressed it through the chest of Zuno. She felt something warm. The salty smell of blood. Zuno's grip came lose. Zuno fell to the ground. His eyes were bulging out, voice became heavy.

"Capture and kill her. Kill her!" He was screaming.

Many more enemy soldiers flew in and surrounded Ella from every side.

She looked up.

"You cannot save your Prince! Neither Queen Eleonora. They will die. So will all of you." Zuno was laughing. With that word, he glided out to the sky as a mist and vanished.

Ella chased him through the air. But Zuno was gone.

Ella raced through the battlefield. The enemy soldiers were dying in vast numbers. Then a flying sword came and pounded her hard. She fell on the mud with her mouth gaping. As she was standing up, another beastly creature came down with axe. But just in time, Lyra's arrow pierced through its chest. The beast dropped dead.

"Where is Tyler?" Ella asked Lyra.

"Must be busy saving the palaces."

Tyler was fighting other beasts that were trying to go over

the moats. He moved swiftly to the top of the palace tower. Another beast flew after him. He did not see it coming. The beast caught his leg and tried to stab him from the back. Both rolled down the palace wall and fell on the ground. Tyler did not know what to do. In one swing, he collected all his strength and managed to hold on to his sword which he almost lost. Next thing his sword went through the beast. The beast left him and fell on the ground.

Tyler turned and moved in another direction. That is when he discovered what was happening in front of the palace gates. Most of the moats were full. Beasts were walking over their dead bodies and gathering in front of the palace gates.

"The palace gates are holding well but they could get compromised." Ella shouted.

Right then a part of the Topaz palace fell apart. Fire broke out in many rooms of Pearl, Amber, and Emerald palace. The Sapphire palace spire fell off.

The beasts tried to start a fire at the front gate of the Ruby palace. The soldiers poured down hot tar from the top to burn them alive.

Thousands of arrows and spears were coming down at the Ruby palace.

The front gate of the Ruby palace was being pounded every minute. The beasts poured in from everywhere in thousands.

Then something strange happened. For some reason, most of the beasts turned around toward the Sapphire palace. There they gathered at the gate. Their flaming arrows were bringing havoc and fire inside the palace. Yet the palace held well against the attack. A bright blue golden light lit up across every corner of the palace.

"Their main target is the Sapphire palace. Notice, how they are aiming it from every direction. And they are in thousands. But why? Why Sapphire?" Tyler screamed at Ella.

"Not sure. But there must be a reason." Ella shouted.

They sailed toward the Sapphire palace and landed at a

corner. The guard recognized them and let them in. As they walked in, they saw only havoc and destruction. People were running through a narrow passage and were disappearing behind a wall.

"Where are they going?" Tyler asked one of the guards.

"To the safety. From here they can get into any palace they want. Except the Diamond palace." Saying this the guard moved on.

"Now it is clear why it is the main target of the enemy." Ella said.

"The Diamond palace is the only one not even being targeted?" Tyler commented looking at Ella.

The soldiers and families went through a hidden passage and retreated behind the next safety wall.

Ella and Tyler watched hundreds of beastly creatures approaching toward the Sapphire palace with huge hammer in their hands. She started shooting arrows. Many dropped dead. A new wave of creatures came roaring. The beasts were tearing apart the bodies of the soldiers fighting. Another fire ball dropped. In huge smoke Ella could barely see anything. With anger and rage, she started shooting arrows and killing every beast.

On sudden reflection of lightning roaring across the horizon, Tyler and Ella spotted Nigam. His tall body was flying in the sky like a shooting arrow. With his six friends he was fighting a terrific fight in front of the Ruby palace. It was like magic. They could fly and camouflage. They could change their shapes and sizes. But the devils outnumbered them.

Hundreds of devil soldiers were fighting with them swinging their blades. Nigam and his friends flew to the top of the treeless granite rock standing next to the Ruby palace lake and started floating in a circle. All stretched their hands upwards. An electric spark came down from the heaven, hit the rock and created a force field. A series of armors appeared from thin air, created a barricade and circled them around.

Nigam and his friends looked up at the sky and tossed their weapons in the air. The weapons produced many copies of its own and came down like a blizzard at the devil soldiers. They died instantly. Blood came out pouring into the dirt. Their body vaporized leaving behind no trace.

Many more enemy soldiers poured in from every direction and flooded the landscape with their face and body covered in white snow.

Nigam and his friends looked around. They heard the laugh of a ghostly creature. The four-legged winged creature had a human face and the body of a hyena. It was the Devil King Scorpion's evil bird Circinus. With high peached voice, armored body, and a sharp look it was screaming, "Silence, kids, silence. I know you can do a few things. But let me take the control now." Circinus was laughing.

Circinus stopped the shooting knives coming out of Nigam by using its own force. The same weapons started shooting back at Nigam and his friends without any warning. By then Nigam and his friends asked for a separate series of knives. The knives came down and raced as shooting star and neutralized all the weapons coming at them. Enraged Circinus turned mad and started chasing with a red face.

"Go, bring me the Chosen Ones." He ordered his fellow soldiers.

The evil faced Circinus screamed with his open jaws and sharp long teeth. He was tossing his tail and throwing out molten lava and fumes. He quickly moved in different directions walking over people, tossing out or killing them.

Circinus was shouting, "hand us over the Chosen Ones, the Prince and Queen. Or face your destiny."

Waves of creatures poured down from every direction. They came in waves after waves.

Nigam and his friends were fighting with their swords, arrows, fire balls, axes, and knives. They were moving swiftly. Then a beast flew in and attacked one of his friends. His friend succumbed to the wound of the axe. With rage, Nigam was trying to figure out who was the killer. In fire and smoke, it was hard to spot the killer. Next, he saw Tyler's sword had separated the head from the body of a beast.

"The assassin." Tyler roared.

Tyler, Bernard and Sharpnil killed many beasts with their weapons. Only a few could escape. Ella, Ashwini and Lyra's arrows brought down havoc among the enemies.

In the meantime, the beasts had circled the Sapphire palace. One tall man sitting on the top of a six-legged Cropion was their leader.

"Destroy! Destroy them. Bring me the Chosen Ones. Bring me the Prince and Queen Eleonora." He ordered with a thunderous scream.

"That is Benjiro, son of the Devil Scorpion King. Unless we destroy him, we can never win this battle." One old lady was shaking out of fear as she was talking to her husband inside the Sapphire palace. The man was listening quietly as he was nodding his head in agreement.

The beasts could not get through the sky of the Shadow Kingdom and the Land of Nines. The moment they tried to breach the defensive force-field; died instantly.

"Enemy soldiers are coming down like rain. The roads, mountains, treetops, houses all turned black. The beasts are merging and flying like a streak of molten lava moving up and down through the ground. They can get anywhere, everywhere." Tyler screamed.

"We need to get to safety. We can never win." Yelled Sharpnil. "Agreed." Shouted Ella.

"No strategy will work. They are too many," Shouted Perseus.

"Turn back to the palaces." He ordered his soldiers.

"Need to warn Nigam and his friends." Screamed Ella."

She flew next to Nigam and his friends. "Turn back to the palace. We cannot win."

"No! They killed my friend. I cannot leave." Shouted Nigam.

"You must. If we are alive, we would be able to take the revenge. Time to talk to our Queen." Ella whispered at Nigam's ears. She took his hand and uttered the words slowly to make sure they sink in.

They all started flying in another direction toward the Ruby palace.

"Where are you going? You cannot leave. The King is waiting for you." It was Circinus laughing. Tyler and Ella flew toward her. But before they could strike, Circinus swung her hands. Thousands of snakes came out of thin air and entangled Tyler and Ella. A dark velvet came down upon the chosen ones. Circinus drew the snake-net with Tyler and Ella trapped and unconscious inside.

"No! Screamed Nigam. He flew toward Circinus. But before he could reach, Circinus disappeared. She was now sitting on the top of the lake next to the Ruby stone.

"Finally! King will be incredibly happy. Bring me the Prince and Queen Eleanora. Circinus ordered his slave snake soldier. The snake made dozens of copies of its own and moved quickly through the battleground. Soon the snakes were sneaking into each palace through the broken parts in search of the Queen and the Prince.

"I will destroy the stone and unlock every force-field. Ha, ha, ha." She started hitting the red wall around the gigantic red stone with her long sword.

Suddenly thousands of golden leaves started coming out of the Ruby palace.

"Find the Chosen Ones. The Queen wants to see them." It was Perseus riding his black horse with his soldiers.

"But we can't find them." Screamed Nigam.

"We must. Queen's order.

Perseus moved in another direction.

Nigam was unaware of the fact that Circinus was sitting over the lake on the pyre next to the Ruby stone. He flew in every direction to locate Circinus.

"There he is" Boltus screamed. "Let us go and get them."

"Wait, we have to be careful." Nigam said.

They all took another turn.

"We must save the Chosen Ones." He whispered at his friends.

They silently flew over the lake, dived in and turned into frilled sharks.

Only a few guards were standing behind the fortification walls defending each palace. The beasts took out pillars from the side and began pounding every palace gate. The huge iron gates buckled under stress.

"Every part of the kingdom is vibrating with a thumping sound. The doors will collapse!" Circinus started laughing.

Nigam and his friends silently reached near the snake-net and cut it open. Unconscious Tyler and Ella slipped out of the net, fell into the lake, and started to drown.

Nigam and his friends dived deep down.

Nigam held Ella and came out to the surface.

"Come on, wake up, wake up!" Frantic Nigam was whispering at Ella's ears. His soft touch woke her up. They came out. Their eyes met. Nigam could not wait to kiss Ella.

"But where was Tyler?" Asked Ella.

Then they saw Tyler and Boltus surfaced at a distance.

"I was with him. He will make it." Said Boltus.

"The Queen wants to see you." Nigam said.

"Let's go then." Screamed Ella.

From the other side of the lake they all flew out toward Ruby palace.

Circinus never realized what had just happened. He was still standing next to the Ruby stone holding the snake-net tightly.

When Ella and Tyler reached the Ruby palace, the palace passages were dimly lit.

"Which way?" Ella asked one of the lady guards.

"Her Majesty is at her chamber. Everyone is waiting for you. Doctors and nurses are there." The lady guard started to sob.

The Queen was lying on a bed. Her glorious beauty started fading. Two bodyguards at the entry moved to let them in. Her left shoulder was bleeding. Two doctors and three nurses were assisting.

"What happened?" Ella asked softy one of the guards standing at the door.

"A flying knife made it through the palace spire while she was standing by the window."

One doctor answered while examining her wound.

The nine ministers standing at a corner of the room were talking to the other doctor.

"The knife is out. I gave the medication. Still, we might lose her unless we get help from the Wizard Saint King. The poison is making its way through her blood stream." The doctor said in a concerned low-pitched voice.

"How much time do we have?" Asked Prithvi.

"Maybe a few days or a few hours. Hard to say." The doctor answered in a soft concerned voice.

"Where are the Chosen ones? Where is Nigam?" The Queen opened her eyes and asked in a soft voice.

"We are right here your Majesty." Answered Nigam. "The Chosen Ones are standing next to me."

"Come close to me. I want to see you." The Queen smiled.

They paced slowly to the Queen.

The Queen looked up. Her eyes fell on Nigam and then moved to Ella and Tyler.

"If anything happens to me, you two fulfill your mission. Save the Prince, save the Kingdom. You two are the Chosen Ones! Remember?"

Ella and Tyler nodded. They held her hands tightly.

"We will. Will do everything we can." Tyler said. Ella's eyes became watery.

"The enemy has breached every safety mechanism of the kingdom." Said Aphiguna. Her voice was shaking.

Right then another part of the Ruby palace fell apart. A fire broke out.

"We have to go." Ella said frantically.

"Me too!" Tyler turned back. So did Nigam.

But the guards stood on their way.

"You cannot leave the palace now. It will not let you." Prithvi commented in a concerned tone.

"At least that's how it looks." Said Afjal. "Unless you truly wish to go out there!"

"No, you cannot go out there. You have another work to do." Minister Imani was saying softly.

"We are losing. The Diamond Palace seems vulnerable." Minister Bidziil said in a grave voice.

"Prince's chamber can fall any minute." Minister Ayoreo said.

"In fact, every palace is in danger." Minister Najeebah worried.

"It is not true. The Kingdom will not fall." Minister Birsa continued, "of course, the enemies are making their way. At least that is what it looks like."

"And yes. Her Majesty is injured. That is critical." Prithvi said slowly.

"What do you mean? We are under attack! We all can die!" Tyler shouted and continued, "Look everywhere. Only ruin and destruction. Our Queen is injured. We have nowhere to hide. And you are saying that is nothing to be worried about?"

"That is an illusion. Illusion created by the Wizard Saint King." Minister Prithvi said very softly. "Illusion to give us time. Illusion to take everyone to safety."

"We need to do something. There must be a way?" Shouted Ella.

"I think we are out of our options." Said Ayoreo. "The Kingdom is on its way to fall. No one can save it anymore."

"Options are only options. Rarely they are fruitful." Afjal was speaking in a mystic tone.

"There is still a way. Only one way." Slowly uttered Hoag.

Everyone looked at Hoag.

The old man was now standing with folded hands.

"Reveal the way!" The Queen gazed at Hoag.

Hoag bowed and said, "There is a price to pay."

Everyone uttered, "there is a price to pay."

With a mode of salutation and closed eyes, he spoke softly:

"The Trishul moves to wheel
Tower gets the light
Stone speaks the truth
Rescue in sight."

Minister Hoag started waving his hands.

In front of them appeared the elephant seal.

"Did you call me? "He bowed at the queen and asked.

"Yes! The time has come. Reveal the way." Hoag smiled in a strained voice.

Emerged Cygnus, the handsome Royal Guard.

"There is a price to pay."

"We are ready to pay any price. Tell us." Tyler said.

"Just say it. Her Majesty would like to know." Shouted Nigam.

"There is a price to pay." His eyes travelled across the room from face to face, and finally fell on the face of the Queen.

The Queen spoke in soft voice with a sad smile:

"You are lucky. We all were lucky. But the time has come. Reveal the way, reveal what you have."

Cygnus slowly took out a paper from his pocket.

"The wizard saint king gave this to me. *'Golden Treatise of Magic' they call it.* A mystic magical paper that can never be destroyed. And how to get to the Land of Nines? It has some clues." His hands were shaking. He paused, started taking deep breath and continued.

"The wizard saint king ordered me, 'read this only when the paper turns red, and the Queen asks you to do so. But there is a price to pay. In time you will know.' Then he explained, 'this paper changes color from golden white to purple, yellow, red, blue, grey, or black. When all is well, the color is bright golden white reflecting the colors of the seven palaces, shifting from one color to another. Normal color: white paper with golden print. Royal celebration: Purple. In time of joy: Golden yellow. A threat to the Kingdom, the Prince, or our Queen. Red. If their lives are in danger: Grey and even worse: Black." He swallowed the lump in his throat and looked around then continued, "not everyone can read this paper either except the Queen and the Prince or the Chosen Ones. It will reveal itself to the people who can see his own reflection on this page. It also has a pair, Golden Dome of magic, a mystic magical cloth. Together they can reveal much more." He paused, then started, "Let me read what it says," started reading softly:

> 'Deep into the stones, lie there a source
> Reach there by wisdom, fire, and the force
> Gate will not open, Devil will not cease
> Light will not come, neither will be peace
> Chosen are the two, face they all the beast
> Let them read the stones, codes in the mist
> Queen sheds blood, death haunts the land
> Huntsman comes through lake, sky, and the sand
> Reveal then the truth, reveal all you could
> Then would be the time, only then you should
> Take the path you must, creature, mist, or stone
> What else could it bring? Do it all alone
> Fire and the wind, are the only force
> Wizard is the guide; wisdom be their source
> Faith be the guide; wisdom be the source'

He handed over the paper to Hoag. Hoag's reflection came up on the paper. He looked at it. The sentences were still there. He moved and gave it to the Queen.

She looked at it. On the top of the golden red paper were still flying the sentences.....

'Wizard is the guide; wisdom be their source
Faith be the guide; wisdom be the source'

The body of Cygnus was slowly transforming into statue.

"This is all he told me. I do not know the meaning." With this as they watched, Cygnus, slowly transformed into a golden red statue.

Tyler and Ella were looking at each other. They did not know what to say.

"The price to pay for revealing the truth." The Queen softly said while glancing at everyone with a desperate look.

"But what does this all mean?" Minister Ayoreo said.

"It does not make any sense." Minister Aphiguna said.

"How do we get the Wizard Saint King? He is already dead." Said Imani. "It is very confusing." Said Birsa.

"I know what the Wizard Saint King wanted to say. But I am not sure if I should say it or if it is the time."

Everyone looked up. It was Bootes. The little boy was listening to their conversation from a corner with his mother and all the other friends. He had a devastating look on his face.

"Say what you have to say." Said Prithvi.

"Not sure, if we have much time." Said Hoag.

Bootes came forward to the Queen, looked at everyone, then said, "And there is a price to pay," he looked up.

Then continued, "He is talking about Tyler and Ella. Ella has the armor of Fire. Tyler has the armor of wind. Asking them to go to the Stone Room in the Temple Tower of Magellan. There lies the Endless Stone next to the mummy of the Wizard Saint King." He finished.

"And then? The Queen Eleonora was listening.

"Once they meet the endless stone, everything will be revealed." Bootes took a deep breath and said after a long pause.

In front of everyone, Bootes turned into a hyacinth blue Macaw and flew away.

"This is the cost he had to pay for revealing the truth." Bootes's mother uttered with watery eyes.

"Is there any way to remove their spells?" Ella asked.

"Only when Prince Anish wakes up and the kingdom is saved." The Queen said softly.

"But how do they get to the stone room?" Prithvi asked.

"Through a hidden way." Afjal said.

Everyone looked at Afjal.

"And there is a price to pay." He bowed to the Queen. This is what I know:

'Remember when you say
Hefty price to pay
At the end of it all
Evil must fall
Seal turns to human
Boy turns to bird
Reveal then the truth
Know it feels absurd
Only then you feel
Trishul moves to wheel
Only then in sight
Tower gets the light
Pay the price you must
Pay the price at last
Or they lose it all
Shatter into the dust

Everyone was staring at him.

Afjal gazed at Tyler and Ella.

"The time has come. Now if you follow me." His face turned red.

"Go with him, carry this with you. Be careful with it. It might serve you a purpose." The Queen handed them over the mystic paper as she looked at Tyler and Ella. Ella took, folded, and tucked it inside the pocket of her armored dress.

Hoag turned to Tyler and Ella. "Follow his leads. We will be waiting here for you." His voice was braking.

Tyler and Ella looked at the Queen. She appeared feeble and exhausted.

They came out of the chamber. A horse drawn carriage was waiting.

Tyler was hesitating, "but leaving the queen in this condition?"

"Get in." Muttered Ella.

"This is the way. Only way." Murmured Afjal.

Three of them got in.

The carriage flew into the air and disappeared like a mist.

In minutes, they landed on the top of the ruin-tower. Ella was surprised.

"I thought we are going to the Temple Tower of Magellan." Ella spoke.

"You are. But the road to the Temple Tower of Magellan starts here." Afjal said. Then he continued, "originally our King built it to give shelter and protect people in time of any invasion. With hidden passages, this place was ideal. People could move or go in any direction across the kingdom if they wanted to. The same thing they can do now from the Sapphire palace. Then the Devil King attacked, everyone died including the two of you." Afjal was speaking softly. "The Wizard Saint King helped a few of us to escape through a secret route to the Temple Tower of Magellan. We stayed there for a long time before we came back to the seven palaces that he built. I do not remember how we got there. All I know is the entry point where the route to the Temple Tower of Magellan starts."

They walked past the terrace and reached a hidden chamber. Ella could not recognize this part. Afjal picked up a burning torch from the wall.

"It should be here." He was carefully examining the white, grey, and dark walls. "Somewhere here. Must be."

They stopped in front of a faint mark of a tree on the wall. Afjal moved forward, hesitated, and then touched it. The tree mark started to spread across. A golden red colorful tree emerged on the wall as a beautiful painting.

"There it is." He smiled. He touched the root of the tree and pushed. A creaking sound started, and a door opened. On the other side of the door, they could see a beautiful lighted tower was standing in the middle of a starlit sky.

"Reveal the way." Shouted Afjal, as he bowed down.

Immediately the walls started to move, the image of the tower disappeared. Another room appeared. On the side was standing the same cabinet that Ella recognized immediately.

"I have been to this room before." She spoke.

She opened the drawers one after another.

All had a yellow map with red dotted lines and star marks lying inside. The same map she saw earlier.

"I have to go." Said Afjal.

Afjal said staring at them before leaving.

"Save the Queen, save the Prince, save the Kingdom..." the last few words came out of his mouth.

He ran out of the open door into the darkness. Lightning struck, and in that light Tyler and Ella watched Afjal turning into mist and disappeared.

The door vanished and only a wall was standing.

Tyler and Ella did not know what to do.

"What do we do now?" Tyler asked.

"We have to read the maps." Said Ella.

She quickly took out all the maps and started to spread them over the table next to the burning torches on the wall.

The corners of the maps moved and joined to each other. Slowly a landmass full of lakes, seven palaces, green meadows and people emerged. Letters, and numbers started emerging and dissolving over the maps. Then they started moving. In the middle a star was standing with a red chakra. Next to the chakra was sitting a Trishul.

A whisper came out of Ella's mouth.

"The Trishul moves to wheel

She slowly moved the Trishul toward the chakra.

Ella continued:

Tower gets the light....

She touched the tower. But nothing happened. She looked at Tyler. Her eyes turned watery......she felt frustrated. They sat there quietly. Then they noticed emerging a tall tower on the map from the base of the tower. And it lighted up with golden light.

Golden red numbers started appearing and dissolving on the map ....0,1,2,3,4,5,6,7,8,9,0,1,2,3,...

Then all the letters and numbers melted away and a soft voice came out of the map:

'Answer comes, comes from the past
Comes from the light, comes from the dust....'

The wall in front of them dissolved and a road emerged from the top of the ruin tower. Sound of hooves started at a distance. Then it became more intense. Appeared nine equestrians on white Pegasus.

"Chosen Ones? Looking for a way to get to the Temple Tower of Magellan ? Hop on." One of them screamed.

Next thing they realized they were soaring high. Light snow was coming down. Bright moon was shining in the night sky. Soon they were standing on the atrium of the Temple Tower of Magellan. Tyler and Ella came off the horses.

The equestrians and their horses started falling apart and turned into dust.

Tyler and Ella rushed out to explore the huge tower and its large rooms. They went and explored floor by floor. In many dimly lit rooms oil lamps were burning on the floors and torches were burning on the walls and in the hallways. People, men, women, and children dressed in saffron, were coming in and out of the rooms. A few rooms had people engaged in meditation. They went through from one room to another. Tired and exhausted Tyler and Ella came to the top floor. This floor was completely empty. Except a few birds were flying in and out. They came to the last room on that top floor. At a distance on the tower spire were shining a Trishul and a Chakra.

Ella and Tyler stood still there in silence. Didn't know how to get in. It was locked with a heavy lock from outside.

"What do we do?" Asked Tyler.

"Reveal the way......" Slowly uttered Ella.

The lock fell off. The massive door opened with a screeching sound.

As the entered, they understood nobody has ever been into this room for many years. It was completely empty. Intense flash of light was coming out of that room. Once their eyes became adjusted to the light, Tyler and Ella saw a box. Next to the box was sitting a large golden bluish red stone on two stone holders. The mysterious stone was changing colors. A strong beam of light was shooting out of the stone that diverged into seven streams of lights. The beams were striking all the seven stones sitting in front of seven palaces. In that light, from the top of the tower, Tyler and Ella could see and hear everything. The havoc and destruction. The beasts were hammering on the palace gates.

Tyler and Ella slowly turned to the Diamond palace. The Prince was asleep. The guards were standing outside the door. The Diamond palace was intact without any major damage. They turned their eyes to the Sapphire, Pearl, Emerald, Amber, and the Topaz palace. The partly damaged palaces were standing strong against the attack. The enemy soldiers were making their way into the palaces. Then they turned to the Ruby palace and saw the Queen. Still waiting for their return. Her beauty was quickly fading away. They could even hear her. She was asking in a feeble voice, "are the Chosen Ones back yet Prithvi?"

They approached the mummy. A fossilized body of a man wrapped in saffron dress was lying inside. He had a calm and peaceful face. He had a distant look with a smile on his face. They bowed down in front of the mummy with folded hands.

Then they gradually walked to the stone and sat down.

"The Stone Room. The Wizard Saint King and the Endless stone." Ella whispered.

"Endless stone, show us the way" Ella prayed softly.

A voice came out of the stone:

> *Read the letters, at slow pace*
> *Look in space for a staircase*
> *End not in sight*
> *At the end there is light*
> *See what love and faith can bring.*
> *Prince will live, so the Queen.......*
> *Follow your instinct...chosen ones."*

Letters and words started to appear on the stone and then dissolve, they kept repeating.....

> *E: Enigma of six*
> *C: Center of power*
> *R: Red Palace*
> *E: Eight lakes*
> *T: The Book of Ten*
> *N: Notorious King*

Ella and Tyler exchanged looks.

"I don't understand." Said Tyler.

Ella nodded her head. "Not sure, what it is all about? But we are close. We need to figure this out." They looked at each other

Then Ella closed her eyes and stayed motionless for a few

moments. She stared at the letters and the words that were still emerging and dropping from the stone.

"Center!" She screamed. That is the only word you could make with these letters: E,C,R,E,T,N. We need to look at the center of every room.

She took Tyler's hand, "Let's go!"

Ella and Tyler rushed out and this time took the elevators. They started from the ground floor. They went in and out to check every room. In one of the rooms people were practicing yoga. In another people were eating and drinking, it was like a cafeteria. In the other, some younger children were reading and chanting their passages from books with a teacher. In another dimly lit room, monks were practicing yoga. They went past people to get to the center. There was nothing, no leads. Frustrated and exhausted Tyler and Ella returned to the same room and sat down on the floor.

"I am not sure if we will be able to do anything or save the queen." Tyler was whispering.

Ella took out her paper. They noticed; the parchment paper has turned from golden red to greyish red.

"Time is ticking." She said as she folded and put the paper back into her pocket.

She was determined and thinking. Tyler stared at every corner of the room. Then the huge table sitting at the center caught his attention.

"Come, come with me." Ella jumped up and screamed at Tyler.

"Where? Where are you going? Asked confused Tyler.

"You will see. Not far."

Ella took Tyler's hand and advanced to the middle of the room. As they advanced to the center, they noticed the words *"Stone Room"* was written on each marble slab of the room. A huge heavy mahogany table was sitting in the middle. On the top was lying a map. The same yellow golden red color, same type of letters and numbers emerging and disappearing on the paper. The kind of map they had seen in the ruin tower. But this one had something extra. It had a wax seal stamp at the bottom with the signature of a queen. 'Queen Eleonora' was printed next to it. It also had a title: *'From the Shadow Kingdom to the Land of Nines'*.

"Help me figure this out." Said Ella. She was holding the map in her hands.

"Must be carrying a clue to get to the Land of Nines from here."

They moved close to the huge table and understood it was not exactly a table. Something different. A thick layer of sand and dust had covered the furniture. The four giant legs were sitting like columns on the marble floor. From the distance, it appeared like a table.

Ella and Tyler started removing the dust and the sand with their bare hands.

Slowly emerged a golden seat in the middle. A few words were emerging and disappearing:

'To the land of Procyon'

"Is it the same throne we have seen in the middle of the ocean?" Tyler whispered.

"Seems that way. Soon we will find out." Ella answered. Then emerged the two handles.

Tyler and Ella gently approached and sat on the chair. Nothing happened. It was all quiet for a few minutes. Then the chair started to change and emerged the ancient throne they had seen in the past in the middle of the ocean.

Golden light started beaming out of the throne. The flash of bright light coming out of the throne sparked across the kingdom for a few seconds. Then it made its way back to the throne and absorbed into it. A whispering voice started emanating and dissolving in the room: *'To the land of Procyon.....* *'To the land of Procyon........ 'To the land of Procyon'*

"Reveal the way." Tyler and Ella said softly.

"Call me if you need, call me must

Call me if you need, Call at last."

A voice came out of the throne.

"How do we call you? What is your name?" Tyler regained his strength and asked.

'Anser is my name,' A voice came out.

Immediately they found themselves standing in an atrium in front of a library. In a nameplate written, *"Land of Knowledge and Light."*

It was a busy place to be. A huge place. Shelves filled with millions of books in many floors. Elevators going up and down from one floor to the other.

Tyler and Ella looked up and down. There was no beginning or end to the library.

"Knowledge has no beginning, neither it has any end." Said Ella.

Library staff were busy serving people. Every floor was packed. Patrons coming in and out, carrying and going to their desks or computers with the books. Two girls were standing at the gate.

"Welcome!" The girl smiled. "I am Immersia and her name is Engrada. Welcome to the path, path to Knowledge, knowledge to humility, …she kept going.

"We are here to read a book." Tyler was annoyed.

"You can ask for the book at the main desk."

Tyler and Ella approached the main desk. One old man and a lady were sitting.

"Nice to meet you. My name is Ichika. What can I do for you?" The lady smiled.

On the desk their nameplates were shining, Hermitage and Ichika.

"We are here to help you." The old man Hermitage smiled.

"Fill up these forms. He handed them over two forms. Tyler and Ella filled up the forms with their names and address. In the address part they wrote, "Shadow Kingdom, Ruby palace."

Hermitage looked at their forms and smiled. "From the

Shadow Kingdom? Very rarely we get any visitor from there. Welcome to the Land of Knowledge and Light. He went to the next table and put in two gold coins into a machine. Came out two coins prepared with photos, names, and stamps from the other side. Ichika took and handed Tyler and Ella the two coins and said, "here are your patron numbers, he looked at Tyler, "your number is 00, and then looked at Ella and said, your number is 01.". They looked at the coins engraved with their photos, names, and numbers. On the other side it had the seal of the library, '*Land of Knowledge and Light, with the picture of the Temple Tower of Magellan.*'

"We want to meet the secretary." Tyler said.

"Let me look at his calendar." Ichika said. Then she checked the calendar and said, "Yes, he has time now. Half an hour break prior to the staff meeting. Please wait here. I will let her know." Smiled Ichika.

She rang her bell., one lady appeared.

"Please let him know he has visitors."

The lady walked out and, in a few seconds, came back with a note.

"He is waiting for you. Go ahead." Ichika said. "Mehr will guide you." She turned at Tyler and Coco.

They walked past the next room and a few other rooms following the ostrich, Amir. Finally, they stopped in front of a spacious room.

A big man was sitting. The name tag said, Caelum: Secretary.

"Can we meet the librarian?" Ella asked him.

"Why? What do you need?" He looked impatient.

"We need the Ten books, I mean book of …book of…" Tyler was stammering.

"Come on, say it what you want." Caelum shouted, "spit it out."

"Book of ten. Yes, the book of ten. That's it." Shouted Ella.

Immediately the face of Caelum turned red. He turned back at them and took a few moments. His face started to sweat. He regained his composer, and said very slowly, yes, The Book of Ten....will be in the rooms of Light and Ash. Hard to get in there. He turned back at Tyler and Ella and started to laugh. Yes, yes, not you. No worries. Yes, you can get in there. Yes, you can. I see it in your face. Now go to your left, then to your right, then take a U turn and enter the Room, *'The Rooms of Light and Ash.'* There lies the Book of ten. You can go in there only if you have the code. Hope you have the code. Anyone going in there without a code, will turn into ashes."

Tyler and Ella slowly walked out of his office. Caelum looked back at them, wiped his sweaty face and hands. Then quickly wrote down in his notebook, 'Visitor came for Rooms of Light and Ash, looking for the Book of Ten-One boy and one girl.'

He went to the window. One parrot with purple, yellow stripes and sharp beak was sitting on the balcony. Caelum quickly slipped his note into the beak of the parrot.

"Shiyoong, Good girl, give it to the master. Go."

Shiyoong immediately flew away and disappeared in the vastness of the sky.

Caelum went back to his chair and sat down. He wrote the same note for himself on his notebook. Looked around everywhere with an irritating smile. Then reached into his lowest drawer, slid his notebook behind a bunch of paper and locked it immediately.

Tyler and Ella went through the aisles and took a left turn. One Blue Macaw was sitting there. With a smile it said, "go to your right."

"Bootes, you?" asked Ella.

"Yes, it is me." I can help you if you need me." Bootes said.

"Do you know where to find the librarian?" Tyler asked.

"Her name is Monishan. She is there all the time. Very rarely we can see her. We call her the invisible knowledge lady." Bootes continued.

"Yes, we barely ever see her or know where she is. But she is there." One girl named Samhriti was standing next to the door said. "If anyone has any question in mind and cannot find the answer no need to worry. They can write the question on a paper and drop it in the drop boxes. They will have the answer within a minute on their way out at the front desk. That's her. People say it the wise soul of the saint sitting in her mind. Others say it is the force of wisdom."

"Could you give me a pen and paper?" Ella asked.

Samhriti brought in a pen and a piece of paper immediately.

"Do not forget to put down name and Number.

In the paper Ella wrote,

> *"Poison runs, runs through fast*
> *Queen dies, save her must*
> *Chosens are here, choose at last*
> *Or we fail, mist or dust"*
> *Ella-01*

"Where should I drop it?" She asked.

"I will take it and drop it in his box. You two can wait here." Samhriti said.

The blue Macaw flew out with the note in his beak. He soared upward high and high and went to the message room. Many message boxes with different labels, *'Patron- 21-answer, Patron 65-answer, empty-waiting, empty-question me,* were dropping from above, appearing and disappearing in front of him. He quickly dropped the message into a box that had a label: *'empty-question me.'*

Then Bootes flew back to Tyler and Ella.

"Your answer must be ready by now. If you go and ask at the front desk, they will hand you out the answer."

Ella went back to the front desk and asked Ichika.

"I have asked a question and waiting for an answer. I am Ella-01."

"Here you go." Ichika immediately handed her a note.

"Thank you."

"Enigma of Six" three words were glittering like gold on the top of the paper when she opened the envelop.

"Come!" They thanked Bootes and Samhriti and started to walk.

"Let me take you there." That room is hard to find and easy to miss." Samhriti said.

They took the elevator, went up and up. Finally, the elevator stopped at the 990th floor. They came out of the elevator, took a few turns, and came in front of a room, "Rooms of Light and Ash." A huge lock was hanging from the door.

"This is the room you are looking for." Samhriti said. "You wait here. Someone will be with you shortly. Now if it is ok, I will leave."

"Yes, of course!" Said Tyler.

They stood there silently for a few moments. This part of the library was completely empty. With very few lights, the area appeared mystic and ghostly.

Then a grumpy old woman appeared in front of them from thin air. All her body was wrapped in white. Only her old yet beautiful face with no wrinkles was visible.

"What do you want? I was having my mid-day nap." She yawned.

"We want to get in here." Tyler said.

"For what?" She questioned.

"To read a book."

"There are many. Which one? And in which part? Light or Ash?" The lady asked.

"The Book of Ten." Ella pondered for a few moments and said, "should be in Light."

"Hmm… in between Light and Ash. I remember." She commented with a grin on her face.

Then after a pause, she questioned, "Have you got your code? Let me look at your patron ids."

"Yes, yes. We have it." Tyler said immediately. They showed her their patron coins.

"Here it is, the Code." Ella slowly handed her over the paper and uttered 'Enigma of Six.'

The old lady took the paper, looked at carefully. "It sounds about right." She took out her keys and started to open the lock with a few misses. "I am getting old. Do you know how old I am?" She asked with a smile.

"No, we don't." Said Ella.

"Hundred maybe?" Said Tyler.

"Noooo…not even close, much mush older than that. I am older than this library. Older than anything you come across. …., not easy nowadays…getting older is never an easy thing….you see…. she continued……."

Finally, she was able to open the lock.

"Come this way." The lady entered leading them into the room.

"Which book you want again?" She asked.

"The Book of Ten." Ella said.

"Are you sure? Check again." The lady said.

"Yes, it is. The book of Ten." Tyler answered.

"That should be isle nine, middle of the shelf-29." Her voice shook, as she advanced with hesitation.

They started walking through the middle. One side had rooms after rooms that had shelves filled with books burning most of them were in fire, half burnt. Smoke was coming out.

"What's going on?" Tyler screamed.

"None of your business. Stay with me. This room has two different sides. One part: room of Light and the other: room of Ash. You are looking at the part of the room of Ash. That is for people who never use their knowledge for good cause, their knowledge ends up into ashes. Never part of any light. Not for you. Come with me."

Soon they were standing in front of the isle nine, shelf-29.

Three books with golden linings and grey cover were sitting on the shelf. The book of Ten was in between two other books.

Left to it was sitting a book named, "Book of Ash. The Book of Light was sitting to its right.

"Here it is." The lady handed them over the book of Ten.

"I must leave now. It is up to you what you want to do with this book. In last thousand years to my memory, never ever anyone had asked for this book. Must be interesting." She paused as she looked at them. Then said again, "you can't check this out. It stays here. Hope you know that. Have fun." Then she turned. Very soon she was gone.

Tyler and Ella slowly went to an empty table and sat down with the book.

An enormous book, on the top cover something was written that they could not read.

"Sanskrit." Ella continued, "an ancient language, I have no idea how to read the book."

"There must be a way." Tyler said.

Ella turned the page. Every page had a picture. As she turned the pages, letters and numbers started flying and moving over from one side to the other in high speed before they could read anything.

"Reveal the way." Ella and Tyler closed their eyes and prayed with folded hands. The book flew out of their hands, started rotating in high speed as it propped open in pages one by one. Soon the book came down with a thumping sound and sat on the table. They looked at the book, a book written in English was sitting in front of them.

The word, 'KNOWLEDGE' was lighting up on the cover.

Ella started to open the book. As she was turning the pages, it opened to only one page and sat there.

"Let me try." Said Tyler.

He held the book in one hand and tried to turn the pages. But the book did the same. It opened to only one page and sat there.

"Not sure what is happening." Ella said. They exchanged looks.

Tyler started to read the page,

'Procyon land, has it all
Unknown stairs, you might fall
You the guide, You the source
You the light, power, and force
Lake has water, stone from the land
Hidden in there, hidden in sand
Take your leap, take with trust
Either you die, or you must

Ella stopped. Slowly as they took their eyes off the book, there was no library. They were holding the same old map they had found in the stone room in their hand and standing on a large black stone that had no support. In front of them was visible a broken white staircase that was hanging from empty space and went down that had no end.

"Come, "whispered Ella. "This is the way."

"Take your weapons out." Tyler said.

Ella had her bow and arrow. Tyler was holding his sword. With full body armor, they looked at the two sets of staircases wrapped around in front of them lying at a distance. In between there was no support.

The staircase was hanging by itself in a completely empty space.

"Are you sure you want to take this route?" Tyler screamed from behind.

"Faith be the guide, wisdom be the source
Knowledge be the light, power, and the force….." she uttered.

"Let me go first." Tyler shouted.

Tyler came and stepped forward to go down the stairs. Behind him was Ella. Suddenly a hyena jumped out at them from thin air. Tyler's sword went through its chest. For every step they took, a stair appeared from nowhere to give them support. But as they advanced taking each step, they were hanging in the balance to fall into the space of infinity. The staircase was creaking, it could fall apart any minute it seemed. In front of them a greenish white and blue ball was appearing and disappearing with maps of lands, oceans and continents…..and next to it was appearing and disappearing another land…Land of Procyon.…..

They went down and down….but the Land of Procyon was still far away. After a while they became tired and exhausted.

"I am tired, cannot go anymore." Said Ella.

"Me too." Said Tyler.

Both sat down on the staircase.

Now they were sitting still. The rotating ball stopped. In front of them was shining…The Land of Procyon.

Suddenly Ella stood up.

"*Anser*, come we need you." She screamed.

Instantly a flying throne appeared beside them.

"Did you just call me?" The throne asked.

"Yes. We need to go to the land of Procyon." Ella said.

"Hop on."

They jumped on the throne.

They realized, they were racing down through many past civilizations, toward an ever green land filled with forest, lakes, gardens, flowers, oceans, mountains…. "The Land Of Procyon.…..." A billboard was shining over the landscape.

The throne slowed down and landed next to a lake.

"The Stone Lake." The words were shining in a billboard made of stones next to the lake. Next to the billboard were sitting many colorful stones and clay pots over the sand.

Ella quickly picked out two pots and filled them with water.

"Let's go back." Said Tyler.

"No. something is missing. Remember what the throne said?

Lake has water, stone from the land
Hidden in there, hidden in sand

We must take the stone from here as well. She rushed to the billboard and looked at the pot of stones next to it.

"Which one?" Tyler asked.

"The color of Ruby. Must be a red stone, the color of Ruby." Ella said.

They searched for a red stone for a while. Many colorful stones were lying on the sand. But none of them was red.

"None of these." Said Ella.

Remember what the book said, Land of Procyon, has it in the sand."

"But where?" Asked Tyler. He looked around. A vast stretch of shoreline covered with sand was lying in front of them.

"Must be somewhere in here." Ella said. She sat down on the sand.

Then their eyes caught a sight. It was the nearby tree.

One baby bird was trying to come out of the nest as it was ready to fly. Finally, the baby bird jumped and took a flight. It could not fly very far and fell on a large stone. It started shaking its wings and soon could not move. It was injured.

Within moments, its mother appeared. She carried the baby bird with her beak, flew to another place on the sandy shoreline. The bird started digging and took out a bright red color stone from the sand. It started to throw the red stones on the injured bird.

Very soon, the baby bird, started moving its wings. Then it jumped and took a flight and nowhere to be seen.

"That is the stone we need." Ella murmured.

The huge bird was still sitting on the sand.

"But it is not leaving." Said Tyler.

"We need the stone. Need to drive the bird away." Ella said.

Tyler and Ella ran to the place. They took out their weapons and tried to scare off the bird.

The bird looked at them. It made a sound, then started to speak in human voice.

"What do you need?"

Tyler and Ella were caught by surprise.

"We are here to collect water and the stone of life." Ella answered. They advanced to the bird with their weapons in hand to scare it away.

"Stop!" The Bird said in a grave tone.

Immediately Tyler and Ella became immobilized. Their weapons fell from their hands. They lost all their powers.

"You must answer my questions. If you give me the correct answer, you can take the water and the stone of life. If you give the wrong answer, you will die instantly. Agreed?"

"No, why should we? Who are you?" Screamed Tyler.

"Yes, we will." Said Ella calmly.

"Ok. Then answer me. What saves you at your darkest hour?"

"Light." Answered Ella.

"What gives you hope when everything is lost?"

"Love." Answered Ella.

"What gives you strength when you have none left in your body or mind?"

"Knowledge."

What is the most important virtue that any human being can have?"

"Trust."

"Who never leaves you?"

"A true friend." Ella said.

"Chosen ones! You have answered all my questions correctly. Now you can take the water and the stone of life."

The Bird flew away into the vastness of the empty sky.

Tyler quickly picked up a few red stones in his bag.

Ella took out the paper that the Queen gave her. It was fading, half of the paper turned black and half grey.

"She is not well. We need to rush." Ella said.

"Hop on" They saw those nine equestrians have arrived. Next thing they realized, they were soaring high into the sky and soon they found themselves standing in the room next to the queen.

"Are they back Prithvi?" The weak voice of the Queen came. "We are here. Your Majesty." Ella said.

She handed over the water to the doctor. Doctor took the water and helped the Queen to sip it slowly. As she finished the water, her wound started to heal. She started to smile. She was still weak and frail. Ella slowly took out the red stone from her pocket and put it on her chest.

A miracle happened. The stone started to glow and then it became absorbed in her body. The Queen lay there motionless for a few moments. Then she moved and stood up. Her dazzling beauty was back. She regained all her strength.

Queen Eleonora stood in silence for a few moments. She made a folded hand. Then she stretched her hands toward the heaven. A spark of red glow started forming on her two palms. The sparks flickered for a few seconds and then jumped out of her palms and flew out toward the sky. Suddenly the Temple Tower of Magellan that was never visible before turned visible. The top of the Temple-Tower of Magellan had a glow and its chakra turned red. Each palace started to glow. The animal statues engraved on outside walls of the palaces came alive. They all opened their mouth to spew out blazes as they moved. Every stone sitting on every lake lit up. The high beam of lights from every stone merged and started hitting the chakra at the Tower of Magellan. The chakra started spinning at high speed as it started to glow. Its light reflected at every corner of the Kingdom. Then the chakra came loose.

The glowing golden red chakra flew out of the tower and came down in full force on the enemy soldiers. It passed through the enemies making its way toward Circinus. The beastly creature was now hiding on the top of the mountain waiting for the fall of the kingdom.

"Bring me Queen Eleonora. Bring me Prince Anish!" He was shouting. He was still holding the snake-net tightly.

The chakra advanced at high speed toward Circinus. Circinus had never seen such a thing. He threw his staff at it. But the chakra advanced. Then he threw his axe. The chakra did not stop. Circinus threw every weapon to stop it, but the chakra advanced cutting the weapons into pieces or burning them. Circinus approached the chakra with his sword. But he was killed immediately in front of its unstoppable force. The glowing chakra was making a havoc. The strong fiery blaze coming out of the statues took out the advancing enemy army and turned them into ashes. The enemy soldiers started running in fear.

The palace guards started shooting their flaming arrows at the beasts. The beasts retreated. The chakra chased them everywhere, and they had nowhere to hide.

The light and fire of the chakra was so intense no one could even look at it. Thousands of enemy soldiers were caught in fire and jumped into the lake or river. Some escaped half burnt. The rest were charred and fell on the streets. Their bodies vaporized. And there was no trace.

"For now, they are gone. But it won't be long before they return." Said Bernard.

"Yes. Soon they will return, and it will be more difficult to beat them." Said the Queen. They saw the Queen talking from behind. She is encircled with her guards and the eight ministers. With a smile together they circled Tyler and Coco and sang,

> *"Chosen ones, you are hope*
> *Chosen ones, downhill slope.*
> *Chosen ones, turn to the sky*
> *Chosen ones, you need to try"*

So, it is not an illusion. It is for real. We need to stay here, live here, and do what we are born for." Uttered Tyler.

"Yes, it is just the beginning." Said Ella.

ABOUT THE AUTHOR

INABIS P.M. was born and raised in West Bengal, India. He is from the field of science. When not working or writing, you can always find him spending time with his friends & family, gardening, or with a book in his hand. He currently resides in Orange County, California near Los Angeles with his wife and two children.

Made in United States
North Haven, CT
23 April 2024

51698046R00168